Aces and Eights

Copyright © 2017 by David Archer.

All right reserved.

Published by: David Archer

David Archer

ACES AND EIGHTS

A SAM PRICHARD MYSTERY

ACES AND EIGHTS

DAVID ARCHER

USA TODAY BESTSELLING AUTHOR

PROLOGUE

The halls of Washington DC are often full of twists and turns, no matter how straight the architects may have meant them to be. The ones in the Nebraska Avenue Complex, where the Department of Homeland Security still rested in the "temporary headquarters" it was assigned when it was created by President Bush, were often the most convoluted of all.

Harry Winslow mused about those convolutions as he walked up the hall to the office of the current director. This would be the last time he would make this walk, he knew, and even though his old bones wouldn't miss the hard marble floor, he knew he was going to feel a loss when he had to get up in the morning and not come to work here.

Or anywhere else, for that matter. Harry was being forced into retirement.

Well, he figured, what could you really expect from these new upstarts who run the world nowadays? Before, when DHS and NSA and CIA and the rest were run by former military and intelligence people who knew what it was like to put their own lives on the line, a guy like Harry was always there in the background, always the one that got called in when things got too messy for the "public persona" to handle. Donovan, Hoover, Bush Sr.—almost every leader since the formation of the FBI and the other alphabet soups had called on Harry, or someone like him, at one time or another.

Sometimes it takes the guy who knows where the bodies are buried to make things work. Especially if he's the same guy who put some of them there, and everyone knows it in an "unofficial" sort of way. Over the span of his long career, Harry had buried an awful lot of them, so when one group had a problem with another one, he was often the one called upon to smooth things over.

But that wasn't why he was on his way to see Danuel Doherty, stomping through the halls for what he was sure would be the very last time. Callie, the girl who served as his office assistant down there in the dungeons they'd tried to bury him in, had come in that morning with a copy of a memo that had gone from personnel to building security, letting them know that Harry was being retired and that his access codes would need to be deleted after the end of the day. She'd been fighting back tears as she showed it to him, even though she knew she could be fired and possibly even imprisoned for possessing a classified interoffice memo.

Harry had read through it, then set it afire with his cigar lighter and dropped it into the dirt that held the fake potted tree some idiot had put in his office. Then he'd called upstairs and told Doherty he needed to see him. Doherty had told him to come up around ten, but Harry didn't like to set appointments.

"Classified Interoffice Memo!" Harry snorted at the very thought that such a thing could ever exist. How the hell could you work with people that you wouldn't trust to know who was being fired and who wasn't? Since when did retiring an old guy come under the heading of National Security?

Since they started using social media as a means of obtaining intel, that's when. Who during the 70s and 80s would ever have believed that the country would consider something like Facebook to be a reliable source of anti-terrorism intelligence? Not Harry Winslow, that's for sure!

Doherty's secretary saw Harry as he entered the office and looked up at him with her smile in place. "Mr. Winslow," she said, "you're a little early. Have a seat and I'll let the director know you're here."

"Why?" Harry demanded in his slow, southern drawl. "He got a girl in there he don't want me to know about?" He walked past her desk as her face took on the expression he liked to call "befloozled" and opened the big oak door into The Inner Sanctum.

Doherty was behind his desk, speaking into a telephone, and looked up at Harry with what actually looked like amusement in his eyes. "What'd I tell you?" he asked. "Just came barging in without even being announced, and he's more than an hour early. I'll call you back."

He set the cordless handset on its base and pointed at a chair in front of his desk. "Harry," he said, "to what do I owe..."

"Cut the bull crap, Danuel," Harry said. "I bounced you on my knee when your momma was in my analysis unit forty years ago, remember? There ain't any pleasure in this and we both know it. I want to know why you're kicking me out on my ass, boy, and I think I'm entitled to an explanation."

There, he'd said it. Harry felt the tiniest bit better as he sat in the chair Doherty had offered.

The director smiled at him. "Harry, I haven't forgotten, and just in case you didn't know, I learned an awful lot from you during those years. You and mom were always talking, ignoring little Danny on the floor, but I was listening. Why do you think she used to say I was destined to become a spy? Any idea what kind of hell I put her through during my teens, using tricks I picked up from you?"

"I ain't got time for reminiscences, boy," Harry said. "I want to know why I'm..."

"You're being retired, Harry," Doherty said, "because we finally figured out that you've been getting someone to manipulate your personnel file for the past fifteen years. That's the only way a man could serve with SEAL Team One more than four years before he supposedly enlisted in the Navy. Did it never occur to you that just changing your birthdate wouldn't hide the fact you've been active in one way or another since before you officially joined up?"

Harry didn't miss a beat. "That's ridiculous, Danuel," he said. "One of your clerks has made an error, that's all. I'm not ready to retire yet, and you still need me, so let's forget all this and go back to work, shall we?"

"Nice try, Harry," Doherty said, "but you're busted, old man. We found the original birth certificate you used the day you joined, showing when you were actually born! You're not going on sixty, Harry, you're already almost seventy-six years old!" He sighed and leaned forward, softening his voice. "Harry, don't make this harder than it has to be. You've served your country for far longer than you should have had to, and I know that we'd have ended up in a world of hurts more than once if it wasn't for you, but this is a younger man's game, nowadays. There was a time when you'd have given James Bond a run for his money, but I've got dozens now who could have run rings around you even then. Don't be bitter about being put out to pasture, Harry; think of it as being able to finally take time for yourself. Let the rest of us shoulder the responsibility, while you go out and enjoy the years you have left."

Harry stared at him for a long moment. "Enjoy the years I have left? Do you have any idea how ridiculous you sound? Danuel, if you had actually read through my file, you'd know why retirement is the last thing I could ever want. What the hell could I do with myself? What is there in this world for me outside of this job?"

Doherty sighed deeply. "Harry, Harry," he said. "Of course I read your file, but there was nothing in it I didn't already know. No one is immune to tragedy, Harry. You were talking about Mom a few minutes ago? Were you even aware that she and my father were on flight eleven when it crashed into the World Trade Center? We all suffer loss, Harry, it's part of living. It's terrible, it sucks, but we still go on."

And that's how it happens, Harry thought later that day, as he cleaned out his desk and packed up the few things that really mattered to him. He had the photo of him and Ian Fleming, taken during a chance meeting at Heathrow Airport a few weeks before the author's death, and another taken with Ronald Reagan during his presidency, but there was little else he might have considered mementos of his career. Those were mostly in his memory, and consisted of faces and names of those he had worked alongside.

Callie couldn't stop sniffling as she tried to help.

"I think it's just so unfair," she said. "These past few months, working with you, they've been fantastic. I love hearing the stories you tell, of all the adventures you had and the things you accomplished. It won't be the same with you gone."

"Well, my dear, just try to make do with whoever replaces me," Harry said. "I'm sure it'll be someone who has stories of his own to tell."

And then it was time to go. Harry picked up the small box he was taking with him and started out his office door, but a young man took it from him and offered to carry it down to his car. Harry only sighed, and gave Callie a smile as he walked down the hallway for the very last time.

He surrendered his badges and keys to the security desk, and the officer there was kind enough to say he was going to miss him. Harry made a point of getting his name—David Wells—and promising to mention him if he ever got around to writing his memoirs, but he thought they all knew that wouldn't happen. He'd have to let CIA go through the manuscript, and by the time they got done redacting parts of it that would reveal things better kept secret, there wouldn't be anything left!

He got into his car, a 1969 Lincoln Mark III that he had found for sale on a collector car website and bought on a whim. It was one of the very few flights of fancy he'd ever taken, but there was something about the car that reminded him of when things were most right in his world. He'd driven one like it when he had been transferred from the SEALs to Naval Intelligence in 1979, and that had been one of the best times he could remember.

He'd been a ladies' man, back then, and was always dating one beautiful woman or another, always had what his friends called "arm candy" hanging off him. They were all superficial relationships, though, not one of them lasting more than a few dates, until he'd met Kathleen. She'd first noticed him because of that car, that Lincoln, telling him that it seemed to be some sort of compensatory possession for a man who didn't have everything he wanted out of life, and it had dawned on him that she was correct. He'd always thought he was doing fine, but her words made him take personal stock, and he realized that he was, to put it bluntly, quite lonely.

Kathleen was only twenty-two, a secretary who had managed to get a high enough clearance to allow her to sit in on the highest-level meetings of the command. Harry's own clearance was just as high, but there was a very strict policy that prohibited dating between employees of the National Maritime Intelligence Center. Still, despite the age difference—Harry was thirty-eight—they carried on a flirtation for most of the first six months they knew one another. But Harry wanted more. One night, when she had to stay late, Harry disabled her car so that it wouldn't start. Then, of course, he "just happened" to be leaving the parking area at the right moment to offer her a ride home.

She'd climbed into the car with a smile, and started looking through his glove box as soon as they left the parking lot.

"Looking for something?" Harry asked her.

"The rotor from my distributor," she said without looking up. "Where did you hide it?"

Never one to avoid the truth, Harry grinned. "Inside the air filter housing on your engine. Figured me out that fast, did you?"

She looked at him and smiled. "Harry, I've been waiting two months for you to get up the nerve to try something like this. I was starting to wonder if I was gonna have to be the one to seduce you."

That had led to a clandestine relationship that lasted three years, culminating in their marriage when Harry was finally transferred to the Joint Military Intelligence Training Center as an instructor, removing the prohibition. Harry knew full well that his superiors had been aware that he spent many of his nights at her apartment, and that she spent equally as many at his, but that was just another area where knowing where the bodies were buried came in handy. As long as they made at least a moderate effort to keep it hidden, nobody wanted to risk having Harry Winslow pissed at them.

And then had come the best news of all: that Kathy was pregnant. No one paid any attention to the fact that Harold David Winslow, Jr. was born only seven-and-a-half months after his parents were married, and Harry couldn't have been a prouder papa. Harry, Jr.'s sister Elizabeth was born the following year, and the family lived happily and comfortably in a suburb of Arlington.

In 1986, only three weeks after their second anniversary, Harry was called up for a special mission into Cambodia. Intel had come across information indicating that there were at least eighteen former American soldiers still being held as POWs in the country, and Harry would lead a mission to go and find out if it was true. The mission would last a month, and he kissed his family goodbye as he left to go and rescue those good American boys who deserved to come home.

The mission was a bust, because it turned out the only American ex-soldiers there were those who had remained after deserting. They were living together in a rural area encompassing several villages, where they'd set themselves up as tin bosses over the people. Harry was so disgusted that he almost killed them, but he called it in and waited for the MPs to arrive from Germany to arrest them all. He couldn't wait to get home to his wife and kids, but while he was waiting to board the transport plane that would start him on the journey home, he was called to the field office and handed a telephone receiver.

"Harry?" said a voice he recognized. It was his best friend, Michael Watkins, another former SEAL who worked as an instructor at the Training Center. "Harry, it's Michael."

There was something in Michael's voice that told him the news wasn't good, and the sensation that went down Harry's spine felt cold, but it wasn't like a chill. It was more of a sudden knowing, a sudden hunch that life as he knew it was about to be over.

"Harry—Listen, they said I should be the one to call you because of what we've been through together, y'know?"

"Is it Kathleen, or one of the kids?" Harry asked.

There was a moment of silence on the line, and then Michael cleared his throat. "Harry, it's all of them. There was a fire, Harry, it looks like something went wrong with your wiring and a short caused a fire..."

He made it home without falling apart, and the funeral was handled quickly with Michael's help. The coffins were all closed, of course, because the bodies were terribly burned, but he'd known that they would be. The only weakness Harry Winslow had ever allowed himself came then, when he looked at the closed caskets and told himself that they weren't really in there, that Kathleen had actually taken the kids and run away for reasons of her own. The bodies inside them weren't his wife and children, they were someone else, just corpses shoved into the burning house to make it appear that his family was dead.

Of course, that only lasted a few days before he got past denial and into acceptance and grief. After that, Harry just didn't talk about them, didn't even think about them if he could avoid it. Michael got transferred to someplace overseas, Harry buried himself in his work and built a name for himself, and when he was tapped in the 1990s to form a new department to watch some upstart terrorist group called "Al Qaeda," he dedicated himself to his duties with every fiber of his being.

Now, on the day of his retirement, Harry let all the memories come back in, and he couldn't help wondering if Kathy and the kids would have been proud of all he'd accomplished. Sure, there were things he'd have never wanted them to know about—every intelligence agent had things he wasn't proud of—but in general? Would they have been proud of the times he'd saved lives, or even helped save the world?

Harry shoved those thoughts aside and came back to the present as he pulled into the parking garage of his apartment building in Annapolis. None of that would help him, now. He had to think of what to do next, and how he was going to make his moments continue to count, or else he'd be one of those who merely wasted away after retirement.

And Harry Winslow didn't like to waste anything.

He carried the box up to his apartment and let himself in, dropping it on the couch and walking on to the kitchen to get a glass and some ice. The whiskey was on the table beside his chair where it always was, the same bottle that had been untouched since the day he'd buried his family. He'd kept it to remind himself that he didn't want to drink and forget, he wanted to always remember them, but today he had decided it was time to get himself rip-roaring drunk.

That ancient bottle of Jim Beam was about to become his best friend. He fetched the glass and added ice, then went into the living room again and picked it up.

The envelope that fell over had been leaning against the bottle, and Harry knew it hadn't been there when he'd left that morning. He set the bottle back down and picked it up, then reached into the drawer of the table and took out the Colt .45 he always kept there. Another pass through the apartment convinced him he was alone, so he sat down on the sofa and looked over the envelope.

It was gray, and obviously old. The only words on it were handwritten, and even after all these years, Harry knew the handwriting was Kathy's. This envelope had been written a long time before and been stored somewhere ever since, but for some reason it had been delivered to him at this time, on this day. What possible cruelty could have been behind such a plot, he wondered?

He stared at it for more than five minutes, but then he had to know what it would mean. He took out the Swiss Army Knife that Kathy had given him as a gift on their anniversary, only a few weeks before he left on that mission, and slid its blade under the edge of the flap. The glue was so old and dry that it popped free instantly, and he opened it to take out the contents.

There were three photos inside, along with a single sheet of paper. He looked at the photos first, and his breath caught when he realized that the first one showed Harry, Jr. He looked at the second and saw Elizabeth, and the third, of course, was Kathleen herself—but something was wrong, because Harry Jr. looked like he must have been at least seven or eight, and Lizzie was around six or so, and Kathy...

Kathleen was sitting on a beach, and there was another man beside her. She had also aged, though it wasn't so obvious in her case. The look on her face said that she was happy, and Harry looked closely at the man beside her.

It was Michael Watkins.

Harry turned to the sheet of paper and unfolded it, and the words he saw written there caused him to forget the bottle and take out his phone. Harry Winslow had a number of calls to make, and there was no time to waste.

Too much of it had already been wasted.

1

"Daddy, wake up," Sam Prichard heard his little daughter say, so he rolled over and grabbed her, pulling her up onto the bed beside him. She shrieked and giggled as he began tickling her, but then she pushed his hands away just enough to gasp out, "Daddy, Uncle Harry's here!"

"Uncle Harry?" he asked, the surprise evident in his face and voice. The announcement brought him to full wakefulness in an instant, for the last time "Uncle Harry" had shown up unannounced, Sam had been involved in an international manhunt for a would-be dictator.

"Yeah," his wife said as she stuck her head into the bedroom. "I told Kenzie to wake you up while I start breakfast. He's in the living room." She glanced down the hallway and then came into the room. "Sam, he's been forced to retire, and I don't think he's handling it very well. Seems upset, you know?"

Sam grabbed her hand and pulled her down for a kiss, then let her go. "Tell him I'll be right there," he said, as he pushed Kenzie gently off the bed and rolled to a sitting position. The two girls got out while he went into the bathroom and took care of morning necessities, then pulled on a pair of athletic pants and a t-shirt he used for when he was hanging around the house.

Harry was on the couch when Sam walked in, and Indie was right; he looked like he'd aged ten years since they'd last seen him a little over a year earlier. There was something about him that almost suggested defeat, but Sam knew with certainty that "defeated" wasn't a word in Harry's vocabulary.

"Harry!" Sam said boisterously, and the old man got to his feet, showing that he was still as spry as ever. The two of them hugged the way men who love and trust one another do, and then Sam sat down beside him. "What's this about retirement? I didn't think you'd ever give up your work."

"Wasn't my choice, Sam," Harry drawled. "Seems some smart-ass with a computer managed to find out that I'd been making some adjustments to my 201 file over the years. Apparently, there was a digital image of my original enlistment that showed my birth certificate, so they no longer believe I was only ten when I joined the Navy."

Sam stared at him. "Just how much of an adjustment had you made, Harry?"

The old man grinned. "Let's just say I managed to stay on the job for eleven years past mandatory retirement age and leave it at that, shall we? And that isn't why I'm here, anyway." He glanced toward the door that led to the dining room and kitchen. "Is there somewhere we can talk privately, Sam? It's not that Indie can't know about this, it's just that I need to go over it with you, first."

Sam looked at his old friend for a moment, then nodded. "Let's go out to the office," he said. "We can talk there for now." He told Indie where they were headed, and the two of them walked down the hall to the room behind the garage.

Sam sat down at his desk and let Harry take the comfy chair in front of it. "Okay, Harry," he said, "what's really going on?"

Harry reached inside the leather jacket he was wearing against the late-autumn chill and extracted an envelope. He held it in his hand and looked at it for a moment, then looked up at Sam again.

"Three days ago, I walked my ass into the Director's office and got handed my walking papers," he said. "He told me about finding out how old I really am, gave me a speech about how I'd done more than my duty and should take the rest of my time to relax, and such, and sent me packing. I've got a pension that'll keep me comfortable for the rest of my life, a couple of hidden nest eggs that even the gubmint doesn't know about, and more free time than I can stand, but I've also got one of the most unusual problems I've ever even heard about. Sam, boy, I need to hire you."

Harry started talking, then, and over the next few minutes he told Sam enough of the story to give him an idea of what he would be going up against: a woman and two children apparently died more than thirty years before, but there was now evidence that their deaths had been falsified. Photos of the children a few years older than they would have been when they died, a photo of the woman with a man who wasn't her husband, and a note in her own handwriting that almost seemed like an attempt to explain but that left more questions than it gave answers.

"Harry," Sam said after hearing the short version of the story, "you have any idea who could have put the envelope into your apartment?"

"Oh, probably about 100 names could easily spring to mind. Remember, Sam, I've spent my life in a world of people who can get in and out of places without leaving a trace. I checked the apartment; there was no sign of any forced entry anywhere, no scratches on the keyholes, absolutely nothing to suggest this could have been the work of any amateur. Whoever put that envelope on that table knew exactly what he or she was doing. We're talking about a spook, Sam. The big question in my mind is the old how and why. How did this person come into possession of it, and why the hell did they bring it to me now?"

"I'm pretty sure that finding the answer to either one of those questions is going to answer the other one," Sam said. "If we can find out the how, we'll get the why; if we find out the why, the how will almost certainly become apparent." He looked at Harry and raised his eyebrows. "What does the note say, Harry?"

Harry was still holding the envelope, turning it over and over in his fingers. He glanced down at it for a moment, then leaned forward and handed it to Sam.

Sam opened it and let the contents fall out onto his desk. An old policeman's instinct made him want to avoid touching the photos and paper, in order to avoid contaminating any fingerprints that might be found, but he was sure Harry had already thought of that. If there were prints on it, Harry would already know whose they were, and he wouldn't be sitting across the desk.

The first photo showed a young boy playing with a small dog. The boy appeared to be somewhere around ten years old, in Sam's estimation. The dog was a dachshund, and the two of them seemed to be dancing around. "You ever own a dachshund?" Sam asked.

"No. Kathy always wanted one, though."

The second photo was of a little girl. It was the kind of photo often taken in a department store, with the child posed in front of a fake backdrop of scenery. This one showed the girl in a bright yellow dress, holding a small parasol. The background was a field of sunflowers. The child had a happy smile on her face.

Sam looked at the third photo. A couple was sitting in beach chairs, and they seemed to be very happy together. The woman, who looked like she might be close to thirty, was looking at the man with eyes that were twinkling. Her hand and his were intertwined, their fingers linked together in the way couples do when they're happy with each other. The man, who had short hair and the build of a professional soldier, was also smiling. The two of them were looking at each other, rather than toward the camera. It appeared to have been a candid shot.

"This is probably a stupid question," Sam said, "but you're certain that this woman is Kathleen? There's no doubt in your mind?"

"Absolutely none," Harry said. "Look at her left thigh, where it's lifted the tiniest bit and you can just see the back. She had a pair of moles right there, and you can see them in the photo. Believe me, as illogical as it would be after seeing the photos of the kids, I've tried to convince myself that Michael just found himself a look-alike, but there's no doubt, Sam. That woman in that photo is my wife."

Sam looked at the photo for another moment, then dropped it on the desk and picked up the note. He unfolded it carefully and looked at the words that had been written almost thirty years earlier.

Harry,

I wish you could see them growing up. Harold is so much like you that it's spooky sometimes, and Lizzie has all the grace and poise of a royal princess. I look at them sometimes and wonder how they could be our children. Let's face it, you and I were both a little rough around the edges in a lot of ways, but these two are about as perfect as perfect can be.

I miss you, Harry. The kids miss you, too, in some ways, though it's been long enough now that they don't truly remember you. Michael tries to keep me happy, and for the most part he does pretty well, but he understands that he can never be Harry Winslow. Let's face it, you were a very tough act to follow.

I don't know what I would have done without him. Michael came to my rescue when the world was falling in on me. He helped me accept that you were gone and when he explained the dangers to me and the kids, how could I refuse his help? It hurts to know that we had to walk away from everything we ever knew, but I guess that's the price you pay for being in our world. I just count my blessings and thank God that I've still got the kids safe and sound, and while Michael knows I still love you, he makes it clear that he's always going to be here for me. I guess I should just be grateful for what I've got.

I guess that's all for now. I'll write you again next month.

Love,

Kathy

Sam looked up at Harry. "I see what you mean," he said. "She wrote this as if it was something she would mail out to you at the time, and yet it almost sounds like she didn't expect you to ever see it at all."

"I'm quite sure she didn't," Harry said. "I've read that note 100 times, and the only way I can make sense of it is to believe that she thought I was dead when she wrote it. That's the only possibility I can see. See how she refers to me in the past tense, and talks about wishing I could see the kids grow up, as if that's not a possibility? Then she mentions Michael helping her accept that I was 'gone' and coming to her rescue when the world was falling in, and something about dangers to her and the kids that she needed his help with. She said after that she had to leave everything they ever knew behind them, which sounds like witness protection or something, and then she talks about how she still loves me, even though she and Michael are obviously together."

"Yeah, I caught all that," Sam said. "And you're right, that's about the only interpretation that makes any sense. I'm just trying to figure out how she could possibly have believed that."

"She believed it because it's almost certainly what she was told, and God alone knows what kind of proof she might've been shown. Nowadays, they can use computers to make a picture look any way you want, but back then we had to do things the hard way. I thought it over, and it wouldn't have been all that difficult for Michael to show her pictures of what looked like my dead body, but it wouldn't even really take that. All he'd have had to do would be to hand her a CCL, a Command Condolence Letter. Nobody ever doubted those. When you got one, it meant your husband or father or brother or whatever was dead."

Sam shook his head. "I see your point," he said. "So, you think this guy Michael made it look to her like you were dead, then—what? Talked her into running away with him? Harry, that would mean she never even got to go to your funeral. How can any of this make any sense?"

"Remember the reference to danger? Every spook knows that there's a risk to his family if the wrong people find out who he is; hell, you've gone through that yourself. Some of my missions were under deep cover, which means I stopped being Harry Winslow when the mission was assigned to me, and became somebody else. Some of those, if the people I went up against learned who I really was, Kathy and the kids really would've been in danger. Michael must have told her that I had been exposed and killed, and that he had to get her and the kids into deep cover of their own. Believe me, seeing me put into the ground wouldn't be nearly as important to her as protecting those children."

"Was there a plan for that kind of thing?" Sam asked. "Let's say your cover identity really was compromised, was there some protocol in place to protect your family?"

Harry shook his head. "No, nothing official," he said. "Needless to say, the first thing I did after I saw all this was to find out whatever happened to Michael Watkins, and that was a very interesting trip down memory lane, let me tell you. While I was in Cambodia looking for POWs, old Michael was transferred to the

Foreign Asset Management section, Brazil Division. I remember that he went to Brazil, but after he had just helped me bury my entire family, he wasn't exactly the guy I wanted to exchange Christmas cards with. We lost track of each other—I should say, I lost track of him rather quickly. When I got to digging into this, though, I found out that about six months after he left, he married a woman named Katherine Baker that he met in Brazil. A month later he retired and dropped off the face of the earth."

"So the woman he married, you think, was actually Kathleen in a new identity. He took her and the kids to Brazil as part of some plan to keep them safe? Harry, forgive me, but it just seems odd that your wife would fall for that."

"It's a different world, Sam, boy," Harry said. "People like me had to live with the knowledge that there was always someone out there who wanted us dead. There were at least two dozen loaded weapons hidden around the inside of my house, so that if the day ever came when some of those people tried to take me out, no matter where I was in the house I'd be able to reach a weapon. Kathleen knew where they were, in special hideaways where the kids couldn't reach them. Now, you think about what it would be like for Indie if she had to live like that, and tell me whether protecting that little girl in there might be more important than seeing your body come home in a box."

Sam chewed his bottom lip as he looked off toward the kitchen. "Okay, I'll give you that point." He turned back to look at Harry. "So, here's the big question, Harry. You said you wanted to hire me. What do you want me to do?"

"Well, hell, Sam," Harry said, staring at him. "What would you want if you were in my shoes?"

Sam looked into his eyes for a long moment, then smiled sadly. "I'd want to know if my wife and children were still living, and I'd want to find them."

2

The two men got up and went into the house for breakfast, and Harry made a point of keeping little Kenzie entertained while they ate. As he often did on his rare visits, he had brought her a present: a set of magic tricks that, despite their simplicity, were actually quite amazing when he demonstrated them. Five-and-a-half-year-old Kenzie was fascinated by them, but got even more excited as she began to learn how they worked. She had mastered a couple of them by the time breakfast was over.

Afterward, with Mackenzie safely installed in front of the television, the three adults remained in the kitchen while Harry brought Indie up to speed. Like Sam, she was initially shocked at the thought of a woman who would vanish under such circumstances, but it wasn't long before she was ready to accept it. "It makes sense, Sam, if you think about it," she said. "I love you, but if it came down to being able to say goodbye to you as you were buried or keeping McKenzie safe? I'd be gone just as fast as she was."

"Okay, I get that," Sam said, "but would you take off with my best friend? If you look at the photo of the two of them, they look pretty cozy."

"Look at the letter, Sam," Indie said. "This is a note written by a woman to a husband she believes is dead and gone. She included some photographs that she would have liked to be able to show him, and since the kids are each several years older than when Harry saw them last, it's a safe bet the picture of her and Michael was taken at around the same time. She's had at least a few years of accepting that Harry is gone, and that her life with Michael is not any kind of betrayal, so as far as she's concerned it's all perfectly acceptable. She was, at least as far as she knew, a widow. Do you think she wouldn't get married again someday? Or that she wouldn't accept the very man who, as far as she knows, gave up his own private life to keep her and her children safe?"

Sam nodded. "I see your point," he said. "Take a look at the last line, too. She talked about sending another letter the next month."

"Yes. Basically, these are little short love letters to a husband she lost, the one she never expects to see again, and she probably intended them to go to her children, sooner or later. Maybe she felt they would help them understand just who their father had been."

"That sounds remarkably like her," Harry said. "That's the sort of thing she would think of…"

"All right," Sam said, "then let's use that as our working hypothesis. Now we've got to figure out what questions need to be answered, and the first one that comes to mind is who could have done this? Who would have known enough about the situation to get hold of this letter and realize that it was meant for Harry? It has to be someone who knew both him and Kathleen, and somebody who knew that she thought he was dead, even though he wasn't."

"And then there's the why," Indie said. "Why bring this to Harry now? He hasn't seen his wife or children in more than thirty years, so why would anyone want to open those wounds afresh? Is this just someone being cruel, or is somebody trying to actually put him back in touch with his family?"

"I've been asking myself that question since the moment I found it," said Harry. "Even assuming whoever it was is trying to do something good, here, what sort of person would think this was a kindness? I've spent the last thirty-one years thinking Kathy and the children were dead, for God's sake, and now this? And why isn't there more information, like where I can find them? This is enough to drive an old man mad."

"We'll find out why," Sam said, "when we find out who, and I think that's going to be critical to the actual desired outcome. We want to know if they're still living, and where. Harry, Kathleen was younger than you? How much?"

"Oh, I was thirty-eight when we met, Sam, and she was twenty-two. What's that, sixteen years? She'd just be sixty now. And Michael was only a few years older than she, so he might be sixty-five or so. They could still be together."

"Yeah," Sam said. "But where? I doubt they ever came back to the States, simply because she'd have almost certainly gone to see your grave, and when she didn't find it..."

"It wouldn't mean a thing, Sam," Harry said. "There are always ways to explain something like that. I was buried under my mission identity as part of the plan to protect my family, or maybe I was lost on the mission, my body never recovered. Michael would have known how to handle such things."

"Okay," Indie said, "but what about the fact your name's been in the news off and on? Wouldn't she have noticed that?

Wouldn't she think it odd that there's a Harry Winslow who's the right age doing all the things you've done for the country?"

"Sweetie, my name has made it to the news stories maybe twice in the last ten years, and before that everything I did was classified to the point it could only be denied. It wouldn't be hard to believe she would have missed it, even if she's in the country. She had no family other than me and the kids. Her parents died in a car crash while she was in college, and she didn't have any other relatives. That's part of the reason she got such a high clearance; she wasn't a potential extortion risk because there was no one who could be threatened in order to make her reveal a secret."

"So she had no reason to come back," Sam finished. "That means we need to start looking where she was last known to be, and that sounds like it was in Brazil."

"Rio, in fact," Harry said. "That's where they were when they were married, and that's where Michael took his retirement. I managed to get the address, an apartment on Rua Garibaldi, but there was a notation that mail sent there was being returned only a few weeks later. No forwarding address was ever received by our government."

"Wait a minute," Indie said. "You said he retired; didn't he get a pension or something?"

"Took a lump settlement," Harry said. "Because he only had eight years in, he was allowed to take his pension fund as a single lump payment of sixty-eight thousand dollars and change. In Brazil, that would have lasted a couple of years and let them live pretty well, or he might have put it into some kind of business venture that they could live on." He sighed. "Listen, as much as it hurt to find out my best friend stole my wife and children, there's no doubt in my mind that once he got them, he'd have been a good provider. Michael could blend in anywhere; he could always find a way to make people like him, no matter who they were. We went into Cuba once on an intel-gathering mission and he had the peasants risking their necks to help us. If he took that money and set himself up in business, he probably got rich at whatever it was."

"Okay, that's something to use in looking for them, then." He looked at Harry, then turned to Indie. "What can Herman do to help on this, Babe?"

His wife smiled as she got up. "I was just working out the search parameters I want to feed him. Be right back." She went out to the office and came back a minute later with her laptop and set it on the table. "I'm giving him the names we've got, Michael Watkins and Katherine Baker, and the address on Garibaldi…"

"It's 422B Rua Garibaldi, number 4," Harry said.

"Okay, and what was the last date you can establish him living there?"

"That would have been December 11th, 1986. The wedding was on November 10th."

"Okay, so I'm also searching anything to do with weddings on November 10th, and any reference to Katherine Baker having children, checking on American children in schools in the area…That's all I can think of for now, but more will occur to me as Herman runs." She tapped a couple more keys and then hit the enter button, and the screen started displaying lines of code.

Harry leaned over and looked at it. "What's it doing?" he asked.

Indie smiled sheepishly. "Things that will get me in trouble if he gets caught," she said. "Right now, he's searching for any web-connected databases that are likely to contain information about residents of Rio during 1986. Once he finds one, he uses a hacking routine to get into it and look for information related to the things I just fed him. It takes a little time, but he's a lot more thorough than any human can be. He looks at almost everything that could possibly be relevant, and then checks it against what he knows to see if it's important. The results come up when he's made some progress, but the program keeps running until it either runs completely out of possible sources of data, or I tell it to stop."

Harry shook his head. "Why is it I never recruited you, I wonder? You seem to be doing things our own computer geeks haven't thought of."

"You didn't need me, you had Gary Stone, remember?" Indie asked. "The kid who helped us with the Grayson Chandler thing, in Rome? He's every bit as good as me when it comes to code."

"Yes, but you're smarter than he when it comes to how to use the programs you've written. Never mind, let's just figure out where we begin on this."

Sam grinned at him. "I'm pretty sure we're going to begin in Rio de Janeiro," he said.

Harry nodded his agreement. "Yes, no doubt. You'll need your passport, of course."

"It's good. Let's see what Herman comes up with and we'll figure out when and where to go from there."

"Agreed," Harry said, and the computer chose that moment to chime.

"Okay," Indie said, "let's see what we've got here." The page that opened up on the screen held about a dozen links, each of them titled by a word or phrase that Herman had deemed relevant to the search he was conducting. The very first one read, "Watkins-Baker marriage."

Indie clicked on it, and a web page appeared. It was on the Globo Daily News website, drawn from its archives, and showed a photo of the couple posed without the children.

Senhor Michael Dale Watkins, an immigrant to Brazil from the United States who is now working as a security advisor to Mayor Saturnino Braga of Rio de Janeiro, will wed Dona Katherine Baker on 10 November. Dona Baker is the widowed mother of two children, Harold, aged 3 years, and Elizabeth, aged 2 years.

"That's it," Indie said, "just the announcement, but it tells us where Michael was working at the time. Let me add that to the parameters...And, while I'm at it, this gives me a good photo of their faces to work with, too." She called up a program and used its tool to indicate the features of the two faces, and then entered a command.

She went back to looking through the links Herman had provided, most of which were only references to the one they'd already looked at. After seeing the same story appear for the fourth time, she skipped a couple links, and the next one that came up caused her to pause.

"Um, guys," she said, "you might want to see this one." Harry and Sam both leaned close and looked at the screen.

It was another news story on the same website, dated a month later, and showed a photo of Michael Watkins wearing a suit. "Security Supervisor and Family Killed in Crash," the headline read.

Senhor M. Watkins, Security Supervisor for Mayor Saturnino Braga, was aboard the airplane that crashed at Roberto Marinho Airport on Monday, along with his wife Katherine and their children, Harold and Elizabeth, and the pilot, Jorge Mendes. The airplane suffered the loss of a wing and crashed into an empty hangar, where it exploded, killing all aboard.

Harry stared at the screen for a moment, but then shook his head. "That's another fake death," he said. "The date shows it has to be. We've got the photos of them all alive and healthy at least five or six years after that." He glared at the computer. "What I want to know is why I didn't find that story when I was looking. I was calling in favors from Company researchers who should be able to find anything at all, especially when it's archived on the internet."

"I can tell you that," Indie said. "It's because of relevance. I told Herman to search anything that contained the name Watkins in Rio for that time period. Your people probably searched for the entire name, Michael Watkins. This one didn't use his first name."

"Then they should know to do it your way. Idiots!"

The computer set off another chime just then, and Indie called up the latest page of search results. This time, there were more than fifty links, and she clicked on the first one.

The page was part of a business section of the same newspaper, and showed a slightly different Michael Watkins, with a different nose and darker hair, smiling into a camera and waving a hand toward a building in the background. The building was two stories high and boasted neo-Roman architecture. A sign over the front entrance proclaimed it to be 'Roma de Angelina,' while the story below described it as 'the finest in Italian cuisine to be found in Leblon!'

Senhor Michael Reed is proud to announce the opening of his new restaurant, which he named for his mother. With his wife, Katherine, he hopes to entice the patrons of Leblon to enjoy a dining experience that can only be equaled, they say, by a journey to Rome.

Harry stared at the picture. "There's nothing about Michael Watkins there," he said. "How did you find it?"

Indie shrugged and winked at him. "Facial recognition program. I copied the four best pictures of them and made a few tweaks of my own. When I told Herman to run their faces through it and look for matches, he seems to have found quite a few."

"I'd say so. Is that restaurant still in existence?"

A quick Google search found that it was not, although the building was still standing. It was now owned and occupied by a clothing retailer.

Harry nodded. "What else do we have?"

3

Across the city, a man sat at a folding table in the tiny room he considered his office. Thick fabric had been hung over the windows to prevent any light from escaping, but the only light in the room came from the bank of computer monitors he was facing.

A man's voice coming through the speakers said, *"There's nothing about Michael Watkins there. How did you find it?"*

A female voice replied. *"Facial recognition program. I copied the four best pictures of them and made a few tweaks of my own. When I told Herman to run their faces through it and look for matches, he seems to have found quite a few."*

The man's voice came once again. *"I'd say so. Is that restaurant still in existence?"*

The man at the table, another local private investigator named Frank Hornsby, was reading the transcript that was scrolling across the screen. The transcription program identified the male voice as "Voice 1," a second male voice as "Voice 2," and the female voice as "Voice 3." When it was completed, Frank would use a simple word processor command to replace those labels with the names of the speakers. He knew Sam Prichard, though not well, and had identified the other two voices simply by listening in to their conversation. The woman's name seemed to be Indie, but the other man was the one he was hired to watch for. That was Harry Winslow, and he was being paid quite well to keep tabs on him while he was at Prichard's place, and to report regularly to his employer.

Frank was getting quite a kick out of this job. He was learning an awful lot about surveillance techniques he'd never even known existed before taking it, and one of them was letting him listen in on this particular conversation. A simple program, essentially a virus, had somehow been inserted into almost every electronic device in Prichard's house. His cell phone, his wife's, all of their computers, even their smart TV were transmitting every sound through the Internet into a server which then sent it to one of the computers on Frank's table.

It was a beautiful system. Frank had made it a point of thanking his employer for providing him with them. He had been watching Prichard's household this way for nearly two months already, following his instructions by copying the entire hard drive of Mrs. Prichard's computer and sending daily transcripts of their conversations and activities. His employer had come to visit once during that time, but the money arrived in his bank account every week on schedule. As long as he was getting paid, Frank would continue to do the job.

Thinking of following instructions, he reached over and picked up his cell phone. He tapped the icon that dialed directly to his employer and smiled when the line was answered. "You were right, sir," he said. "Mr. Winslow showed up this morning."

"Of course," his employer said. "And what do you think brought him to Denver?"

"Well, personally I think he's nuts. He's been telling the Prichards this really wild story about how his best friend up and stole his wife thirty years ago by convincing her he was dead. You don't think there's any truth to it, do you?"

"Of course not. This is why we hired you, Mr. Hornsby. When a former espionage asset like Mr. Winslow reaches such an advanced age, the risk of dementia causing him to release classified information is too high to ignore. He's been telling some unusual stories like this off and on for some time now, which is what alerted us to his condition. Just keep me posted on any new developments, especially if Prichard decides to involve himself in any of it."

"Yes, sir," Frank said. "Happy to oblige."

He cut off the call and laid the phone back on the table, then allowed himself a moment to gloat. Everybody knew that Prichard had worked for the Feds a few times, and it seemed like he was some sort of superstar among the PIs in the area. Well, just wait till they found out that the National Security Agency had hired none other than Frank Hornsby to watch Prichard. According to the agent he was working under, there was a lot of suspicion in Washington that Prichard had been manipulating old Winslow for some time. Naturally, that would be a pretty major crime, and required that they find a man of Frank's skills and character to come up with a solution.

Besides, Prichard had only been in the PI game for a couple of years, if that. Frank had been at it for more than three decades, paying his dues by chasing the cheaters and doing the skip traces that were the bread-and-butter of the business. He had come up the hard way, and it was rewarding to know that Uncle Sam had finally noticed just what he was capable of.

Prichard, on the other hand, had blundered into something high-profile in his very first case, finding a missing child and bringing her home safely, and then busting a pretty large drug ring as a result. He'd gotten a lot of good press, something that didn't usually happen to a private eye. That was the reason he got tapped for some of those government jobs, Frank figured. It certainly didn't have anything to do with experience or skills.

That was all right. Now that Frank was working with NSA, the country would be a whole lot safer.

* * * * *

The man who had answered Frank's call tucked his own phone back into a pocket and kept his eyes on the street in front of him. He'd been working on this plan, or at least thinking about it, for more than a year now, and it was all about to come together. Using Frank had been a stroke of genius, he thought. There were a number of private investigators in the Denver area, but he had specifically sought out the one who seemed to be the most disreputable gumshoe of them all.

Frank had given him a sales pitch, claiming to have solved a number of major cases in his career, but the truth was a lot simpler. He was the guy people called on when they thought their spouses were cheating, the one men called when the wife they had abused for so long finally got fed up and ran away. He would tail or track down anyone as long as he was getting paid, and he never let himself be bothered with wondering what might happen after his report was made and delivered. In two cases, women he located for angry husbands had ended up dead, but Frank never felt any remorse. As far as he was concerned, it wasn't up to him to worry about what the clients did with the information they received. His job was just to report it. After all, they didn't hold the carmakers responsible when a drunk driver killed somebody, right?

He was definitely making money on this job. His current client was paying him nearly three times his usual daily rate, and all he really had to do was sit in front of a computer. The machine was doing all the work, but the client considered it well worth the money. When the job was over, hopefully soon, Frank was also the kind of PI whose death wouldn't be considered too great a surprise. Arrangements for his elimination had already been made and paid for, and he thought that they might be implemented rather soon, now. Frank had outlived his usefulness, or he would as soon as Harry made his next move.

He put those thoughts out of his mind and made the turn into the apartment complex that was his destination, then got out of the car and walked into Building A. There weren't any elevators in the old structure, but he took the stairs two at a time and quickly found himself in front of Apartment 214. He knocked twice, then once more, and the door was opened by a man who seemed rather glad to see him.

"I was wondering when you'd turn up again," the man in the apartment said. "We're getting pretty close, so if this is going to happen..."

"It is," said his visitor. "Everything's in place now, should all come to a head in the next few days. I can't say exactly when just yet, but keep yourself at the ready. And, Ron, I want you to know how much I appreciate this."

Ron chuckled, but there was a sarcasm to it. "You don't appreciate it nearly as much as my family does," he said. "As crazy as your little scheme might be, it's been a godsend for us. The worst part of this whole ordeal has been worrying about my kids going hungry, but now they never will."

The visitor watched his eyes for a moment. "You haven't told them anything, have you? I told you, no one can know anything about our arrangement."

Ron shook his head and grinned. "No, no, they don't know anything. In fact, whenever I go to visit them, the wife keeps telling me how much better I look, how well I'm handling it all. It's amazing how much stress you've taken off of me, and I mean that. You've been like a miracle to us. To me."

"Well, you're doing an awful lot for me, too. You're giving me a whole new lease on life, you know? I'm sure this hasn't been the easiest job to cope with, but you're certainly the right man for it. I'm more than happy to pay what it's worth, and if that gives your family the security they need, then it's all been worth it."

Ron nodded. "Definitely worth it on my end," he said. "I don't know if I ever told you, but I was honestly contemplating suicide the day we met. I just didn't know how to handle everything that was happening to me, just couldn't cope with it all. When you told me what you wanted me to do, it was like the weight of the world fell off of my shoulders. This job has been the best thing that's ever happened to me, especially under the circumstances."

"I'm very glad. Listen, it's like I told you, and we may have to move quickly. I thought I'd go ahead and bring the suit over, so when I call you can be ready and dressed for the part." He handed over the suit bag that he had draped over his shoulder as he got out of his car. "It's Armani, so don't let it get messed up between now and then."

Ron took it and pulled the zipper halfway down to look at the suit inside. It was gray and probably one of the finest suits he had ever seen. "No problemo," he said. "Soon as you call, I'll get into it and grab a cab your direction."

"No, no, don't take a cab to the house. Do you know where the Gator House Restaurant is, at Sunset Point and North Fort Harrison? There's a boat dock just across from it; meet me there, and I'll take you over by boat."

"Gator House, yeah. No problemo, just say when."

The visitor smiled. "Sounds good, Ron. We're all paid up for now, right? The most recent payment came through okay?"

Ron nodded enthusiastically. "It sure did, sir, and I'm ready. I'll grant you this job seemed a little odd at first, but with all you're doing for my family, and with me coming up to my own deadline, I'm really quite comfortable with it."

The two men shook hands and the visitor turned to leave. Ron watched him for a moment until he disappeared down the stairs and then closed the door.

The other man got into his car and drove away, heading back to his office. Seeing Ron so seemingly ready to play his part had brightened his day, but he still had work to do. Uncle Sam wanted him to babysit someone on a long trip the next day, but with everything coming together the way it was, he didn't want to be leaving the country. It wasn't that big a problem; he had plenty of people he could assign to the task.

Hell, if he hurried he might even have time for a little fun with the secretary.

4

"One of the things Herman can do that most search-bots can't," Indie had continued, "is learn as he goes. When he found a couple of stories about Michael Reed that had photos of Michael Watkins attached, he added that name to his parameters. I've got a number of small articles that mention the name, but I'm not certain they refer to the same one. There are a couple that are definite, though. Here's one that talks about Reed selling the restaurant in 1990, and another from the same year saying that he and Katherine are proud of Harold, who won some sort of award at school. Unfortunately there are none mentioning him after that, so I'm expanding the search to the rest of Brazil."

"It just amazes me that I couldn't find anything about Reed," Harry said. "One of the things our government is famous for is keeping track of former agents, and Michael went on some very deep missions. There should have been a file on him more than a mile thick, but there was nothing after he got married. I didn't even find the report of his death, and that's just about out of the realm of reasonable possibility. There's no way it wouldn't have been recorded and added to his file."

"What about if he was still working for the government, but under cover?" Sam asked. "Would they have kept that out so he could start a new life under another name?"

Harry looked at Sam for a moment without saying anything, then shook his head. "There should have been at least a mention of his reported death, and possibly even a cross-reference to a new file. No, I get the feeling that Michael had the files laundered. There's always someone in the Company who can do such things, and will if the price is right. That's how I kept getting my files altered, so I could stay on active duty."

The computer chimed. Indie called up the results page and looked at the five links that appeared.

"This first one is a newspaper article from Sao Paulo saying that Reed was just opening another restaurant there. Date is June 16th, 1990. Next, we have an article about the restaurant—it's called Katherine's, by the way—and here's another one saying it was rated the best restaurant for tourists in the city. A few more mention it, always with something about Reed, and there are a couple of photos of him. This restaurant was smaller, but a lot nicer than the one in Rio."

Harry nodded. "As I said, Michael would be some sort of success at anything he chose to do. And he loved to cook, I might add, so I suppose I should not be surprised that he went into restaurants."

"The last article I've got here is dated in August of 1995. He sold out again, and this one says he and his family are moving to Italy, specifically to Rome."

"Scratch Brazil," Sam said. "We need to think about going back to Rome, I guess."

"Don't start packing yet," Indie said. "I'm feeding all this to Herman. I'm gonna tell him to search the whole country, though, cause this guy is slippery. And I'm having him do the facial recognition again, just in case of another name change."

"Harry," Sam said, "if we find them, what are you planning to do?"

"Are you asking me if I'm going to kill Michael, Sam, boy? You can relax on that score. First off, I think the fact that Kathy will find out he lied to her all those years ago will be enough punishment, but even without that, I wouldn't want to put my children through the trauma. It is quite possible they believe he's their father, and they didn't do anything wrong." He ran a hand over his white hair. "As for Kathleen, I really just want to see her and know that she's alive, if she is. I spent most of the last thirty-one years regretting the fact that I never got to say goodbye, you know? I need some closure, I suppose."

* * * * *

Herman was running a much larger search, and it took almost twenty minutes before he chimed. Indie took a look and groaned.

"What's wrong, babe?" Sam asked.

"Nothing," she said. "I mean, Herman got nothing. There are no accessible files related to Reed and family in Italy at all, and no photos of him or her."

"So we're back to square one," Sam said. "Try running just the photo recognition back in Brazil again. Maybe he changed names and stayed in the country."

"I'm already on it," she replied. "I'm running them through Google, so it'll be a worldwide search. Every image you upload anywhere gets indexed, and Herman can look at one in just a few nanoseconds to see if there's a match. Still gonna take a few hours, but we'll see what he finds." She hit the enter key and turned to Harry. "You do know I have to call our moms, right? They'll kill us if they find out you were here and I didn't tell them."

"Bring them on," Harry said. "And invite the old soldier, too, if he's still making the occasional appearance. Maybe he can shed some light on this mystery."

Sam groaned. "Beauregard," he said. "That alter ego of my mother-in-law scares the hell outa me at times, but he certainly can make life interesting."

"And longer," Indie said. "Don't forget how many lives he's saved working with you, including your own!"

"I know," Sam said, "but I still refuse to believe in him, just on principle! I do not believe in ghosts, and especially ones who claim to have known me in a past life, which is something else I just plain don't believe in!"

Indie chuckled at him, as she picked up the phone and dialed. "Hey, Mom? What are you and Grace doing this morning?" She listened for a moment, and then went on. "Well, Sam and I just thought you'd like to know that we've got company. Harry Winslow showed up on our doorstep bright and early, and he'd love to see you both."

She chatted with her mother for a couple of minutes and then hung up the phone. They'd be right over, she reported, and Harry smiled.

The computer suddenly chimed, and Indie looked surprised. "That was awfully fast," she said, but she looked at the results page. "Sometimes, if there's a lot of results coming up, he'll give them to me in groups. Let's see what he's found so far.

Most of the links that came up were from the names being searched, and Indie could dismiss most of them easily. Apparently, there were a number of Michael Reed's in the world, but none of them seemed to be the one she was looking for. She went through about eighty of them in under three minutes, but the next link was to a photograph.

The picture was of both Michael and Kathleen, but they were both noticeably older. Their hair was graying, and there were lines visible in their faces, but they were still quite recognizable. In the photo, they were sitting in the stern of what appeared to be a large sailboat, and smiling happily.

"Hang on," Indie said, "I'm sourcing the photo. Oh, this one came off of MySpace back in 2005. The page itself is gone, but let's try the Way-Back Machine." She went to archive.org and entered the link that had come up in the metadata of the photo.

A copy of the page appeared on the screen, and they were able to read the caption that had been typed under the photo. "Taking the yacht out on her maiden voyage. Cruising down to St. Kitts for the weekend."

"That entry was added on May 20th of 2005, but here's the interesting thing. The page is obviously Kathleen's, but it's not under the name of Katherine Reed. She's going by the name of Kathleen again, Kathleen Reed. I'm seeing a lot of references to Mike, the kind a woman makes to her husband. Hey, here's a photo of both of them, and the caption says she and Mike are going to buy a new car for their daughter, Beth. That one's in June. The last entry I can find is on January 22nd of 2007." She went back to the results page and began scanning the links, then broke into a smile.

"January of 2007, she switched over to Facebook. Here's the page, and it's still active." She turned the computer a bit so that Harry could see it clearly, and he was suddenly looking at a clear photo of Kathleen that had been taken quite recently.

"Oh, dear heavens," he whispered. "How long ago…"

"That selfie was posted a week ago, Harry," Indie said softly. "Look at this." She clicked a link, and the page changed, showing her home location as Clearwater Beach, Florida. A telephone number was displayed, as well. "She's still alive, Harry, but she seems to still be with Michael. There are pictures of the two of them, and she refers to him as Mike now and then."

Harry stared at the screen for several seconds, then looked up at Indie with tears in his eyes. "I came here expecting to be starting a months-long search that might never turn up any real results," he said, "and you found her in a matter of minutes. I don't how to thank you, Indiana." He looked back at the screen.

"Harry," Sam said softly, "What are you going to do?"

The old man looked at him and smiled. "Why, Sam, boy, I'm going to burden you with my lazy presence for a few hours, so that I can come to grips with this incredible turn of events, and then I'm going to go to Florida and see my wife." He turned back to Indie. "Is there any mention of the children?"

"Well, let's scan her posts," Indie replied. "There are a lot of mentions of a daughter named Beth and a son named Harold. Harold Reed and Beth Reed, and Beth is short for Elizabeth, no doubt. Each name is linked to a profile, so…" She clicked on one of the links to Beth, and they were suddenly looking at the profile of a lovely woman in her early thirties, surrounded by four kids who looked as though they ranged from about ten to mid-teens. There were three girls and a boy, and the boy seemed to be the eldest.

"Great jumping Jehoshaphat," Harry said with his eyes wide, "I've got grandchildren! Does it tell their names?"

Indie laughed out loud. "Well, I'm just looking through the things she's posted," she said, "but it looks like the boy is Reggie, then there's Vicki, Susie and Danielle. Last name for all of the kids is Jacobs, and that's her name, too." She smiled over at Harry. "Elizabeth grew up into a fine woman, Harry."

"She sure did," he said. "Any sign of a husband?"

"Well, I don't see one mentioned. Wait, here's a reference to the kids going to spend a week with their father, so it sounds like maybe she's divorced."

Harry shrugged, but he was still grinning. "That's the world we live in today," he said. "What about Harold?"

Indie popped back to Kathleen's page and clicked on a link to Harold. His page came up, but there was very little information on it. Most of the photos were of cars and motorcycles, but there were a few that showed a man who looked the way Indie figured Harry must've looked when he was younger. Some of the older photos included shots of him in a Navy uniform.

"It looks like he's living in Largo," Indie said. "Elizabeth, or Beth, is in Florida, too, in Tampa."

Harry was nodding his head. "Well, naturally, I can't wait to see them," he said, "but I think it should wait until after I've spoken with their mother. I'm not sure how well that's going to go over, you understand."

Sam nodded his head. "Yeah, that might be intense," he said. "It's definitely going to be a shock to her, and probably to Michael. From the look of things, he's gone to great lengths to cover his tracks, trying to make sure you couldn't track them down."

"Did a hell of a job of it, too, didn't he? All the resources of the Department of Homeland Security, and I couldn't even find a picture of him after he left the Company. If our government had anything comparable to Herman, we might be a viable player in the field of cyber intelligence. As it is, I think we're just a big joke."

Indie motioned for Harry to pull his chair closer to hers, and helped him navigate through the various Facebook pages. Gradually, Harry learned that his daughter had been divorced for the past three years, and that she wrote young adult novels for a living and loved taking her kids to visit her parents now and then. Harold, they found, had spent twelve years in the Navy as an airframe mechanic, serving several tours on aircraft carriers. Since receiving an honorable discharge, he had turned his mechanical aptitude to restoring antique automobiles and motorcycles. He was still single, but there were quite a few posts about his live-in girlfriend, whose name was Janine. The two of them had one child together, a three-year-old boy named Christopher.

They were still perusing the pages when Grace and Kim came in, and both of them hurried to the old man who had so often helped to protect them and their children. Fortunately, Harry enjoyed being hugged.

5

Harry had decided to let the ladies in on his situation, so Indie let them take over the table with Harry and Sam while she got up to make lunch. She was interrupted periodically when Harry asked her to show them one picture or another, but she didn't mind. There was something in the way Harry was acting that made her feel good. It was like he had been on the verge of giving up on life, but suddenly had a reason to keep living.

Of course, a lot of that would depend on how Kathleen reacted. If they were right in their suspicion that she didn't know Harry was alive, then she probably wouldn't have any objection to him making contact with their children. On the other hand, there was always the possibility that she would want to avoid that contact, rather than have the children find out what their stepfather had done. Little Kenzie's father had died some years before, and she wasn't sure how she would feel if he suddenly turned up alive today. Kenzie never actually knew him, and Sam was the only daddy she'd ever had, as far she was concerned. Trying to explain the truth now, even without all of the backstabbing drama of Harry's situation, could confuse the child to no end.

"Oh, God," she suddenly heard Grace say, and she turned quickly to see what was going on. Her mother was swaying in her chair, with her eyes closed and her head thrown back. This was a sure sign that Beauregard was about to drop in for a visit.

Kim suddenly stopped swaying and brought her head up, opening her eyes and looking straight at Harry.

"Hello, old buddy," Kim said in a voice that sounded a lot like Harry's own. "Good to see you again."

Harry grinned and nodded hello. "Beauregard," he said. "It's been a little while."

Sam was rolling his eyes, but Harry held up a hand to shush him before he could say anything. "What brings you out, Beauregard?" Harry asked.

"This whole mess of yours. I was listening in, hope you don't mind, and it suddenly dawned on me that I know a little bit about this. It's not much, you understand, but it could be important."

"I'm listening," Harry said. "Go ahead."

"Well, it's good you get to see your wife and little ones again, but you need to understand that not every story has a happy ending. I don't know how this will all turn out, but it's not going to be an easy one. I think you're going to get what you want, but it's going to be up to Sam to make sure you live long enough to enjoy it."

Kim turned her face to look at Sam, who was staring at her with his own eyes wide. "Samuel, you're going to play some poker, but each hand you lose is going to cost a life. I wish I could tell you more, but that's all I can see."

"Whose lives are we talking about?" Sam demanded, but Kim's eyes had slowly fallen closed again. Her head fell forward as if she was dozing off, then snapped upright. She blinked as she looked around, then quickly looked at Grace.

"Beauregard?"

"Oh, God, yes," Grace said. "He said Sam has to keep Harry alive, and he's got to play poker to save other lives!"

Kim blinked a couple of times. "Poker?"

"Metaphorically, I'm sure," Harry said. "As for keeping me alive, Sam, that could have many meanings. At my age, it could simply mean keeping your phone ready to call 911 if I'm overwhelmed."

"Or it could mean your old pal Michael is still dangerous," Sam shot back. "After all, Harry, we're talking about a man who stole your wife and kids right out from under your nose, in a way. He made each of you believe the other was dead for decades, and he's been enjoying them as if they were his own family for all these years. He may put up a fight."

Harry looked at Sam with a sadness that made him look even older for a moment. "He won't have anything to fight, Sam," he said at last. "The evidence of his sins will be standing before him. I can't imagine that Kathy will accept what he's done without shock and anger. Even if she loves him today, this will mean a betrayal of the deepest kind, and women don't handle betrayal well."

"But it could be," Kim said softly, "if she does love him, she might see your sudden return as a danger to the life she's lived all these years, too. She might not want to put the kids through it, Harry."

"I've considered that possibility," Harry said. "I'm afraid I'm not going to leave that choice to her, for that reason. I may be willing to refrain from taking any action against Michael, if that is what she wishes, but I want at the very least to come to know my children, and for them to come to know me, if they're willing."

Sam sighed. "Okay," he said. "I'm with you. How do you want to handle it, Harry?"

Harry grinned, and looked a bit more like his old self. "Well, I need a little bit of time to process this," he said, "and I think it might be wise to at least look into the legal ramifications, but I expect we'll leave tonight sometime for Florida."

"Okay, that sounds good," Sam said, "but I meant, how do you want to handle letting Kathleen know that you're still alive, and that she was lied to all these years. That doesn't seem like the sort of thing you do on a phone call, but it might be too much of a shock to her if you just ring her doorbell, don't you think?"

"He's got a good point," Grace said. "She's how old now?"

"She's sixty."

"I'm getting close to that, and I can tell you it's no picnic! Doctors are always talking about slowing down, watching your heart, all that stuff. She answers the door to find a ghost standing there, it could be too much for her."

"She's strong," Harry said. "And I need to see her face when she realizes it's me, I'm afraid. As much as it appears she didn't know I was alive, I have to see her face to be certain. Can you understand that? I have to know."

There was silence at the table for several seconds, and then Indie laid a hand on his shoulder. "Of course we do," she said softly. "And we're with you, Harry."

The conversation turned then to the legal ramifications Harry had mentioned, and he took out his phone. He scrolled through the contacts for a moment until he found the number he wanted, then hit the send button. He waited a moment, and then grinned.

"Jared, you old goat," he said. "Harry Winslow...Fine, but I got kicked out, you know. Seems they got upset about me fudging my date of birth to remain on active duty longer than allowed. Yeah, but I know where too many bodies are buried, they're not about to try to prosecute me. Listen, I've got a situation, and I need the kind of legal advice I can only get from someone as despicable as you. Well, it's like this..."

Harry told Jared, who was a lawyer used by Homeland Security when their actions appeared to overstep the bounds of the law and their authority, about what they had uncovered, and how convoluted it seemed to be. When he was finished, the lawyer asked several questions, then said he'd call back in an hour. Harry thanked him and ended the call.

"Now I wait," he said. "Hey, did I hear something about lunch?"

Indie laughed. "I'm working on it," she said. "Leftover roast beef from Sunday's dinner, okay? Mashed potatoes and gravy, and I'm heating up some corn to go along with it. Mom, you want to make some tea, please?"

Kim got up to help her daughter, and Grace reached across the table and put a hand on one of Harry's. "Listen, Harry, I know you're going through a rough time," she said, "but if there's anything I can do, just let me know."

"Why, thank you, Grace," Harry replied. "I do appreciate it. At this point, though, I'm still just trying to come to grips with the fact I've been a fool all these years. I recall at the funeral, something was telling me that it wasn't right, that my family wasn't dead, but I didn't listen. If I had, maybe things would have gone a different way."

"Yeah," Sam growled, "you'd have ended up dead!"

"Dead? How do you figure that, Sam?"

"Simple. You had Michael telling you that your entire family had died in a house fire, right? Thing is, he knew it wasn't true because he already had them stashed away somewhere safe in Brazil or someplace. He couldn't run the risk of Kathleen finding out what he'd done, that would mean full exposure and probably get him a long term in prison, so if you had refused to accept what he told you, he would have been forced to kill you to protect himself. And if you'd gotten to Kathleen before he could stop you, he probably would have killed her and the kids, too."

Harry's eyes took on a sadness again. "I don't want to believe that, Sam, boy," he said slowly, "but you're probably right. Good Lord, he could be just as dangerous today. Perhaps that's what Beauregard meant about you keeping me alive."

"Could be, and I'm going with that for the moment. I'm your bodyguard for the next few days, 'til we see how the dust is going to settle on this mess. Agreed? You'll duck when I yell?"

"You can count on it, Sam," Harry said. "After all, I came to you for help, didn't I?"

Lunch was ready a few minutes later, and they all sat down to eat. Sam had to go to the garage and bring in the two extra chairs so there would be enough, and Harry was on the phone when he came back in.

"Yes, Jared," Harry was saying. He listened for a moment, then interrupted the lawyer. "Jared, wait a minute," he said. "I'm with a private investigator friend of mine who'll be working with me on this, and I want him to hear what you're saying. I'm going to put you on speaker." He poked the speaker icon, and set the phone on the table. "All right, say that again, please."

Jared seemed to take a deep breath. "I've been saying that there is no legal action that can be taken against Michael Watkins at this time, because the federal statute of limitations would apply. There is nothing about this case that would negate the statute. Harry can file a civil suit for being deprived of his family, but there are no criminal charges that can be brought against Watkins after so many years."

"Wait," Sam said, "what about kidnapping? He took Harry's children completely out of the country, and kidnapping has no statute of limitations."

"Actually, Watkins didn't kidnap them. The children left the country in the company of their mother, who almost certainly would have thought she was taking them away for their own protection. Since she thought Harry was dead, we can't even say that she wasn't within her rights to do so. And since Watkins was not a beneficiary of any of the life insurance Harry collected, there isn't any fraud charge that can be brought against him over faking their deaths."

"Changing their names and faking his own death? What about that?"

"Watkins is a former field agent of the CIA," Jared said. "As Harry can tell you, there are situations when such a person can change his or her identity with impunity, and it's likely he'll have set up one of those situations to cover his ass on this."

"Okay, then what about the remains found in the ashes?" Sam asked. "There were apparently some bodies there. Would there be any applicable charges from that?"

"Not unless there is evidence that Watkins actually murdered whoever they were in order to place them there. The only charge that might stick in this case would be a murder charge, but then only if we can prove he killed or arranged the killing of the people whose bodies were found. I'm sorry, but that's just how it is."

Sam shook his head, and Harry thanked Jared and said goodbye.

"Well, isn't that just ducky," Sam said. "I guess we just need to go and take this head on, Harry, but the way it looks so far, it stinks to high heaven."

"Doesn't it, though?" Harry asked.

6

Harry, it turned out, had flown in from DC late the night before, and had simply hung out at a coffee shop until he figured they'd be awake and caught a taxi to their home. By the time lunch was over, the lack of sleep was showing. Indie overruled his arguments and led him upstairs to their guest room, threatened to undress him herself if he didn't cooperate, and then left him alone. When she checked on him ten minutes later, he was snoring peacefully.

She went back down to Sam and their mothers, who were all playing Old Maid with Kenzie. The little girl was winning, and all three adults swore she was cheating, which only made Kenzie laugh. Indie convinced her that they should all watch a movie instead, and they moved to the living room.

As *Turbo* played on the TV for the fiftieth time, Sam and Indie snuggled in his overstuffed recliner and talked about Harry's problem.

"Sam," Indie began, "I'm worried. As much as I know you hate Beauregard, he's usually right and you know it. This thing about playing poker for people's lives is scary."

"I know," Sam said. "The thing that frustrates me most about that old soldier is that he's always so vague. If he'd say things clearly enough to make sense, it'd help a lot." He sighed deeply, and Indie caressed his face in sympathy. "The only way I can take the first part, about keeping Harry alive, is to assume that Michael is gonna be a problem. Even if they can't prosecute him for what he did back then, what's to keep him from trying to blame it all on Harry?"

"On Harry? How could he, he's the one who lied to Kathleen..."

"I've been thinking about it, trying to figure out how I'd handle it if I were in his shoes, and if I was that kind of liar. Seems to me the only move he could make would be to try to convince Kathleen that Harry put him up to it. If Harry had told him he wanted out of his life, for example, and gave Michael an outline of how to pull it off, then old Michael might claim he saw it as a chance to find his own happiness. All he'd have to do is swear up and down that Harry threatened him if he ever told the truth, and with Harry's reputation back then, a threat like that would be one to take seriously. It's possible Kathleen would believe him, and turn against Harry."

"I guess that's possible," Indie said. "Or it could be even more subtle than that. We don't know who put that letter in Harry's apartment; what if Michael arranged it? Sent it to Harry to make him do exactly what he's doing, then just follow him or lay in wait until he shows up and shoot him as a stalker or something?"

"The problem with that would be that Harry's body would be identified, so Kathleen would find out. That would start the whole thing Michael wants to avoid..."

"Yes, but then he can use the scenario you came up with. Harry wanted out of his marriage, Harry gave me the whole plan, Harry convinced me I should be with you, et cetera. If Harry showed up after all these years and Michael said he was being threatening, she might fall for it, then. It'd be a lot easier to convince her with Harry dead and unable to deny it, right?"

Sam looked at his wife and, not for the first time, was thankful she hadn't decided to go into a life of crime. With her brains, she'd have been a criminal mastermind unlike any the world had ever known. "You do have a point," he said. "This is going to be a mess, I know that. I wish there was a way to know in advance what's going to happen." He cocked his head to one side and looked at her again. "What about Herman? Could he find anything that might give us some idea of what Michael is like nowadays?"

Indie blinked, then jumped off him and hurried to the kitchen. She grabbed her laptop off the counter and brought it back, crawled onto him again and started typing. "I'm just going to go after him for a full background check, the way we would any other suspect. We saw what Kathleen talks about on Facebook and such, so I'll set Herman to look for any posts by Michael Reed, so we can see what kinds of things he puts out for the world to see. We should be able to track down his email address, and then Herman can hack his way into it. Between all of those, we should be able to get a picture of what kind of man he's turned into."

"Go for it," Sam said, and Indie hit the enter key.

The computer program that was Herman began crunching data, and Sam let his attention be caught by the movie for a moment while they waited, and found himself laughing softly at "the

White Shadow." He returned his attention to the computer when it chimed a moment later.

"Sam," Indie said, "this is weird."

"What?" he asked, and she turned the computer so he could see the screen. There was a page from the National Security Agency website displayed, and it contained a warning that the person viewing it was not authorized to access the information requested.

"One of the things Herman always looks for is hidden links, because a lot of people—especially black hats and criminal types—try to hide things that way. He found a post Michael made to a message board about yachting," she said, "and when I clicked it, this came up."

Sam scowled. "That means he's still connected to the government, and that link must be some sort of hidden access to something they use. What about other links?"

She clicked the back button and chose another one. It opened up to a website for Gulfwind Yachts, a company that sold luxury boats ranging from thirty-foot sailboats to five hundred million-dollar private ships that need a crew of fifty just to go from one place to another. Michael Reed was listed on the front page as the Sales Manager, and the bio with the photo said he'd been in the business for eight years. There was a whole list of awards he'd won for Sales Excellence.

She went back and clicked on another. This one led to a Facebook post, with a picture of Michael standing in front of a motorcycle. Harold was standing beside him, and they were both grinning at the camera.

Look what I got for my birthday, the post said. *Harry found this old Indian rusting away in a barn and completely restored it for me. What an awesome kid!*

"He obviously gets on well with them all," Sam said. "This is going to come as a shock to the whole family, I'm sure."

"Yeah," Indie said, going back and clicking on another link.

This one led to a news story. There was a photo of Michael, as Michael Reed, standing in front of two policemen.

Michael Reed of Clearwater Beach was arrested early this morning after police were summoned to the home of his daughter, Elizabeth Reed Jacobs. Ms. Jacobs had called police after an altercation with her former husband, Daniel, but they arrived to find Daniel unconscious and Michael Reed standing over him. Paramedics were called, and Daniel told police that Reed had assaulted him while he was trying to talk to his ex-wife. Ms. Jacobs denied his version of events, saying that Daniel had threatened her with his fists as Reed arrived, and that her father had intervened. The resulting fight left Jacobs with non-life-threatening injuries. Reed was taken to the county jail, where he was released on his own recognizance.

Indie looked at Sam. "That sounds like he's got a violent streak," she said.

"Or a protective one," Sam said. "I'd probably react the same way if I saw a man threatening my daughter. What else?"

The next link was to another blog post on a yachting site, but it went directly to the actual page it was supposed to. The post was about his Beneteau Oceanis forty-six-foot sailboat, and was posted in answer to another person's question about the vessels. Michael wrote that the boat was the best he'd ever owned, and that he'd sailed it throughout the Caribbean for the past seven years. It required far less maintenance than other boats he was familiar with, and was always comfortable for his family, including kids and grandkids.

"Hmpf," Sam said. "He definitely loves boating, doesn't he."

"Well, he was Navy at one time or another. Makes sense, I guess."

There were no other links that indicated any kind of violence in his nature, but Sam was bothered most by the link that had redirected to the NSA site. Indie suggested letting Herman try to find a way inside, to see what kind of thing Michael might be involved in with them, but Sam didn't like the idea. "The last thing we need is for the NSA to spot you trying to get into their clandestine site," he said. "That could get pretty ugly real fast."

Indie rolled her eyes. "Sam, do you know how many times I've hacked the NSA? Herman won't get caught, even if they see him trying to get in. I wrote some of the most comprehensive defensive subroutines that have ever existed; if he's spotted, he starts backing out and leaving smokescreens all over the place, and since he goes through more than forty different ghost servers along the way, it's impossible to track us back to here. Trust me, Sam, he can get in there! Whatever Michael's up to with the government, Harry needs to know about it!"

Sam tried to get another word in, but Indie wasn't having it, so he finally threw his hands into the air and gave in. She spent the next forty minutes typing, as Sam watched the conclusion of the movie that saw a snail become one of the fastest racers in the world.

"It's gonna take a while," Indie said when she finally finished, "but sometime tomorrow I'll know what that back door leads to.

If you and Harry leave tonight, I can call you as soon as I get it, okay?"

"I'm betting he'll want to leave as soon as he's up," Sam said, "so I think I should go and get packed now. My gut says he isn't going to wait until later tonight." They climbed out of the chair and left Kenzie explaining the movie to her grandmothers while they went to the bedroom.

Indie grabbed Sam's favorite carry-on from the closet while he got out his Glock and checked it over. He loaded three extra magazines and slipped them into one of the big pockets on the bag, then added a box of ammunition. The gun itself went into a holster that would be clipped to his waistband and hidden under a light jacket.

Sam still had valid DHS credentials, which would allow him to carry the weapon even on a commercial airplane. Harry's, on the other hand, would have recently been revoked, since he was retired. The old man could probably handle a gun better than ninety-nine percent of the population, but he wouldn't be allowed to take one on an airliner.

There were some things, Sam felt, that just shouldn't be allowed to happen as you got old.

Forcible retirement was one of them. As long as a man could contribute to the field he had chosen, he should be allowed to do so, in Sam Prichard's opinion.

Indie took charge of packing his clothes, so Sam went to his office and dug out the little Kel-Tec P-32 Harry had once given him. The little gun was light but powerful, and had the added benefit of having been fitted with a silencer that cut its noise down to barely above the sound of an asthma inhaler. The silencer was both thicker and longer than the gun itself, but if it came down to a need for a stealth shot, Sam would trust it over any other gun he'd ever used. He dismounted the silencer and shoved it into his shaving kit, then added the pistol to the pocket with his extra magazines and ammo. Two extra seven-round mags and a box of .32 ACP for the P-32 went in, as well. He could slip the gun to Harry later.

A noise caught his attention and he stuck his head out of the bedroom. Harry had just come down the stairs and was looking for him.

"Down here, Harry," Sam called out, and the old man turned toward him and smiled.

"I suspect you might be anticipating me," he said when he came into the room and saw the bag on the bed. "I'm afraid I can't seem to stay asleep, so I think we might as well start planning on leaving this afternoon."

"Yeah, I figured," Sam said. "Indie and I thought you'd feel that way, so we went ahead and packed my stuff."

Harry smiled sadly. "Does it make sense to you, Sam," he asked slowly, "that a part of me dreads this journey? As much as I have missed Kathy and the kids all these years, I've at least known where I stood and who I was. Now, I'm not so certain anymore. Will this trip give me peace and answers, or will it cause me to doubt who I've been for so long?"

Sam shook his head. "Harry, I can't imagine what you must be going through," he said. "To me, this would be the worst nightmare I could ever have, and I don't know if I could handle it at all, let alone as well as you're doing. Don't look to me for advice or opinions on this one; I wouldn't know what to say."

Harry nodded. "Of course, Sam," he said, "but at least I know I've got the best man possible at my side."

"Thanks," Sam said, "but I'm no Navy SEAL or secret agent, which reminds me. While you were sleeping, Indie and I tried to find out a bit more about your old buddy Michael, what he's like these days, and we stumbled across something interesting. There was a hidden link in something he posted on a yachting board that turned out to be some kind of back door into the NSA website. Indie's got Herman working on finding out what it's for, but it'll take a while. Maybe a day or so."

Harry's eyes became brighter suddenly, but they didn't actually register surprise.

"So," he said, "the bastard's still running with the spooks, is he?" He was silent for a moment, then grinned at Sam. "Sam, it could mean anything, but I have a feeling, a gut feeling, that we may have just stumbled upon the first hand of that poker game Beauregard mentioned. Play your cards close to your vest, Sam, and don't be afraid to bluff if you have to."

7

Sam had expected to have to book a flight, but Harry surprised him. "I didn't want to have to fight with airline security," he said, "and the TSA is a royal pain to anyone who ever worked in intelligence, so I chartered a private jet. It's not one of the really big ones, just a six-passenger job, but it'll get us there. A lot faster than a Delta flight, too, by the way."

"Harry, I know you said you're not hurting for money, but isn't that a bit over the top? A private jet can't be cheap."

"No, they're not, but the owner is an old friend who owes me a favor or two. I've got it for a week, and all he's charging me is the operating costs. It's not as bad as you might think." He took out his phone and called the pilot, who agreed to have the plane fueled and ready by four that afternoon.

Sam told Indie they'd be leaving at three, and she insisted on getting some pictures of them all together in the backyard before then. Harry was delighted to sit with little Kenzie on his lap in her swing, with Sam and Indie standing alongside him while Grace and Kim took the photos, and then he demanded one with the two older ladies, as well. Grace and Kim both giggled and blushed, but then they got into a minor fracas about who got to stand on which side. Indie settled it by grabbing her mother and putting her on Harry's left, while Grace stood on his right.

Neither of them was silly enough to argue, and the picture came out fine.

Once the pictures and the goodbyes were over, Sam and Harry climbed into the Corvette and drove away. It was a twenty-mile drive to the airport, but Sam knew how to avoid the busiest roads and got them there in less than forty minutes. The small jet and its crew would be waiting, Harry had told him, on the tarmac beside the terminal, and they were able to find a parking spot in the long-term lot that was not too far away.

Sam carried both bags slung over his shoulder, despite Harry's protests, and they made good time. His hip was giving him a little trouble, probably because the sky was so overcast, but he simply leaned a little harder on his cane and ignored it, as usual.

"Mr. Winslow," said the pilot as they got to the plane. "We're ready to go as soon as you're on board."

"Thanks, Sam," Harry said, then pointed at his companion. "This fellow is also a Sam," he said. "Sam Prichard, meet Sam Kilgore, our pilot. If you need someone to hustle a plane around the sky, Kilgore's the best there is. And Sam Prichard is the best private detective I've ever known. You guys ought to trade phone numbers or something, find a way to keep in touch. Never know when one of you might need the other one!"

Sam and Sam laughed, but then swapped business cards. The co-pilot, Jerry Wolford, took the bags from Sam and carried them inside while Sam and Harry climbed up the small flight of steps that folded down.

The hatch was closed, and the flight crew went into the cockpit. A moment later they heard the sound of the starter motor whining on the left engine, and once it had caught and was running smoothly, the left one fired up. Kilgore's voice came over a speaker in the ceiling.

"All right, gentlemen," he said, "we're going to taxi out to the runway now. We're number four for takeoff, so we'll be in the air in about five minutes. Seat belts on, please, and stay put 'til we level off, then there's soft drinks and snacks in the cooler up here by the cockpit."

Sam and Harry were sitting on opposite sides of the small craft, so they each had a window. They watched out through them as the plane made its way out to the runway, and a few minutes later they were pressed back into their seats as the plane accelerated and launched itself into the air.

Sam loved to watch the city recede as a plane took him up into the sky, so he watched it for the brief few minutes before they were too far away to see any more, then turned to Harry. He started to say something, but then realized that the old man was asleep again, so he leaned back in his seat and smiled.

The flight lasted just under four hours, but with the time zone factored in, it was almost nine PM by the time they landed. Harry had awakened as they descended, and Sam wondered if it was something that came from all the flying he must have done in his years of service.

"Absolutely," Harry said when he asked. "We all learn it, eventually. Rest while the plane is on the way, then make sure you're wide awake by the time it's on the ground again, because you can't be sure what kind of welcome you're going to get. Been more than once I got off a plane ducking, because someone really objected to my arrival."

"Well, hopefully we won't run into that this time," Sam said. "And that reminds me..." He picked up his bag from the seat in front of him and withdrew the Kel-Tec. "Brought along a friend for you," he said as he handed it and the spare loaded magazines to Harry. The old man looked at it for only a second before making it vanish into an inside pocket of his jacket. The mags went into another one, and he didn't look at all like he was carrying a weapon.

"What's the plan, Harry?" Sam asked as they disembarked and walked toward the car rental agencies near the front of the terminal building.

"Well, a part of me wants to go straight to their house, get it all over with, you know? Another part says we should do this fresh in the morning. What do you think, Sam?"

"Tomorrow morning would suit me better," Sam said, "but I can understand your need to get some kind of closure. It's your call, Harry. You tell me."

Harry let out a sigh that sounded even older than he was. "Tomorrow morning, then," he said. "I want to get some rest tonight and get up early, though. I want this face to be the very first thing they see when they open the door in the morning."

They rented a Buick Enclave and Sam googled directions to a local motel. By ten o'clock, they were checked into a room and Sam was on the phone with Indie.

"Any news on Herman?" he asked.

"Nothing yet," she replied, "but I can tell you that whatever it is, it's buried pretty deep. Herman's gone through a few dozen proxies already, so there's no telling where the server is located. Could literally be anywhere."

"And it could be tied to just about anything. Are you sure it can't be traced back to you, if they see Herman trying to get in?"

"Yes, babe, I'm sure," Indie said, and he could hear the grin. "Herman takes good care of me, he won't let anyone trace him back home. But while I've got you on the phone, I did think of something else, and it didn't take long to find what I was looking for."

"Okay," Sam said. "And what was that?"

"Well, when we were looking at Michael earlier, I didn't think about maybe running a similar background check on Kathleen, because we've been thinking of her as another victim in all of this, right? So I started one, just to see if there's anything you and Harry ought to know, and I found something interesting. Kathleen has a habit of taking trips without Michael, and she's been doing it under her daughter's name. I can tell it's her, because the trips happen at times when Beth is somewhere else, and the ID she's using has Kathleen's picture on it, rather than her daughter's. She's been making these trips for about a year and a half, at least, and always when he's out of town on business, like when he has to go somewhere to deal with a big boat sale."

Sam grinned into the phone. "You're not gonna suggest we start taking separate vacations, are you?"

"No, butthead," she said, but he could hear the giggle. "No, the thing is, she always goes to the same place. Care to take a guess where?"

"Um...Disney World?"

Indie sighed. "You could have at least tried, Sam," she said. "No, she goes to Annapolis, Maryland. Sam, that's where Harry lives, and guess where she was at last weekend."

Sam looked over to where Harry was flopping around and trying to get comfortable. "I'm going with the same place, right?"

"Yes. She flew in on a Delta flight last Friday evening and came back on United Monday night. That was the day Harry was told he was out, Sam. And it was the day that envelope was left in his apartment."

"Okay," Sam said. "Let me think about this for a bit, and I'll decide what to do with it." They talked for a few minutes more, most of it in romantic whispers, and then Sam hung up the phone and turned to Harry to tell him what Indie had found, but Harry hadn't waited for an update; he was snoring.

Sam smiled and got ready for bed. It was actually still a little early for him, since it was only around eight back home, but he felt like he could stand a little extra sleep.

The alarm Sam had set on his phone woke him at six-thirty local time in Florida, and he sat up to find Harry already awake and in the shower. Sam waited until he finished, thinking over his conversation with Indie the night before, but the cold light of morning made it seem that her trips to Annapolis were coincidental. She was probably going there to visit a friend, or for some purpose completely unrelated to Harry. That had to be it, Sam thought, for surely if she knew the truth, she would have actually made contact with him rather than break into his apartment and leave a single letter from years before.

He couldn't bring himself to say anything to Harry, to get his hopes up that she was reaching out to him. The mystery of the way the letter had been left was just too vague. When the old man came out, he smiled at him as he went to take care of his own morning necessities, and then the two of them went to the continental breakfast room for waffles and coffee.

"I've often said," Sam said as they ate, "that waffles should be considered their own food group. I mean, they've got to be the most nourishing and energizing breakfast food there is, right? And they must have existed in the wild at some point, because I can tell you that my nose came from some ancestor that evolved to hunt them. I can smell a waffle from a mile away, even inside a closed vehicle with the air running and moving at forty miles an hour."

Harry laughed. "Well, I'm not sure about hunting them in the wild," he said, "but I'll concede they're about the best thing you can eat when you're on the road. I've eaten waffles in just about every country I've ever been to, can you believe that? Even some of the best hotels in the Ukraine serve them at one time of day or another." He pushed the last bite of his waffle into his mouth, then grinned at Sam. "I think I'll have another."

It was close to seven-thirty by the time they checked out and got into the Buick. Sam hadn't called Indie yet, because it would have been only four-thirty back home, but he figured she'd call him as soon as Herman gave her anything to report. For the moment, he was merely steeling himself for whatever the coming confrontation might bring.

Sam googled the address Indie had found and poked the icon for directions, and they took off. The ride was shorter than he'd expected, and it was only a quarter of seven by the time he pulled onto Bay Esplanade where it met Iris Street. A moment later, he parked in front of a beautiful Spanish-style house, with white stucco walls and red tile roof. They got out of the car and made their way slowly up the curved walkway, and then Harry reached out and rang the doorbell.

How many ways can a man prepare himself to see someone he thought was dead for so many years? Sam wondered. Harry seemed completely at ease, but Sam suspected he was trembling underneath. After so many years of playing one part after another, though, it was probably second nature to him to put his emotions on hold while he assessed a situation.

The door was opened after only a minute, and a lovely woman with dark hair stood there. For a moment her face bore a smile of welcome, but then there was a sudden transformation to surprise, and her mouth made a perfect "O" as she stared at Harry.

"Hello, Kathleen," Harry said. "It's been an awfully long time."

8

"Oh, dear God," Kathleen whispered. "How in the world did you find me?"

Harry's smile faltered a bit, and he cocked his head to one side as he stared at the face that had held the highest place in his memory for more than three decades. "That's odd," he said. "I would've expected something more on the lines of, 'Harry, you're alive?' Never would have thought of 'How the hell did you find me?' Tell me, is Michael here?"

She swallowed a couple of times, then shook her head. "No," she said. "He had to leave early this morning for Japan, and won't be back until next week." She shook herself, and then stepped back a pace. "Would you like to come in? I'm sure you have a lot of questions."

"I do," Harry said, watching her closely as he stepped into her home. Sam followed him, keeping his eyes open, and she closed the door, then led them into the large living room. She invited them to sit on a white leather sofa, and asked if they'd like coffee. Both of them declined.

"Well," she said softly. "Where would you like to begin?"

"The truth is always a good place," Harry said. "I need to know, Kathy—did you know that I thought you were dead all these years?"

She looked him directly in the eye and shook her head. "Not all along, no," she said. "I only found out you were alive a couple of years ago, when I saw a news story about the terrorists who tried to set off a nuclear bomb in Lake Mead. It mentioned 'Homeland Security Station Chief Harry Winslow,' and my first thought was that it was an awfully wild coincidence. But then I saw a photo, and I knew instantly that it was you."

Harry's eyes were sad. "And you didn't contact me?"

Kathleen's own eyes suddenly went wide. "Contact you? Harry, I didn't dare! Michael—Michael was right here beside me when I saw the news, and I turned around to ask him what the hell was going on, and that's when he told me everything. He told me he'd faked everything about you dying, because he said you didn't really love me or the kids, and how he faked our deaths so you wouldn't ever look for us. He told me that Russian death squads had killed you in Cambodia, Harry, and that they'd broken your cover and were going to come for me and the kids, that that was what they did. If they caught or killed an agent, they always killed his family, too, so that other agents might think twice, he said. He had all these documents, papers that gave us new names and identities in Brazil, and I was so afraid I—I just went with him when he said he'd been sent to get me and the kids out of the country."

She had tears streaming down her cheeks, and Harry's eyes had softened. "Kathleen," he said, indicating Sam, "This is Sam Prichard. He's the man who actually stopped that bomb from getting into the lake and saved a good part of the country. He's also my dearest friend in the world, and the best private eye there is. He and his wife managed to figure out most of this, and I'm comforted to find that they were correct."

"Oh, Harry," she said, sobbing softly. "I wanted to get in touch with you as soon as I saw that story, but Michael said I couldn't. When I asked him why not, he said it was because he wasn't going to give up the life he'd built over you. If I made any kind of contact, he said, he'd know and he'd have you killed. Harry, I didn't dare let you know."

"But you did," Sam said suddenly. "You've been going to Annapolis whenever Michael was out of town, haven't you? You've been watching Harry, trying to think of some way to let him know you're alive, and so you thought of the letters you wrote to him when the kids were young."

"Letters?" she asked, and Sam felt a sinking sensation in the pit of his stomach.

He turned to Harry. "Show it to her," he said, and Harry took the envelope out of his jacket pocket and passed it over.

Kathleen looked at it for a moment, then almost tore it to get at its contents. "Oh, my God," she said, "how did you get this?"

Harry had been staring at Sam as he spoke of her trips to Annapolis, but now he was locked on Kathleen. "I found that on an end table in my living room last Monday night," he said. "Someone had gotten into my apartment and left it on the same day I was forced to accept retirement from government service."

Kathleen was staring at the pictures and the note. "When I wrote this," she said, "I thought you were dead and gone, and it was just a way to try to keep you alive in my memories. I always thought that someday I'd let the kids see them, tell them about you, but they were so close to Mi-Michael, and they were so young when it all happened that they thought he was their father. I didn't want to dishonor your memory, Harry, but I was dealing with a reality none of us could ever have predicted, so I never told them..."

"I can understand that," Harry said. "What I want to know about now is what he said to you about having me killed."

She nodded. "He said if I contacted you, if you found out I was alive and what he'd done, he'd have no choice but to kill you, and that he loved me, but he'd kill me, too, in order to protect what he's got. Harry, I didn't know what to do..."

"You could have come to me!" Harry said suddenly. "Did you think I couldn't protect myself, or protect you and the children? Kathy, do you know how long I have thought, over and over, about how if I'd only turned down that mission, you might still be with me?" He forced himself to calm down and softened his voice. "Kathleen, did you know that Michael is still with the government? Sam's wife Indiana found evidence that he's still involved with the NSA."

"Yes," she said, nodding. "He's never actually been out. It was all part of the deal he made with them to let him take charge of me and the kids, he said, that he had to remain on call for special missions, for NSA, CIA, whoever needs him. I knew that some of his business trips were actually on those jobs, but it was just like you and me. We never talked about what happened when he went out on one, because knowing could put me in danger."

Sam leaned forward. "Okay, we understand the position you were in at that point," he said, "but now the situation is different. We know the truth, now, and it won't be long before he knows we know. As it turns out, there's no legal action Harry can take, but we can definitely get you and your kids out of danger."

Kathleen looked at him. "Mr. Prichard, is it? Yes, I remember your name from those same news stories. Mr. Prichard, forgive me if I doubt you, but I don't think you know the kind of man Michael has become. There was a time when he was a lot like Harry. But he has changed, and some of the changes began long before I found out about Harry being alive. There have been times—there have been times when I thought I was likely to be found dead in some accident, because his anger would flare over something so trivial that I couldn't believe it made him mad. I'd try to laugh it off, but that turned out to be a mistake, and I finally learned to be very quiet when he reached that point. He would stay angry for hours, sometimes, and I'd have to listen to him rant and rave until he got it all out of his system." She sighed, then, and a fleeting smile came across her face. "And then he'd suddenly be the sweetest man you could imagine. He would tell me how sorry he was, and the next few days would be absolutely wonderful."

"Is that what it was like when you found out about me? About what he'd done?"

"Oh, yes," she said. "When I questioned him about how you could still be alive, he became colder and angrier than I'd ever seen him. He pushed me down on the sofa and put his hands on my throat, and told me that if I said one word, even one word, to anyone else about it, that he'd kill me. He said if I tried to contact you, he'd know, and then he'd just make one phone call and you would be killed. I promised not to do anything, Harry, so that he'd calm down, but it took another two days before he let me get up off that sofa." The tears were falling again as she spoke and she closed her eyes. "He wouldn't even let me go to the bathroom, Harry. When the kids called, I had to tell them I wasn't feeling well and they couldn't come over. I sat right there where you're sitting right now, stinking and filthy, until he got past it all."

"Dear God, Kathy..."

"And then it was over. He started crying and telling me how much he loved me, how he hated the things I'd made him say and do, and all I could do was beg him to forgive me. He took me to the bathroom, then, and he washed me so lovingly that I honestly wondered if I was losing my mind, if I'd imagined the whole episode, but I knew better." She reached across a small table beside the chair she was in and found a tissue. She wiped her eyes with it, but the tears didn't actually stop. "I made myself a promise, then, that I'd find a way to see you, even if I couldn't talk to you. I stole some tricks from his own book, and got myself a credit card he didn't know about, so I could travel without him seeing the bills. I put it in Beth's name, and even got a driver's license with her name and my photo, and it took a hell of a lot of makeup to convince the examiner that I was only thirty-three, let me tell you! And I went to look for you, and I found you. I followed you sometimes, Harry, followed you and hoped you'd feel it, hoped you'd know I was there, but you never saw me." She grinned at him through the tears. "Guess I was too good at it."

Sam waited for her to go on, but she didn't. After a few seconds, he leaned toward her again. "But you're saying you didn't put this envelope in his apartment?"

She seemed to suddenly remember that she was holding the photos and note, and the look on her face became frightened. "No," she said. "No, I didn't. I hadn't even seen any of these letters for the longest time, I had put them all away when we came back to the US. As far as I know, they're all in a box in the attic..." She looked up at Sam suddenly. "Michael was in the attic last week, looking for some old paperwork on one of our boats. Harry, if he put this there, then he's figured out I've been going to watch you."

Sam nodded. "I came to the same conclusion a few minutes ago. You said he's gone to Japan. Is there any way to verify that he actually left?"

"The plane was due to take off at three this morning," Kathleen said. "I know the plane was fueled and ready, because we drove out and spoke to the pilot last night." She thought hard for a moment. "I can't reach anyone until it lands, and that won't be until about six this evening, our time."

"Where was he last Monday?" Sam asked.

"He was in England, as far as I know," Kathleen said. "He didn't get back until Wednesday night."

Sam turned to Harry. "Harry, if he put that in your place, then this whole thing has been a setup. He's undoubtedly been watching you ever since, or having someone else do it. That means he knows you came to me, and..."

Sam's phone rang at that moment, and he snatched it out of his pocket. "Indie?"

"Yeah, it's me! Sam, listen..."

He cut her off. "Indie, grab Kenzie and get out of there, right now! Take cash out of the safe and go, anywhere you can think of where no one would find you! Michael may have been the one to put the letter into Harry's place, and if so, then he's probably had him followed. He'd know Harry came to us, so I want you and Kenzie out of there now."

"What? Okay, Sam, I'll go, but I've got to tell you something now! Herman went off a little bit ago, and it woke me up, so I looked. That website, the one from that alphabet group? It's an assignment board, I guess you'd call it. There are links on it with different codes, and each one looks like maybe it's a mission outline. The one he seems to have looked at most recently is a mission to get someone, some foreign person, out of the US and into Japan."

"Okay, that fits," Sam said, "because we just heard he was supposed to be on a flight to Japan right now. If he's using the business flight as a way to smuggle someone over there, that would all fit pretty well. Now, get Kenzie and go, and call me from a burner when you can."

"Okay, Sam, I will," Indie said, and the line went dead. Sam looked at Harry and Kathleen.

"Michael is on an assignment to smuggle some foreign national out of the US and into Japan. I'd say the odds are good that that person is the real passenger on that flight, and Michael—"

"Is standing right behind you, Mr. Prichard," a voice said, "with a gun aimed at your head."

9

Frank Hornsby had almost panicked. Sitting there and listening to the conversations at Prichard's house was boring, so he had a tendency to get up and wander around periodically. It wasn't like he could conceivably sit there twenty-four hours a day, anyway, right? A man's got to have a break now and then. For Frank, that meant letting the computer run while he went into the living room and watched TV, or drove down to Excelsior, his favorite strip club. A few drinks and the chance to stuff some of his newfound wealth into the G-strings of some pretty girls was all it took to relax him so that he could spend another few hours.

The day before, after listening to half an hour of some animated movie, the boredom had hit like a nine-pound sledge. That old man had been up all night and was sleeping, so it wasn't like he was going to be jumping up and starting any kind of trouble anytime soon. Frank figured it was safe to take a break, so he headed for Excelsior.

The girls were particularly friendly all afternoon, and the drinks were cold. It was after eleven by the time Frank got back to his house, staggering into his office and falling into the chair. He stubbed out the cigarette he'd been smoking into his overflowing ashtray and forced his eyes to focus on the screen.

The most recent recorded voice had been Mrs. Prichard, and it sounded like she had been on the phone with her husband. Frank shook his head a couple of times and forced himself to focus, then scrolled back in the recording and listened at various points. Sam Prichard's voice was missing until he got back to the early afternoon.

Prichard had told his wife that he and the old man, Winslow, would be leaving at three o'clock in the chartered jet the old man was using. Their destination was Clearwater, Florida, which meant they would have already arrived. Frank dug through his pockets until he found his phone and called his employer immediately.

"Yes, Mr. Hornsby?"

"Sir, I..." Frank stammered. "I think my blood sugar got a little low, sir, I think I passed out for a little while this afternoon. I've been going over the recordings since then, and I needed to let you know that Prichard and Winslow have left on a plane for Clearwater, Florida. They're probably already there. Sir, I'm really sorry about this, I won't let it happen—"

"Relax, Mr. Hornsby," his employer said. "These things happen. Have you checked Prichard's phone yet?"

Frank breathed a sigh of relief. "I'm actually doing that right now, sir," he said. He grabbed the mouse and clicked on the window that would show him the recording from Sam Prichard's cell phone, and played the most recent file. It was the phone conversation between Prichard and his wife.

"The only thing I'm hearing right now is snoring," he said. "Prichard's wife called him just a little while ago and said something about the old man's wife sneaking around and taking trips to where he lives, but then there's nothing but snores."

"What about location? What does the GPS reader say about where the phone is at?"

Frank clicked on the GPS coordinates that were displayed and then grinned. "They're at the Sunset Motel on West Waters Avenue in Tampa."

"All right," said the man on the other end of the line. "No harm done. It's pretty late, why don't you go and get some sleep. Just be sure to let me know about their movements tomorrow, okay?"

Frank nodded, the relief overcoming the momentary sobriety that anxiety had brought on. "Yes sir," he said, his words slightly slurring. "Yes sir, I'll be back on it in the morning."

The call ended, and Frank sat there for a few more minutes as he scanned through the recordings from Prichard's house. Being able to listen in on someone this way, even through their cell phones when they weren't even in use, this was almost a godlike power. Frank grinned to himself as he thought of the ways he would be able to use it in the future.

Damn, what a crazy story. This old man actually believed that someone had conned his old lady into leaving him years before. Frank scoffed at the idea, because his own experience had taught him that women are fickle. If his wife ran off with his best friend, it wasn't because his buddy pulled a scam; it was because she was a woman, and women couldn't be trusted.

A soft sound from another part of the house managed to get through the alcohol-soaked regions of his brain. Frank looked through the office door but saw nothing, so he got carefully to his feet and slowly staggered toward the living room. Whatever he had heard had come from that direction, so it was probably nothing but that blasted mouse he'd been unable to lure into one of his traps.

He stepped into the living room and reached for the switch on the table lamp beside the door, but that's when the arm went around his throat. Frank grabbed at it and pulled frantically, but it was too strong. He felt another hand on the back of his head, and then a brief moment of searing pain in his neck, and then his body seemed to have faded away. His head struck the floor, facing upwards, and he looked up at a large man standing over him. His mind was already foggy from the booze, but he could tell that it was getting even foggier as he looked up at the man he suddenly realized was his killer.

His neck was broken. That was the pain he felt, he knew, and despite the ravages of alcohol in his brain Frank realized that he was already dead. Snapping the spinal cord meant that his heart was not beating, so blood was not getting to his brain—that's why he was feeling so foggy...

Without fresh blood coming to the brain, unconsciousness set in within forty seconds. Frank's vision faded out, and he slid into a slumber from which he would never awaken.

The man who had killed him looked down at his body in disgust as Frank's sphincters relaxed in death. Foul odors began to permeate the room, but the killer simply stepped over him and made his way to Frank's office. He sat down in the chair and carefully wiped all of the files off of the computers, then cleared the IP address of the relay server from its history. When he was finished, he picked up Frank's phone and redialed the last number Frank had called.

"It's done," he said. "No traces left."

"Excellent. I've already transferred the money to your account. Keep yourself ready for another job; I'm not sure how things are going to go at the moment. It might be necessary to use Prichard's wife and daughter as leverage."

"I'll be ready," the killer said. "Just give me the word."

He ended the call and dropped the phone back on the desk. He'd worn gloves through the entire operation so there were no prints to worry about. He got up and walked through the house again, pinching his nose as he stepped over the body, then walked right out the front door. He strolled quietly down the street until he got to the place where he'd left his car, then got in and drove toward his own home.

After the last phone call had ended, Frank's employer had rolled over and gone back to sleep. His alarm was set for three AM, and he knew that the morning was going to bring a busy day. One of the things he had in common with Harry Winslow was the ability to simply shut down and go to sleep, especially when he knew it might be a while before he could truly rest again.

When the alarm went off, he rolled over and kissed his wife goodbye, told her he'd see her in a few days and got out of bed. His clothes were already laid out so he put them on quietly, then made his way through the darkened house to the garage. He pushed the button to open the overhead door, got into his Lamborghini and backed out, carefully closing the door behind him. He drove down the street a short distance and turned into another driveway, using a second remote to open the garage door on this house. He pulled the car inside and got out, then walked around the other car, a nondescript Chevy sedan, and got behind the wheel. He drove out and used the remote once more to close the door behind him.

The trip across the causeway was uneventful at this time of morning, and he found the Sunset Motel with no trouble. The parking lot wasn't very full, so he pulled into a slot toward the back and picked up a tablet from the center console. He tapped on it a few times, and it displayed a page of information. Harry Winslow had rented a Buick Enclave a few hours before, and he looked up to see it sitting just a dozen spaces away.

Like most motels lately, this one had security cameras on the parking lot. A few more taps on the tablet got him into the servers that recorded the video from them, and it was the work of only a few minutes to turn them off and delete the last hour of video from them. He put the tablet down, reached into the glove box and pulled out a small magnetic device, then got out of the car and walked up to the Buick.

The biggest problem was where to put it. So many parts of the car were nothing but plastic that he finally had to reach up underneath and stick the magnet to a piece of its frame. His thumb pressed a button on the side, and the little tracking device began transmitting its location every eight seconds. He stood up and walked back to his car, leaned the power seat back as far as it would go, and went back to sleep.

When the sun finally began to peek over the horizon at a quarter to seven and tickled his eyelids, he woke again. The Buick was still sitting where he had left it, but he was sure Winslow and Prichard would be up and about.

He opened a small case from the console and pulled out two small, plastic rings. He squeezed them and put them into his nostrils, which caused his nose to flare and look bigger, then put on a pair of fake glasses and got out of the car.

This was one of those motels that offered a free continental breakfast, and the nice thing about those was that the people on duty in the mornings hardly ever recognized the guests who had come in the night before. He walked into the breakfast room like he owned it, and went directly to the waffle maker. By the time it signaled that his waffle was done, Prichard and Winslow had entered the room.

He sat down at a table and proceeded to eat, watching them only with his peripheral vision. The two of them sat at a table close by and he heard some ridiculous conversation about waffles in the wild. A couple of times, it was all he could do not to chuckle, but that would draw their attention. They weren't expecting to see him, so the simple disguise was more than sufficient as long as they didn't look closely.

He finished his breakfast and rose quickly, turning his back to them as he did so. It wouldn't be long before they were ready to leave, and he wanted to be in his car by then so he went directly out the front door without looking back.

Sure enough, they came walking out at just a little past seven-thirty, bags in hand. They loaded them into the back of the Buick and Prichard slid behind the wheel. He started the car up and backed out of his slot, then left the parking lot and pointed the car toward their destination.

The man who was watching them didn't bother to hurry to follow. The tablet beside him would let him know every turn they made, so he waited another few seconds before starting his own car and going out onto the street.

It was just as he had expected. The Buick was headed for his house. He cruised along at the speed limit, ready to set this portion of the plan into action.

Apparently, he was having better luck with traffic lights than Prichard was, because as they got onto the causeway, he was only three cars back. He let a few more cars get between them, then took a couple of slight detours in order to give them a few more minutes of lead time. By the time he got back into his neighborhood, the Buick was parked in his driveway and the two men were nowhere in sight.

Excellent. That meant she had let them in, which was one of the variables he could not predict with 100 percent certainty. Yes, he was fairly sure she would invite them in, but there was always that small possibility that fear would make her insist that they leave. If that had happened, he had backup plans in place, but he was glad to see that he wouldn't need to use them.

He parked the car in the garage of the vacant house a block away, one that he had quietly purchased through a dummy company. Like his own home, the backyard opened on the water and there were privacy fences that prevented any of the neighbors from seeing what he was doing back there. He left the Chevy in the garage beside the Lamborghini, then went through the house in the backyard and stepped into the boathouse. He carefully climbed into the fishing boat he kept there, then slipped on the hoodie he'd left in it. The electric trolling motor took him out of the boathouse silently, and he cruised along the coastline until he got to his own boathouse at home and silently entered it. He tied up the boat inside and dropped the hoodie back into it as he started toward the house.

They were all too occupied to notice the slight drop in air pressure that resulted from him opening the back door, and he was able to slip inside and make his way through the kitchen and bathroom to get into position.

"Michael is on an assignment," he heard Prichard say, "to smuggle some foreign national out of the US and into Japan. I'd say the odds are good that that person is the real passenger on that flight, and Michael—"

"Is standing right behind you, Mr. Prichard," he said suddenly, "with a gun pointed at your head."

Now, if only Prichard could be half as smart as his reputation seemed to suggest. It was all up to him.

10

Kathleen was the first to react physically, leaping to her feet. "Michael!" she said in shock. "Michael, don't—"

"Sit down and be quiet, Kate," he said. His eyes were on Harry and Sam, and the barrel of his gun remained aimed where it had been. "You didn't actually think I wasn't watching you, did you? I knew the moment you got your fake ID, and I knew right then why you wanted it. I'm no fool, you know."

He moved around to stand close to her, but his eyes and his pistol stayed on Sam. Slowly he sank into the chair beside the one she was in, and Sam began taking stock of the situation.

I'm facing a cold-blooded killer who has a gun aimed at my face, and it's one hell of a gun. What is that, a small machine gun? He's the same man who manipulated an entire family more than thirty years ago to satisfy his own desires, putting them all through the hell of thinking they had lost loved ones in order to gain what he wanted. He's the same man who told his wife he'd kill her and Harry if she tried to contact him, and now he's looking at the two of them together in his own living room. He has no intention of allowing Harry or me to leave here alive, but he probably hasn't decided what to do about her yet.

Poker, Beauregard said I'd have to play poker! Those are the cards I've been dealt, so how do I play them to win?

The thoughts flew through his mind in the space of a single breath, and Sam fought the urge to go for his gun. With Michael already aiming a gun at him, there was no chance he could draw and fire before being shot. A trained gunman can react to sudden movement and squeeze a trigger in less than an eighth of a second, but it would take more than half a second for Sam to lean forward, reach back under his jacket and grab the butt of the Glock, snatch it free of the holster, swing it around and point it at Michael and fire. He'd be dead before his hand closed on the grips.

Old police training kicked in, and Sam started thinking. One of the first things he had been taught to do in a confrontation like this was to evaluate his opponent. He looked closely at Michael, trying to examine every facet of the man.

This man is thin and wiry, but there are muscles hidden in there. He's about the same height and build as Harry, but about twelve years younger. His suit is clean and expensive, probably uses a professional drycleaner who can keep the creases nice and sharp. Hair is thick and still showing some color, even though the sides have gone pretty gray. Hands are clean, nails neatly trimmed—looks like he's had a manicure. His shoes are sharp and freshly polished. All of this says he's a man who stays in control of himself, doesn't ever like to let someone else have the upper hand. If I make the wrong move, he will react instantly. Got to think everything through, can't make a mistake with this guy.

"I've been expecting this to happen for more than a year now," Michael said. "Ever since your face showed up on CNN, Harry, she's been acting out, and I knew it was only a matter of time before she'd defy me and make contact with you. That could have so many, well, unpleasant consequences that I thought I'd better nip it in the bud, right?"

"Michael," Kathleen said, "I wouldn't have contacted him. All I wanted was to see him, from a distance, just know he was alive and okay."

"I know, Kate, and that would have been enough for a while," Michael said. "But you said it yourself, you kept hoping he'd notice you, spot you. Sooner or later you would have started getting bolder, you would've begun stepping out in front of him, and if that didn't work, you'd finally just bump into him. I know how this goes, Kate. I had it all figured out that night we saw him on TV, and I knew what was going to happen."

He turned and looked at Sam. "Prichard, I've got to commend you. After that Lake Mead incident, I followed your career. Hell, I even bought some of your CDs and went to two of your concerts in Denver. You should have stayed in music. As a private detective, though, you are very, very good. I'm not surprised Harry went to you once he found out about all this. I will confess that I'm surprised you found us so fast. That wife of yours, she's really quite good with a computer, isn't she?"

"You had him followed," Sam said, with a sinking feeling building in his chest. "You had an accomplice watching my house?"

"Of course not," Michael said, grinning at him. "I bugged your house months ago; all I had to do was have someone listen in to the recordings now and then, send me transcripts, things like that. I heard all about your discussions with Harry yesterday, and with your wife, so I knew you were coming. I had to scramble a bit yesterday to rearrange my 'business trip' and make a few changes, but Kate didn't suspect anything, so it didn't matter. And yes, since I know you're wondering, I heard you tell her to take your daughter and leave this morning. It won't matter, though, because I've got trackers on all of your vehicles. I have them in some of your daughter's toys, in your wife's computer, your mothers' cars. No matter where she goes, I'll find her."

Time to ante up, Sam thought, and he grinned. "Assuming you can," he said. "I've wondered for a while if we were bugged, so I tend to make some arrangements away from the house and on a burner phone. You didn't think we'd come in here with no backup, did you?"

Michael smiled and let out a loud laugh. "Oh, Mr. Prichard," he gasped through his laughter, "you and I would have been friends if we'd met under other circumstances. That was one of the boldest bluffs I've ever heard." He took a second to get himself under control. "I know you're alone, Pri—may I call you Sam? I know you're alone, Sam, because I followed you from your hotel. And Harry, I've got to say you're slipping. I sat two tables away while you ate breakfast, and all it took to disguise myself was a couple of nostril pluckers and a pair of cheap reading glasses. No, Sam, you can't bluff your way out of this one. We just have to make a few hard decisions, the four of us, and then we'll find out how this will all end."

"What kind of decisions?" Sam asked. Harry sat beside him, his mouth shut and his face blank. At the moment, that was exactly what Sam wanted him to do. "And what kind of endings are you seeing for this mess? What kind of ending is there that lets us all walk out of here alive, Michael?"

"Oh, I can see one, perhaps two. That's something we learn in the intelligence services, Sam, how to look at the current situation and extrapolate from it the possible outcomes. I can see six distinct possible outcomes from where we are at this moment, and two of them leave us all alive. One leaves only me alive, one leaves only me dead, one has me and Kate surviving, and one has Kate and Harry being the only ones left alive."

Sam nodded. "Okay," he said. "Let's talk about the ones that leave us all alive and well. What needs to happen to bring one of those to pass?"

"That's easy," Michael said. "You need to understand that I've got a life I enjoy, and I don't plan to give it up. All it will take is for the two of you to walk away, right now, and never come back here, never tell anyone what you've learned, and never, ever attempt to contact me or my wife again. Of course, the real problem isn't getting you to agree to do those things; the real problem is how you're going to convince me I can believe you when you do. Any suggestions?" He looked from Sam to Harry and back. "Now, you, Sam, I can probably get your cooperation pretty easily. All I've got to do is remind you that I can reach out and touch your wife and daughter at any time, and that there's no way in the world you can protect them from me. I can find you no matter where you go, and I can kill all of you without ever being close enough for you to see me. I think that would be sufficient, don't you?"

He turned to Harry. "You're being awfully quiet, old friend. I find it very difficult to believe you don't have anything to say about all this. Maybe we should leave the possible futures alone for a bit and let you vent. What do you want to say to me, Harry?"

Harry sat and looked into his eyes for a long moment, then leaned forward slowly. "I once thought you were my best friend,

Michael. I trusted you with everything, literally with my life on more than one occasion, and I trusted you with my wife, even though I was fully aware that you were infatuated with her. I knew, down deep inside me, that you would never betray me, not while I was alive. I also knew that if anything happened to me, you'd be there for Kathy and the kids, you'd see that they made it through everything and you'd take care of them. I even suspected that, should that ever happen, you might even win her heart one day and end up with her, but since it would mean I was dead, I saw that as a good thing." He sighed and shook his head. "What I never suspected was that you might try deception to make her vulnerable to your charms. You had to have convinced her I was dead, and that wouldn't have been all that hard to do, since we weren't allowed any contact with home when on a mission. I'm sure you brought her a condolence letter, properly signed by the director and the president, and told her that she was in danger and had to leave the country immediately. You took her to Brazil, I know, and left her in some kind of safe house or something, while you came back and arranged for my house to burn down with three bodies that would be identified as those of my wife and children, so that you could hand me the final report and walk me through their funerals. And then you took a transfer, went away and left me all alone, but that was what I needed for a time. I needed to be alone and come to terms with the grief and the anger and the bitterness, and I did so, over time."

He sat back again, and shook his head once more. "No, I never believed you could be capable of something like this."

Michael looked at him and had the decency not to smile. "You want to know the ironic thing, Harry? I got the whole idea from you. Remember the German woman, her husband was a leader of the Red Army Faction and we wanted to get her away, turn her against him? You suggested a plan just like this. You would go in deep and befriend them, then have him sent away and convince her he'd been killed, and that she'd be next if you didn't hide her away somewhere, remember that?"

Harry's face became dark, and it was clear to Sam that he did indeed remember. "That was in seventy-six," he said. "The director turned down the idea and you went in to assassinate him, instead."

"Yes, but I never forgot about it. It sort of sat in my mind, and one day I just fantasized about using it to make Kate mine, and it took root. Eventually, I realized that I had worked out every little detail, and I put it into action. Ever wonder why you were called up for the Cambodia mission? You had been out of that kind of work for four years, but suddenly only you could be trusted with it, did you never wonder why? It was because I just happened to be on the planning committee for it, and I made the comment that I wished you were available, because you were by far the best man for the job, and the director overheard me. I made sure he did, Harry, because he was such a guppie it was easy to lead him around like a little kid. He decided to call you up, and I knew you'd follow orders without a single protest. You were gone, and eight days later I put through a CCL for someone else. It was a simple matter to wash out the original name and put yours in, and then Kate was so scared she'd have done anything I wanted her to do. After all, I was the only thing protecting her and her children, right?"

Michael shook his head at Harry and turned back to Sam. "See my problem, Sam? I can get you to go along with me, but Harry's got thirty-odd years of grief and anger to let out. He's never going to agree to my demands, and if he did, it would last as long as it took him to get to a gun."

"Let's talk about something else," Sam said. "You put the letter in Harry's apartment to lure him here, right? Why? All you had to do was let Kathleen know you were onto her, and she would have stopped what she was doing. Harry would have been none the wiser, and we wouldn't be sitting here playing games. Why did you do that?"

Michael looked at him for a moment, and Sam sensed some doubt in the man, as if he hadn't really figured out himself why he'd done it. "I needed to bring it all to an end. Harry was a big shot in the intelligence community, and I spent years worrying that he and I might run into each other. Suppose he wanted to renew the old friendship? I couldn't exactly take him home to meet the family, now, could I? And then there was Kate; like I said, sooner or later she would have taken things a step too far, and Harry would have seen her. He'd have found out all about what I'd done, and it all would have blown up in my face. I couldn't afford that. While there might not be any legal charges to bring against me, the government alphabet groups I work with would take a dim view of it, I'm sure. Do you know how much documentation I had to forge in order to keep the government from figuring out that my wife was the same woman who died in that fire? Yeah, I think they might have been just a little upset if it all came out, now. I'd have lost everything, even if they didn't decide I was rogue enough to justify termination." He looked at Harry. "And I owed Harry something, even if it was only a glimpse of the truth. He had the right to know Kate and the kids were alive, and to die with that knowledge was the greatest favor I could do him. It was a fitting end to his long life and career, I thought.

When I heard the word he was being retired, I knew the time had come."

11

"Michael," Kathleen said, but he cut her off.

"Don't," he said. "Don't you beg for his life, I won't have that! Harry did damned well for himself, and he's a hero several times over. He doesn't need anyone to beg for his life. That would demean him, make him less than he is, so don't do it."

"Then what's next?" Sam asked. "What are we going to do now? I can't imagine you want to kill us right here in front of your wife, do you? That would be messy, and it might lead to police being called in."

"You're right about that," Michael replied. "I can't have that sort of thing, even though I could easily make it appear that you were intruders. I could even say that you murdered my wife, and I was acting in self-defense when I shot the two of you."

Kathleen's eyes were wide, and Sam realized that she knew they were all likely to die. Unfortunately, at the moment he didn't see any way to avoid it.

Poker! I'm playing poker, and the cards have been stacked against me, but there's always a way to win. I'm in the game, so what's the next bet?

"But you're supposed to be in Japan," Sam said. "Wouldn't it seem odd if you just happened to be here when these intruders broke in?"

Michael shrugged. "Plans get changed all the time," he said. "As it happens, I ended up sending a new employee at the last minute. Kate and I had been fighting, you see, and I just felt that it would be best for me to be at home, right now. Imagine my shock when I came in to find her bleeding on the floor, with two strange men standing over her. One of you was holding a gun, so I grabbed one of my own and managed to take you both in a shootout. Do you really think that will be hard to sell? Especially with three dead bodies as evidence? I'm certain at least one of you is carrying a weapon, so it wouldn't be difficult to kill both of you, find it and use it to kill Kate."

"Michael, please..." Kathleen said, her voice cracking. "You don't have to do any of this! All I wanted was to see Harry, to know he was all right, I won't do it again, I swear! Harry, tell him you'll let this go, tell him..."

"Harry can't do that," Michael said. "He's seen the truth now, and nothing will do for him but to reclaim you from me. Isn't that right, Harry?"

Harry looked him in the eye. "If I could kill you right now," he said, "I'd do so with not a moment's hesitation. I'd face the kids and tell them the truth, and leave the choice of whether they wanted me in their lives to them, but yes. I want Kathleen back. She is *my* wife, Michael, not yours. She always was."

"That's debatable, Harry, but it's no longer important. I have always cared for her, but I confess that watching her lie to me about what she's doing when I know she's been shadowing you has worn my feelings thin. If she dies today, I'll still have the kids.

They honestly love me, you know; I'm the only father they've ever really known, after all."

Harry tensed, but Sam put a hand on his arm. "Easy, Harry, he's trying to goad you into making a foolish move. He wants to kill us, but he wants it be our own fault." Sam thought for a moment as Harry settled back again, then turned to Michael.

"How about if I make a proposition," he asked, "one that you haven't considered?"

"And what would that be?"

"You want to keep all this from coming out, I understand that. Still, there's no reason to kill anyone if you can do that without resorting to violence, and I think I may know a way. You're a spook; as Harry says, you can do things that no one else can. You've already started over more than once. Why not just create another new identity and walk away? The intelligence people won't care who you are, and I can get Harry to keep his mouth shut, if for no other reason than to protect Kathleen."

Michael's eyes went wide. "Are you insane, Sam? Do you know how much I'm worth in this life? I've been buying and selling yachts for twenty years, and now I'm the number one salesman for all of the biggest yacht builders in the whole world! I make more on one sale sometimes than you'll earn in your entire life. I'm not walking away from that. Try again, maybe there's something else in that crazy brain of yours that could make me laugh. I could use a good laugh about now."

"Then let's try another variation," Sam said. "How about if Kathleen leaves you? She found another man, you caught her cheating, but she agreed to let you have everything in the divorce? Harry won't talk, because he knows you could always come back and hurt her. It's a way out that lets you keep everything you really want. How about it?"

Michael rolled his eyes. "And you honestly think Harry Winslow could honor that sort of deal? That he'd let me get away with what I've done, just so he can have his last few months or years with her?"

"He's right, Michael," Harry said. "We both know you were always better than me; there's no way I'd ever risk you taking your vengeance out on Kathleen. If you agree to Sam's idea, we all win, and we all survive. I give you my word, and you know I never break my word. If you'll go along with this plan, I won't ever tell anyone what I know about you."

Michael looked at him for a long moment, and then turned to Kathleen. "What about you?" he asked her. "Would you want to go along with this scheme? Leave me and go off with Harry? You couldn't ever tell anyone the truth, you know. I'd know instantly if you did, and all bets would be off. Both of you would die, and within hours. Would you agree to keep your mouth shut for the rest of your life?"

Kathleen stared at him, her eyes revealing just how scared she was. Did she dare say she'd agree to it, or would that push him to the point of killing them all? "I—If it's what you want, Michael, of course I'd agree. But it's up to you, of course."

He stared at her for a moment, then looked back at Sam. "I know you're armed. Take it out, carefully, and toss it over here onto the carpet."

Sam reached slowly behind his back and took hold of the Glock with two fingers. He had to tug a bit to get it to come free of the tension holster, but then he withdrew his hand and let

Michael see the gun dangling from it. He swung it once and let go, and it landed on the carpet near Michael's feet.

Michael turned his gun on Harry. "What about you? Let's have yours."

Harry didn't even try to claim he was unarmed. He reached into his jacket and took the Kel-Tec out the same way Sam had done, with two fingers, and gave it a toss to land beside the Glock. "That's all I have," he said.

Michael slowly lowered his own gun, but kept it in his hand as he narrowed his eyes and looked at the three of them. "Okay, now, let's talk about this. Kate, even the kids have felt the tension between us lately. They've asked me about it. I always say it's just that we're both getting old, but I think they know there's something. If you were to admit to having an affair and deciding to leave me for your"—he smirked—"much-older boyfriend, that would be believable. Are you willing to do that, let the kids think that was all it was? You couldn't ever tell them the truth, you know. They can never know who Harry really is."

Kathleen licked her lips nervously. "If that's what you want, Michael, I'll do it. And I'd never tell them, I swear. Just promise me you'd never hurt them, will you do that?"

"Of course," Michael said. "None of this is their fault, now, is it? They probably wouldn't believe it, anyway, but they'd come and ask me about it, so I'd know. So, we're agreed on that, then?"

She nodded her head vigorously. "Yes, no problem, if this is what you want."

Michael looked at Harry. "And you? No problems later, down the road? Are you going to come after me yourself, or send someone else to try to kill me?"

"As I said, you have my word," Harry replied, looking Michael straight in the eye. "I won't bother you as long as you don't bother us. The kids will only know me as their mother's new husband. You won't ever have a reason to harm any of us."

Michael looked him in the eye for a few seconds before turning to Sam. "You won't be a problem, will you, Sam? Knowing how easily I can find your family?"

"Look, it was my idea," Sam said. "All I'm trying to do is get us all out of this alive, Michael, and this is the best shot I could come up with. You keep your money and everything else, and you can stop worrying about any of this ever coming to light. It'll be a non-existent problem."

"Uncontested divorce," he said, turning back to Kathleen. "I keep the business, the houses, the yachts, everything. No alimony, but I suppose the court will insist on some kind of a settlement, so I'll give you five hundred thousand dollars, and you can keep the Bentley, I suppose. Other than that, you take nothing but your own clothes and mementos. Deal?"

She was still wide-eyed, but there was hope beginning to show in her face. "Uncontested, you can have it all. Yes, Michael, I agree to all of it."

He stared at her for another moment, then pointed with his pistol at the guns lying near his feet. "Pick those up, carefully, and put them in the cabinet under the entertainment center." He kept his gun angled at the floor, ready in case she decided to try anything, but she did exactly as she was told and then came back to her chair and sat down.

"Okay, here's how we're going to do this," he said. "Kate, you're going to call the kids and ask them to come over. I think the time to do this is now, don't you?"

She looked at him for a moment, then reached down and picked up a cordless phone from the end table beside her. "All right, Michael," she said, and then pressed a button on the phone and put it to her ear. A moment later, she smiled cautiously.

"Beth? It's Mom. Listen, are you busy with anything right at the moment? Well, um—your dad and I would like you to come over, please. Yes, I'm afraid it's pretty important. Please? All right, honey, we'll see you then." She hung up, and then pressed another button. "Harry? It's Mom, honey. Dad and I need you to come over. It's something important, Harry, and Beth is already on the way, so please? Okay, thank you, honey. Okay, we'll be waiting." She hung up again and looked at Michael. "They're both coming. Harry says it'll take him an extra few minutes, he's got to run by his place and drop something off, but he should be here by the time Beth arrives."

"Good. The more I think about this wild idea of yours, Sam, the more I like it, and the sooner we get it started, the better." He turned to Kathleen. "You'll leave today, you and Harry. You can make arrangements to come and pack your things next week, one day while I'm at the office. I'll have someone here to watch, of course, but that's just to keep up the pretense that we're having hostilities between us over your affair with old Harry, here."

"That's fine," Kathleen said. "I'll want to pack a bag, of course."

Michael nodded. "Go on," he said. "I know you're not gonna try anything, Kate. Go pack what you need for a few days, you can get more later if you need to."

She looked at him for a moment, then slowly rose from her seat and walked out of the room.

Michael looked at Harry. "You never remarried, did you? Still in love with Kathleen?"

"I always was," Harry said. "Did you think that would change?"

"Everything changes with enough time. I was crazy about her myself, even though she was married to you. Crazy enough to go to some wild extremes to have her, obviously. But that was then, and let me tell you, this is now. She's been difficult, and since long before she found out about you being alive and kicking. She was always trying to hold me back, keep me from building the business. Her whining about me being gone all the time cost me two of the finest restaurants, but I put my foot down on the yacht business. Built it up from nothing, buying older sailing yachts and restoring them, then selling them for a big profit. Got one that had sunk in the bay, an old hundred-eighty-foot Perini Navi from back in the '90s, and raised it all by myself, then rebuilt her from stem to stern. Turned fifty grand invested into eight million in profit, and I was made. I could give her anything she wanted, but was she ever happy? Not even a bit. Still whined all the time about me working too much, but you know damn well, if you're gonna make it in business, you can't be loafing around. You've gotta keep at it, right, Sam?"

The more he talks, the crazier he comes across, Sam thought. *This is a man who has driven himself mad with the things he's done and his own fear of being caught out. He drives himself in order to feel like he's still in control, and that's the way I've got to play him now. He has to be in control, or he'll decide it's all going wrong. That's when things will get really bad.*

"Sometimes you do, yeah," he said. "Listen, should I be gone when the kids get here? I don't really fit into this scenario, you know."

Michael grinned. "Oh, the hell you don't," he said. "You are a famous private investigator. You're the thing that's going to pull this all together and make it work. See, I was suspicious that Kate might be having an affair, but I didn't have any proof. What does a husband do in a case like that? He hires a private eye to follow her around. That's you, Sam. You been following her around for the last couple of months, and you were able to tell me when to catch the two of them together here at the house. I had you come along as a witness, to make sure nothing got out of hand. That's your story, and you'd better stick to it."

Sam swallowed, but he managed to keep his expression straight. "Okay," he shrugged, "I'll play my part. Let's just get this over with."

12

Indie had hung up the phone and hurried up the stairs to wake Kenzie. When Sam said to move, she had learned, there was usually no time to waste. She wanted to be out of the house within ten minutes.

Fortunately, she had gotten into the habit of keeping what she called 'bug-out bags' ready to go at all times. These were small sports duffels that were always packed with clothing for one of them, just in case of circumstances like this one. She had Kenzie up and dressed in only two minutes, and had snatched up her and Kenzie's bags on her way back downstairs.

She set the still half-asleep Kenzie on her bed and hurriedly dressed herself, then grabbed her purse and computer, slung the bags over her shoulder again and took Kenzie's hand. They were out the door and in the Ridgeline with only seconds to spare on her original deadline.

The truck started instantly, and she backed out and headed down the street. Her eyes were scanning the street and the rearview mirrors, watching for any sign that they were being followed or observed. From what she could tell, no one was paying them any attention.

After some recent events, Indie had begun keeping a cheap, throwaway phone in her purse, charged up and activated, but never used. She'd left her own cell phone lying on the bed, and would use this one only when she needed to. At the moment, she wanted to let Kenzie's grandmothers know what was going on. She dialed her mother's number and listened for an answer.

"Hello?" Kim said, half-asleep. "Indiana? Is that you?"

"Yes, it's me. Mom, get Grace up and both of you stuff some extra clothes into something fast. Leave your phones at home, I'm coming to get you now." She didn't bother waiting for a response. While it was possible to trace a cell phone even after the call ended, keeping it short might mean it wouldn't even be noticed by anyone watching her mother's phone activity.

She raced through the streets of Denver, barely keeping her speed close enough to the limit to avoid getting pulled over, and made it to Grace's house without any problem. Her mother rented a room from Grace, and the two had become best friends. They were standing on the porch, waiting, when she roared into the driveway.

"Get in," she yelled through her open window, and neither of them stopped to ask questions. Kenzie was in her car seat in the back, and Kim slid in beside her while Grace took the front passenger side. Indie spun the truck around and took off down a side street, trying to randomize her path so no one would be able to anticipate it and get ahead of her. She filled the women in as she drove.

"Oh, my God," Grace said. "How does he always get into these kinds of messes?"

"Well, sometimes it comes with the territory," Indie said. "I mean, he's dealing with spies and secret agents at the moment, so you really don't know what to expect, you know?"

"But this is no way to be raising a family! I'm going to talk to him. He's just got to give up all this private eye stuff, that's all there is to it!"

Indie rolled her eyes. "Grace? Shut up, would you? I'm trying to think of where to go, and you're not helping anything with your mouth running off with oral diarrhea!"

Grace turned and stared at her, but didn't say anything. Indie kept driving, and then turned onto I-70 and pointed the truck west.

Kim cleared her throat from the back seat. "Um..."

"What, Mom?" Indie asked, her face turning sour as she dreaded the answer she knew was going to come.

"Um—Beauregard says we need to go back to your place."

Indie's eyes went wide, and she looked at her mother in the rearview mirror. "Sam just told me to get out of there," she said. "The guy they're dealing with is probably the one who left that letter for Harry, so he probably was following him and knows he came to our house..."

"Yes, but Beauregard says we're not in any immediate danger. Something's going to happen with Sam and Harry, though, and you'll need to be at home when it does."

Indie rolled her eyes. "Oh, Lord," she said. "He better be right, or I'm going to find a way to kill him. He can go and haunt all the other ghosts." She took a left turn into a parking lot and then headed back toward home.

* * * * *

Harold arrived a few minutes before his sister, and was surprised to find his parents sitting there with two other men. He tried to find out what was going on, but Michael told him to wait until Beth arrived. She obliged by showing up only a few minutes later, and then the six of them were all seated in the living room.

Michael had put his gun beside the cushion of the chair he was sitting in, so there were no weapons visible. Once both of the kids had settled themselves onto one of the sofas, he leaned forward and clasped his hands together as if he was upset.

"Kids, what we are about to tell you is probably going to upset you," he began, "but something is happening that—no, I'd better let your mother tell it." He looked at Kathleen, and nodded.

She lowered her eyes to the floor for a moment, then looked up at her grown children. She took a deep breath, then opened her mouth to speak. "I think you guys have both known that your dad and I were having problems," she said. "What you didn't know is that—that I've been having an affair." She indicated Harry with a wave of her hand. "This is—this is an old friend of mine, from years ago. He and I ran into each other a while back, and we started talking about old times, and that's when we both realized that the old attraction we had felt long ago was still there. We started seeing each other, quietly, and sometimes I would take trips to be able to see him, and..."

"Mom!" Beth yelled. "Mom, how could you do this?"

Kathleen swallowed, and looked her daughter in the eye. "I know you may not understand," she said, thinking fast. *How would a woman having an actual affair say this?* she asked herself, and the answer came out of romance novels she'd read years before. "The truth is, things haven't been all that good between me and your dad for some time. When I ran into Harry and we started seeing each other, I started to feel better. I felt better about myself, and I've come to the conclusion that I want to be with Harry. Your dad—well, I guess he was suspicious, because he hired this other man who's a private investigator to follow me, and that's how he found out Harry was coming to see me today while he was supposed be out of the country. He pretended to leave for Japan, then came home and walked in on us."

Harold was looking from one face to the other, and his eyes seemed to linger on Harry's. "Do we know you?" he asked. "Me and Beth, I mean?"

"Your mother and I knew each other when you were very young," Harry said with a straight face. "I can remember seeing you both many, many times. If I look familiar, that's probably all it is."

Beth scoffed, shaking her head. "And were the two of you having an affair back then? Kind of hard not to notice that he and my brother have the same name. Is that just a coincidence?"

Michael held up a hand to interrupt the conversation. "Not entirely," he said. "See, Harry and I used to be good friends. We were so close that we named our son after him."

"Fine," Harold said. "So what happens now? You guys getting a divorce?"

"Yes," Kathleen said. "With it all out in the open now, your father and I have agreed. I'm leaving the house today, and it will be an uncontested divorce. I don't want to drag our names through the mud, so we'll do this quietly. I hope you guys can understand, and not hate me over this."

Beth only glared at her, but Harold gave her a lopsided grin. "No one's going to hate you, Mom," he said. "I'm sure this isn't going to be easy on anyone, but you're still our mother." He looked at his sister and scowled. "Lighten up, Beth," he said. "You and Danny got divorced, and Mom stood by you the whole time, even though a lot of it was your fault. Don't forget that."

"I never had an affair," Beth grumbled.

"And I'm sure Mom never thought she would, either, but sometimes life throws you a curveball." He turned and looked at Michael. "Dad? How are you handling this?"

Michael looked at the man he had raised as his own son for a moment, then shrugged. "Of course it hurts," he said, "but if your mother is that unhappy, then I'm not going to try to make her stay. If she wants to be with Harry, so be it. I just don't want it to affect our relationship."

"It won't," Beth said emphatically. "We'll both be here for you, Dad." She turned and glared at Harry. "Forgive me," she said, "you may be a great guy, but I have a hard time finding any respect for someone who would steal another man's wife. Don't expect me to like you anytime soon."

Sam tensed, half-expecting Harry to explode, but the old man simply nodded to his daughter. "I understand," he said.

"Beth!" Harold said sharply. "Come on, you're better than this! Remember that old line about not judging someone until you've walked a mile in their shoes?"

"Sorry, Bro," she shot back, "but civil is about the best I'm going to be able to manage for a while. Take it or leave it, I really don't care." She looked at her mother. "Your mind is made up?"

Kathleen nodded. "Yes," she said simply.

Beth got to her feet. "Dad, I'll call you later. I just can't stay here right at the moment." She turned and walked out of the room, and they heard the front door open and close a moment later. Her car started and drove away, while the rest of them sat in silence.

"She'll get over it," Harold said. "I know my sister, she can't stay pissed off forever." he turned and looked at Michael again. "Divorce isn't the end of the world, Dad," he said. "Don't worry about any problems between us, there won't be any."

He turned and looked at Harry. "Harry, I'll say the only thing a son can say in this situation. If Mom loves you, then all I ask is that you don't hurt her. If you do, you'll find I can be one mean son-of-a-bitch."

"I would expect nothing less—especially considering who your father is," Harry said. "And I can assure you that I never will."

The younger man stood and said his goodbyes, then left. The motorcycle he had ridden in on roared to life when he got outside, and then faded into the distance as he rode away.

"Well," Michael said, "I think that went very well, don't you? And as long as everybody remembers the conditions of this little arrangement, everybody stays happy." He turned to Kathleen. "You can go now," he said, and then he rose from his chair, picking up his machine pistol and tucking it into the waistband of his pants. He walked over to the entertainment center and withdrew the two guns Kathleen had put there earlier, quickly removed their magazines and cleared them, then handed them to Sam.

"I imagine these are yours," he said. "You can have them back, but I'll hang on to the magazines. Kate can pick them up next week for you when she comes to pack her things."

"No problem," Sam said as he and Harry stood.

Kathleen picked up the small suitcase she had hidden behind her chair and walked toward them. She turned and looked at

Michael, and managed a small smile. "Michael," she said, "thank you. This really is the best solution, I think."

The look he gave her could only be termed a smirk. "It certainly works for me," he said. "And Heather is likely to be happy."

Sam lowered his eyebrows. "Heather?"

Kathleen looked at Michael for a moment, then turned her eyes to Sam. "Heather Keller is his secretary," she said. "If I remember correctly, she's about twenty." She reached out and took Harry's hand, and started toward the front door.

Sam looked at Michael for another moment, then turned and followed them. He couldn't help wondering whether a bullet was going to hit the center of his back at any second, but then he closed the front door behind him and slid behind the wheel of the rented Buick. Harry and Kathleen were in the backseat, and Sam smiled at them in the rearview mirror as he backed the car out of the driveway.

"That was some good thinking, Sam," Harry said. "You got us out of there in one piece. If I had suggested the same thing, Michael probably would have started shooting."

"Or me," Kathleen said. "Yes, Sam, thank you so much. But what's going to happen now?"

"Now, we're all going to hold up our ends of this bargain," Harry said. "Michael is right about one thing, and that's the fact that he could easily harm any of us if he chose to. I'm afraid we have locked ourselves into a lifetime commitment. As long as we do what we've agreed and never let the kids, or anyone else, know the truth, then we ought to be safe."

"Well, that sucks for you, Harry," Sam said. "I think it would kill me to never be able to let my own children know I was their father."

"Yes, but you'd do it under the circumstances. Sam, boy, there's no doubt in my mind that Michael would kill me and Kathy, and probably you and your entire family, if those kids ever find out the reality behind this. If they ever meet your family, which isn't outside the realm of possibility once they get used to me being in their mother's life, you've got to make absolutely certain that Indie and your mothers don't let anything slip. And, for God's sake, make sure Beauregard understands that."

"Beauregard?" Kathleen asked.

"You don't want to know," said both Sam and Harry at the same time.

13

Indie was keeping herself busy in the kitchen while Sam's mother, Grace, was watching television with Kenzie in the living room. Her own mother, Kim, was sitting at the table and watching her as she scrubbed and cleaned.

"Indiana," she said hesitantly, "how are you and Sam doing?"

Indie looked up at her in surprise. "Me and Sam? Fine, why?"

"Well, what I mean is—are you getting along okay? Are there any problems between the two of you?"

"Problems? Mom, where is this coming from? Why are you asking something like that? And no, we're not having any problems, we get along great." She actually giggled. "I think we both fall more in love with each other every single day."

Kim smiled at her. "Oh, I'm so glad," she said. "But then, with situations like this coming up all the time, I just worry that there might be some stress in your relationship. You could tell me if there was, you know. You can talk to me about anything."

Indie carried her dishcloth to the sink and wrung it out, then dropped it into the sink and sat down at the table across from her mother. "Okay, stop beating around the bush," she said. "Tell me where this is really coming from. And if you say Beauregard..."

Kim grimaced, and Indie groaned. "It's not what you think," Kim said. "You know, bad news isn't all Beauregard ever gives. Sometimes there's—sometimes there's good news, but good news isn't always good news if it isn't news you're ready for."

Indie shook her head. "Wait, what? What on earth is that supposed to mean?"

Kim let out a deep sigh and looked her daughter in the eye. "Beauregard told me last night that you're going to go from three to four."

Her daughter made a face and squinted at her. "Three to four? Mom, stop being so vague and tell me what on earth this is..." Indie's eyes suddenly shot wide open, and her mouth stopped moving in the shape of an O. She tried to speak a couple of times, but nothing would come out and then she almost seemed to collapse onto the table. She caught herself on her elbows and stared at her mother.

"Three? To four? Mom, come on, how could Beauregard possibly know..." Once again, her mouth stopped wide open, but it didn't take her as long to regain her composure this time. "You're telling me that he says Sam and I are going to have a baby?"

Kim nodded slowly. "He wanted me to call and tell you last night, but I was chicken. I mean, don't get me wrong, I love Sam to pieces. He's been wonderful to you, and he's a great daddy to Kenzie, there's no doubt about that. I'm just wondering, you know, how it's going to affect him if he actually has a child of his own?"

Indie stared at her for a long moment, then finally closed her mouth. "First, let's get one thing straight," she said. "Sam Prichard already has a child of his own. Her name is Mackenzie, and she's in the living room right now watching Scooby Doo. Believe me, Mom, that child is his through and through, and anyone who tries to suggest otherwise is liable to be looking down the barrel of his gun." She paused to take a breath and cleared her throat. "Now, as for this—prediction of Beauregard's, all I can tell you is that we recently talked about maybe trying to have a baby brother or sister for Kenzie, and—so I stopped taking the pill."

Kim's face suddenly broke into a huge smile. "You did? You are? Oh, Indiana, that's wonderful! If you already talked about it and decided to try, then there's really nothing to worry about, is there?"

"Mom, there wouldn't have been anything to worry about even if it happened by surprise. Trust me, Sam and I love each other very much, and we love Kenzie with all our hearts, but there's plenty of love in this family to go around." She dipped her head and looked at her mother from under her eyebrows. "I don't suppose Beauregard happened to mention what we'd be having, did he?"

"Now you come on, Indie," Kim said. "When does he ever give any clear, concise information? Besides, I think it ruins everything when you find out early what sex the baby is. It used to be that you never knew until it was born, and that sounds to me like the best way to handle it."

"Yeah, well, that was before the days of ultrasound. I don't know anybody who waits for the surprise anymore. Besides, if you know what you're going to have, it's easier to get the nursery all decorated in advance."

"Nursery? And where would you put a nursery?"

Indie giggled at her. "I told you, Sam and I have talked about this. Our bedroom has two huge closets, and either one of them would be plenty big enough to make a nursery. Neither Sam nor

I have enough clothes to fill one of them out, so we'd just move all our stuff into one and Sam said I can decorate the other one anyway I want. If it's true and I do get pregnant, I want to know what it's going to be so I can decorate properly."

Kim laughed. "Indiana, I can't tell you how relieved I am to hear that you'd be happy about it. I honestly worried about this all night long, and all day today. I can't wait, now, to hear what Sam has to say."

"Oh, I think we'll wait on telling Sam until I can show him a plus sign on a stick. Somehow, I don't think he'd take too kindly to Beauregard being the one to make the announcement."

Kim's face seemed to fall a bit. "That's something else," she said. "Beauregard says Sam thinks he isn't real, like he's something I just made up. Is that true? I mean, why would I make up something like that? I certainly don't have any way to know the things he tells me, especially when he talks about things that haven't even happened yet."

Indie tried to lighten the mood. "Oh, Mom, Sam always says things like that, but he doesn't mean any harm by it. And for the record, all he ever really said was that he thinks it's really you that can see the future, and that you subconsciously made up Beauregard so you wouldn't have to admit that to yourself."

Kim leaned on the table and fidgeted with a napkin. "Is that what you think? That it's really me?"

Sighing, Indie reached over and laid a hand on her mother's arm. "I think it doesn't matter. No matter where it comes from, the things Beauregard says have saved so many lives that I'm just thankful. I don't know that anyone could say for sure if he was real or not, but the only thing that really matters, I guess, is what you think. Have you ever wondered?"

Kim flicked her eyes up at her daughter for a second, then lowered them back to the napkin in her fingers. "Maybe. I mean, I admit there's been a few times when I thought I was just going crazy. But then it always turns out he's right, no matter what he says, so that makes it pretty hard to not believe in him. And it isn't like I ever really got into any of that Spiritualism stuff, I never played with Ouija boards or séances or anything like that. Beauregard just sort of showed up one day, back when you were just a baby."

Indie cocked her head to the side and looked at her mother. "Really? I thought he was always with you, your whole life."

Kim shook her head. "No, the first time I ever heard him was right after we moved into that old house in Kentucky. Do you even remember that place? It was like almost 200 years old, all the wiring was just stapled to the walls right out in the open. The only reason we moved into it is because the rent was cheap enough I could afford it, or I never would've bothered." She shrugged and grinned at Indie. "Anyway, I had you in a playpen in the living room while I was in the kitchen trying to cook something, I can't remember what, now, and all of a sudden this voice told me that if I didn't take you out of the playpen you were going to get hurt. Well, at first I thought it was God talking, so I ran in the living room and snatched you up, and I was just walking around and cuddling you when all of a sudden a big chunk of plaster fell out of the ceiling and landed right smack in the middle of your playpen. I was so shocked I couldn't even think, but I got down my knees and started praying and saying thank you to God, and all of a sudden I heard that voice again."

Ken fell silent for a moment, and Indie motioned for her to go on.

"It said, 'How do you do, Madam? My name is Beauregard, and I welcome you to my home.' Well, it was so clear that I spun around, trying to find out who was talking, and I think I yelled out something about who was there or something, and then he said, 'Please forgive me if I startled you, I just thought it would be terrible if something happened to your adorable baby girl.' Now, by that time, I was pretty sure I was going crazy, but he kept on talking and telling me that he had been waiting for more than 120 years for someone who could hear him, and I was the first one that ever did. Other people who had lived in the house had claimed it was haunted, I knew that when we moved in, but I never believed in ghosts before that. I just ignored those stories because the rent was so low, but once I got to know Beauregard, none of it ever scared me anymore. And you know, yourself, he's always warned us about problems and even helped us solve a lot of them."

Indie had a slight grin on her face. "Yeah, he has. I remember that one Christmas, I was what, maybe ten? We didn't have any money for Christmas presents or even a Christmas dinner, but he told you about some old house in the woods where he said you would find what you needed to make Christmas perfect. Remember that?"

"Oh, I certainly do. You and I went stomping out through the snow and found that old abandoned house, and we looked all through it for whatever it was he was telling us about. And then, just as I was ready to give up, you looked through a hole in the floor into the old storm cellar and found a big old wooden box. We drug it out and I remember I had to use an old broom handle to pry the lid up, and we found all those old silver plates." She chuckled. "You know, after we sold those, I worried for over a month that some cop was going to show up and say we stole them, but Beauregard kept telling me not to worry. He said he had found out about them from the ghost of the old woman who had died there eighty years before, and that no one ever found them because they had been covered up with old rags. I guess the rags rotted away by the time we got there, right?"

"I guess so. All I really remember is that it was one fantastic Christmas. That was the year you bought me my first computer, do you remember that?"

Kim nodded. "And just for the record, I don't think I ever told you, but Beauregard told me I should buy you—as he put it—one of those new information boxes."

The two of them sat there for a moment and reminisced about that Christmas, but Indie wasn't finished. "Mom," she said, "how do you feel about being a grandma again?"

Kim gave her the biggest smile Indie had seen in many years on her mother's face. "I would be thrilled," she said, "and I can guarantee you that Grace would be in heaven. Trust me, she loves Kenzie to pieces herself, but every woman looks forward to the day when she'll be a real grandmother. I think that she would be absolutely overjoyed."

"You haven't said anything to her yet, right?" Indie asked.

"Of course not," Kim said. "An announcement like that needs to come from the proud parents. Trust me when I say I would never try to steal that joy away from you."

14

Sam drove back into Clearwater until he spotted hotels, then turned into the parking lot of the Marriott on Harry's instruction. They went inside and Harry secured two rooms, and then Sam left Harry and Kathleen alone so that they could talk. He went into his own room and was about to call Indie when he remembered that he had told her to hide. He wouldn't be able to reach her until she called him from a throwaway phone.

No sooner had that thought crossed his mind than his phone rang, and he glanced at its display to see that it was Indie's usual number calling. He answered quickly, almost afraid of what she might have to say. "Indie?"

"It's me, Sam," Indie said. "Listen, I don't want you to get upset, but we're back at the house. I thought that if somebody was maybe watching us, they might go after our mothers as well, so I called Mom and went by and grabbed them, and—well, Beauregard..."

"It's okay," Sam said. "Things are working out a lot better than we expected. We ended up in a confrontation with Michael, literally with a gun pointed at us, but I was able to talk him into letting us go. He's made himself a fortune in the yacht business and doesn't want to give it up. I made a deal with him to let Kathleen go with Harry, on the condition that she gives him an uncontested divorce and he gets to keep everything."

"Oh my God, Sam," Indie said, "are you serious? What a jerk!"

"Listen, Harry and Kathleen were happy to agree to it. The only problem is that they aren't allowed to let their kids know the truth. The official story is that Kathleen has been having an affair with Harry, and Michael hired me to find out what was going on. When he confronted Kathleen, she admitted that she wanted a divorce and wanted to be with Harry, so he's letting her go. He made her call the kids to come over and hear all this directly from her."

Indie was quiet for a moment. "Sam," she said finally, "I don't think things are going to go as smoothly as that. Beauregard says you're about to have some kind of problems there, and that I needed to be here in order to help you. That's why we came back to the house."

Sam sighed, and flopped backward onto the bed. "Did he say what kind of problems?"

"Does he ever? No, just that something is going to happen and you're going to need me here. He did say that we are not in any danger. As much as I hate it, the fact is that he's just never wrong."

"Okay," Sam said tiredly. "I'm not sure at the moment what the plan is, but Kathleen has to wait until next week to go and pack her things up. I would imagine Harry is going to stay here, but unless he needs me for something I'm going to try to come on home. Harry doesn't think Michael will be any kind of problem, and he was so happy about getting to keep everything that

I doubt he's going to cause any trouble in the near future. I'll talk to Harry and Kathleen in a little bit, and call you back then. Right now I think I'm going to go find me a cup of coffee."

"Okay, Babe," Indie said. "Call me when you know something, or I'll call you if that stupid ghost decides to give me any more information."

"I still don't believe in ghosts," Sam said. "I think maybe it's time we get your mom to talk to one of those ESP experts. I'm not saying she can't see the future, because she obviously does; I just don't believe in Beauregard."

"Yeah, well, I'll let you have that conversation with her when you get home, okay?"

"Trust me, I will," Sam said. "Love you, Babe."

"Love you, too. Bye-bye, Baby."

Sam ended the call and dropped the phone on the bed beside him. This was the first time Beauregard had ever tried to countermand Sam's instructions, and he was frankly really upset about it. Unfortunately, there wasn't much he could do unless he could convince Kim to seek professional help, and he wasn't sure that was going to happen.

Sam lay back for a few minutes and let the events of the morning run through his mind. The whole thing had been crazy, and he couldn't help worrying about the fact they seemed to be dealing with a man who was not entirely sane. Michael Watkins had broken an awful lot of laws in his plot to steal Harry's wife and family, and though he couldn't be prosecuted over it now, the risks must surely have weighed on his mind for years. That weight had, somewhere along the line, become too much and some part of him had snapped.

Hopefully, the arrangement they had come to would keep him happy, but even though he didn't express it to Harry, Sam had his doubts. This was a man who showed clear signs of paranoia, and he was obviously terrified of losing everything he had achieved. Even without being prosecuted, he would be fully aware that if the truth ever came out, his reputation would be gone as quickly as if it had been flushed down the toilet. To Sam, that made him every bit as dangerous now as he had seemed to be before. He had the feeling that, sooner or later, he and Harry were going to have to deal with Michael.

A tap on the door roused him, and Sam realized that he had drifted off to sleep. He glanced at his phone as he picked it up and saw that it was almost half-past noon as he went to answer the door.

Harry and Kathleen stood there, and despite the stress they had gone through earlier, there was a glow of happiness about both of them. Sam couldn't help smiling. "Well," he said, "you two seem to be getting along well."

"In some ways, Sam, boy," Harry said, "it's like we were never apart. This is probably the most unusual reunion that ever took place, but it's been well worth the wait." The old man winked at him. "And according to my blushing new bride, here, I'm every bit the man I ever was."

Kathleen gasped and looked shocked, but she was definitely blushing as she gently slapped Harry on the shoulder. Sam chuckled as Harry pretended to wince, and then Harry went on.

"Well, anyway," he said, "now that we've worked up a bit of an appetite, we thought we might ask you to join us for some lunch in the restaurant downstairs. Feeling hungry, old boy?"

"Now that you mention it," Sam said, "I am. Give me just a minute to freshen up and I'll meet you at the elevator."

"Sounds good. We'll be waiting."

Sam went into the bathroom and made use of it, then splashed some water on his face and headed out the door. Harry and Kathleen were waiting beside the elevator as promised, and Harry pushed the down button when Sam appeared in the hallway. He caught up with them just as the doors slid open.

"Sam," Harry said, "I'm under orders to tell you that my earlier comment was made in jest. I hope you didn't take any offense at my sense of humor."

Sam barely managed to keep his face straight. "Not a problem, Harry," he said. "I suspected as much."

The restaurant just off the lobby of the hotel was a very nice one, and a maître d' looked down his nose at Sam and Harry as he showed them to the table. Neither of them were wearing a tie, and the light sport jacket Sam had on had definitely seen better days. They ignored him until he walked away, then Harry turned to Sam.

"Was it my imagination," he began, "or was that fellow just a bit on the snooty side?"

Sam grinned at him. "I suspect he's used to a more elegant type of clientele than he sees in us, Harry. In fact, I think that if Kathleen had not been with us, he might not have let us in."

"Then that would have been his loss, because I intend to have the biggest steak they have available. I haven't eaten very well the last few days, with the exception of breakfast at your house, and I'm feeling so much better now I'm ready to make up for lost time."

"Medium rare," Kathleen said, "with grilled onions and Worcestershire sauce. Am I right?"

"Of course," Harry replied. "You still remember so much after all these years?"

"Well, I remember how you like a steak. Let's see, you're having steak, so you'll want an iced lager, and you'll have a baked potato and a small salad with Italian dressing."

"Right again. Now, let's see if I can do as well. It's only lunchtime, so you'll probably choose a petite New York strip, medium, with a salad and, oh, let me think, raspberry vinaigrette dressing. How'd I do?"

"Not bad, actually," she replied. "That sounds exactly like what I want."

Sam was looking over the menu, and the prices were a lot higher than what he was used to back home. Still, he got the impression that this was more of a celebratory lunch than anything else, so he decided to go all out. "I'm going for the prime rib," he said. "You can never go wrong with prime rib."

Harry blinked. "Now, don't hold back, Sam," he said. "Have two of them if you want, this is on me."

"Harry, don't tempt me. I happen to love prime rib, and I haven't forgotten that you're covering the expenses of this trip."

A waiter came and took their orders, and the three of them had coffee while they waited. Harry and Kathleen were still catching up, but while they tried to include Sam in a lot of the conversation, it was pretty obvious that they were quite wrapped up in one another.

It wasn't until their food arrived that Sam managed to steer the conversation to what was going to happen next.

"My concern," he said, "is that Michael is going to eventually start worrying that someone is going to talk. To be honest, he strikes me as being somewhat paranoid. I don't want him to decide he needs to give one of us an object lesson to make sure we hold up our end of this deal."

"He seemed quite relieved," Kathleen said. "To be honest, I don't think he really cares that much about us, as long as he gets to keep his good name intact and all his money. I'm going to do all I can to assure him there won't be any problems. I'll wait until Monday to give him a call and see when I can go pack up my things, but I think the only thing that might cause a problem is if we said anything to the kids."

"I agree," Harry said. "I'll admit, Sam, it grates me to not be able to tell my children who I am, but for now it's probably the best way to handle things. Sooner or later the truth will come out. When it does, we'll deal with Michael however we have to."

"Well, I'm not leaving you here by yourselves," Sam said. "I'll stay as long as you do, and then..."

"Actually," Harry said in his slow drawl, "I'm not planning on staying, either. Kathy and I have talked it over, and we both feel it would be a good idea to get out of the area. We'll stay the night, since I've already paid for the rooms, but then tomorrow morning I was planning on flying us back to Denver. We can get a hotel there, and then fly back next week when it's time for her to pack up."

Sam grinned. "We can fly back to Denver," he said, "but if you think for one minute that Indie is going to let you stay in a hotel, you've obviously forgotten just how tough my little wife is. You and Kathy are more than welcome to use our guest room, and that way I can keep an eye on you. Remember, Beauregard says it's up to me to keep you alive and healthy."

"Okay, that's it," Kathy said. "That's the second or third time you've mentioned somebody named Beauregard. Who on earth is Beauregard?"

Sam sighed and grinned at Harry. "Should we tell her?"

"We might as well," Harry replied. "Knowing Beauregard, he's bound to put in an appearance while we're there."

Sam turned to Kathleen. "Beauregard is a figment of my mother-in-law's imagination," he said. "Unfortunately, he seems to be an alter-ego she created to deal with the fact that she can occasionally see bits and pieces of the future. I don't know how she does it, but she insists that Beauregard is an old Civil War ghost she calls her spirit guide. Whenever she gets a glimpse of the future, she insists that Beauregard told her whatever it is, and she's even been known to lapse into a Beauregard personality now and then."

Kathleen was staring at him. "Your mother-in-law is schizoid?"

Grimacing, Sam said, "I don't know if schizoid is the right term, but she does seem to have a second personality. Whenever Beauregard, what's the word, manifests himself, it's actually a little difficult not to believe she's possessed. I mean, it's weird, she talks like an old Southern gentleman and even her face looks—I don't know, different."

"Why are you so sure it isn't a Civil War ghost?" Kathleen asked. "I've seen some pretty strange things, especially when we were living in Brazil. I knew an old woman down there who could talk to all kinds of ghosts, and sometimes you can actually see them. I saw that with my own eyes, so I'm not quite as skeptical, I guess."

Sam smiled, but shrugged. "The only ghost I've ever seen is Beauregard, but only when Kim is supposedly possessed by him. I guess I'm just not willing to give up a lifetime of not believing in ghosts or the supernatural."

Kathleen turned to Harry. "You don't believe in Beauregard either?"

Harry pursed his lips and looked at her for a moment, then shrugged his shoulders. "I honestly don't know," he said. "He once gave Kim a message for me, something about not having seen me since we fought together at Valley Forge, and something about it gave me a chill. I've always been fascinated by Valley Forge and what the Continental Army went through, there, I've literally read everything I could get my hands on about it, and I have to confess that I've always felt as though I could almost remember being there. Some of the things I read seemed so familiar that I toyed with the idea of reincarnation, but I never really took it seriously."

He let out a sigh. "Then one day, about ten years ago, I met this old woman in Europe. I was there to interview some witnesses to a terror attack, and she was one of them. I sat down with her and we started to talk, and she suddenly looked at me and said, 'You are an old soul.' I asked her what she meant, and she went on to tell me that I had lived several different lives, and that I was always involved in some kind of espionage work. I tried to brush it off, but then she put her hand on mine and said, 'You were Tallmadge. When Nathan was hanged, Washington turned to you.'"

"Tallmadge?" Kathleen asked. "Did that mean something to you?"

Harry nodded. "Yes. At Valley Forge, General George Washington sent a spy, Captain Nathan Hale, into New York to gather information on British fortifications. He was captured and hung, of course, and gave us his famous line about only having one life to give for his country, but Washington then turned to Major Benjamin Tallmadge, Hale's best friend, and asked him to organize a spy network. I recognized the names when she uttered them, but didn't put any stock in it—not until Beauregard said that about not seeing me since Valley Forge. I'll confess it sent a shiver down my spine at the time."

Kathleen turned to Sam. "See? There are many things in the world that may be hard to understand, Sam, but that doesn't mean they aren't real."

Sam shrugged and managed to grin. "I'll let you make up your own mind when you meet her."

"I'm looking forward to it," Kathleen said with a grin of her own, and Harry laughed softly.

"Sam, Kathleen mentioned a bit ago that she needs a few things," Harry said when lunch was finished, so Sam gave him the key to the Buick and went back up to his room. He was still tired, and the stressful morning had only added to that fatigue, so he stripped down to just his slacks and stretched out on the bed. He called Indie to let her know he'd be home the next day, then drifted off to sleep.

The phone in the room woke him a few hours later, and he reached out to grab the handset. "Hello?"

"Sam? It's Kathleen," he heard, and instantly became alert as he heard what sounded like panic in her voice. "Is Harry over there?"

Sam glanced around the room quickly, then turned back to the phone. "No," he said, "why? Isn't he there?"

"No, he left about an hour and a half ago because we forgot to get in some cigars while we were out," she said, "and said he'd be right back, but Sam—I just got a call on my cell from the police. Michael's been murdered!"

15

"Did you try his cell phone?" Sam asked, his mind and heart both racing.

"Yes, but he left it here. Sam, I'm worried. You don't think he..."

"No, I don't," Sam said. "If Harry had wanted Michael dead, he never would have come to me. Did he take the car?"

"I don't know. I—I just know he said he was going to get cigars, so I would imagine he had to drive somewhere. Sam, the police are coming here to talk to me, what do I do?"

"I'll be right there," Sam said. "Hopefully, Harry will show up and we can get this sorted out."

"Okay," Kathleen said. Sam hung up the phone and grabbed his cell while quickly getting dressed again. He hit the speed dial button for Indie and she answered on the second ring.

"Babe, we've got problems," he said. "Harry's gone AWOL and we just found out that Michael has been murdered."

"Oh, God," Indie said. "Sam, you don't think Harry would..."

"That's what Kathleen just asked me, but no, I don't think so, but she said Harry went out a while ago to get some cigars, and hasn't been back. The police contacted her on her cell phone and are on the way to talk to her now. I'm guessing he had to take our rental car; is there any way you can track it? Don't those rental car companies put GPS in all of them nowadays?"

"Some of them do," she said. "Which company did you use?"

Sam told her, and could hear her tapping on her computer's keyboard. "No, unfortunately they don't. Let me see if I can get a ping on his cell phone."

"Don't bother," Sam said, "he left it in the room. Babe, I'll call you back in a bit, I better get over next door before the police show up."

"Okay," Indie said, "but, Sam? Beauregard said something bad was going to happen down there, and that you were going to need me here in order to help. I can't help but think this might be it."

Sam grumbled under his breath. "Yeah," he said. "I think it probably has to be."

He ended the call and left his room, then tapped on the door to Harry's. Kathleen opened it instantly and stepped back to let him in, just as the elevator chimed its arrival. Sam looked toward it, and was relieved to see Harry step out and head toward the room. He had a paper bag in his hand and a smile on his face.

"Harry, where the hell have you been?" Sam asked, and Harry's smile vanished instantly.

"The nearest decent cigar store is way across town," he said. "Why? What's going on?"

"Kathleen got a call on her cell from the police. Michael's been murdered."

The look of utter surprise on Harry's face was convincing, but Sam couldn't help remembering that Harry had played many roles in his life. In his short stint as an international agent a year or so before, Sam had learned that acting ability was a prerequisite of the profession. While he didn't actually believe Harry would have murdered Michael at this point, his investigative mind automatically identified him as the most likely suspect.

"What? When?"

"I'm sure we'll find out shortly," Sam said. "The police should be here about any minute. I was just coming over to wait with Kathleen, but we've been going nuts wondering where you were."

Harry hurried along and Sam moved to let him into the room first. He tossed the bag onto the bed and immediately put his arms around Kathleen.

"First, are you okay?" he asked her.

"Harry, I don't know what to think," she said. "You didn't—you didn't go back there, did you?"

"No, I did not. That was going to be the second thing I said." He turned and looked at Sam. "What do we do, Sam?"

Sam had entered the room and shut the door behind him. He picked up the bag Harry had tossed on the bed and dumped it out. Five thick cigars landed on the bed, and Sam looked up at Harry. "Where's the receipt?"

Harry shrugged. "I paid cash, I don't think I got one."

"Okay, what was the name of the store? We need to be able to establish exactly when you were there, just in case Michael was killed while you were gone."

"It was Clearwater Pipe and Cigar, on McMullen Booth Road. Like I said, all the way across town."

Sam snatched out his phone and googled the number, then dialed it immediately. A man's voice answered.

"Hi," Sam said, trying to mimic Harry's drawl. "I was there just a bit ago, and I think I may have dropped my wallet. I'm an old white-haired fellow with a goatee, you remember me?"

"Um, not really," the man said. "How long ago were you here? I mean, like, I've been really swamped all day today."

"Oh, it would've been in the last forty-five minutes or so. I look like a skinny Colonel Sanders, are you sure you don't remember?"

"Nah, I'm sorry, dude. I get so many people in here I just can't remember faces too well. And I haven't seen any wallets lying around. Are you sure you didn't drop it somewhere else?"

Sam sighed. "Maybe I did," he said. "Thanks, anyway."

He turned to Harry. "Sounds like a young kid, and maybe smoking something other than tobacco. He says he doesn't remember you."

Harry shrugged. "The place was pretty busy," he said, "and he was running it all by himself. I frankly would have been surprised if he did. Still, I shouldn't be needing an alibi, should I?"

"Of course not," Kathleen said. "You were here with me the whole time."

Harry turned and looked at her. "Darling, while I appreciate the vote of confidence, I will not have you lying to the police. I didn't kill Michael and I haven't been anywhere near him since we left that house this morning, so there shouldn't be any problem. We'll just wait and see..."

There was a tap on the door, and Sam turned to open it. A casually dressed man stood there, holding a police ID case out in front of him. "I'm Detective Lawton, Clearwater PD. I'm looking for Kathleen Reed."

"Yes," Sam said, "please come in. She's right here."

Lawton looked at Sam for a moment. "And you would be?"

Sam reached into his pocket for his badge case and showed his ID. "My name is Sam Prichard," he said, "and I'm a licensed private investigator from Denver, Colorado." He turned and pointed to Harry. "This is Mr. Harry Winslow, he's my client."

Lawton glanced at Sam's ID, then at Harry before turning back to Kathleen. "Mrs. Reed?" he asked as he entered the room.

"I'm Detective Jerry Lawton. I called you a bit ago about your husband."

"Yes, Detective," Kathleen said. "How can I help you?"

Lawton cocked his head and looked at her. "Well, first, you could tell me why you seem pretty calm about your husband's death," he said bluntly. "You told me on the phone that the two of you were separated and getting a divorce, but you certainly don't seem to be very troubled by learning that he was murdered."

Kathleen looked him in the eye. "My husband and I have not been close for some time, Detective, though we've only just agreed to divorce. Can I ask what happened?"

Lawton watched her face for a few seconds more, then nodded. "Couple hours ago, we got a call from one of his neighbors saying they'd heard gunshots coming from the house. A unit responded and found the front door partially open. They knocked and announced themselves but received no response, so they entered the house and found Mr. Reed on the kitchen floor, surrounded by blood. One of the officers felt for a pulse, but that's when they realized that he had apparently been shot through the head. I was called out and put on the case, and I called you immediately to find out if you were all right."

Despite her statement of a moment earlier, Kathleen went pale and put a hand to her face. "I'm fine," she said. "I left the house with these gentlemen about mid-morning and haven't been back yet. My agreement with my husband was that I would return one day next week to start packing my things."

"Wait a minute," Lawton said. "Are you saying you and your husband decided on divorce today?"

Kathleen nodded grimly. "Yes," she said. "There's a very long story behind it, but I suspect it's all going to come out now." She looked at Harry. "Perhaps we should give him the short version for the moment?"

"As you wish, my dear," Harry said. He turned to Lawton. "Detective, I'll arrange to show my bona fides a little later, but I am a retired agent of the United States government. Thirty years ago this lady was my wife, but we were each led—by the man you know as Mr. Reed, I might add—to believe the other was dead. Reed convinced her that she and her children were in danger, and helped her to hide and change her identity. He kept her from learning the truth and they eventually married. I learned of this only in the last few days, and hired Mr. Prichard to help me find her. We arrived at their home this morning, at which time Mr. Reed held us at gunpoint until we reached an agreement involving his retention of all of their marital assets. At that point we left the house and came here."

Lawton's face was a study in incredulity. He stared at Harry for a moment, then turned his eyes to Sam. "Is this for real?" he asked.

Sam nodded slowly. "He's told you the exact truth," Sam said. "The man you know as Michael Reed was actually born Michael Watkins. He and Mr. Winslow worked together in the intelligence field thirty years ago, but Watkins seems to have had some feelings for Mrs. Winslow. While Mr. Winslow was out of the country on a clandestine mission, Watkins convinced Mrs. Winslow that he had been killed and that foreign agencies knew who she was and were a danger to herself and her children. She can fill you in on the details, but he took her to Brazil for several years and helped her to build a new identity. Later, he brought them back to the United States and began building his yacht business. About a year and a half ago, Mr. Winslow and I were instrumental in stopping a terrorist attack out West, and he made the news. Mrs. Reed learned at that point that he was alive, and that created tensions between her and Watkins, or Reed, as you know him. All of this came to a head when Harry found out she was alive, and we showed up at their house this morning."

Lawton's mouth was hanging slightly open. "And now Reed is dead. I'm pretty sure you can understand how this whole thing looks to me, at the moment, right?"

Sam sucked in his bottom lip and nodded his head slowly. "I'm quite sure I can," he said. "However, you should be aware that Mr. Watkins, or Mr. Reed, was still doing some work for the National Security Agency. I'm quite sure there were a number of people who would've wanted him dead. Considering the fact that Mr. Winslow had his wife back, I have my doubts that he would be on that list at this moment."

Lawton looked from Sam to Harry and back. "And I'm quite certain you're going to tell me that Mr. Winslow has been here with you the whole time, right?"

"Actually, no," Harry interrupted. "Kathleen and I went and did a little shopping earlier, and then I actually just returned to the hotel from a trip across town to purchase some cigars. Kathleen and Sam remained here while I did so."

Lawton whipped around to look at him. "How long ago did you leave the hotel?" he asked.

Harry gave him a sad grin. "I'd say I was gone about an hour and a half," he said. "I had looked up the tobacco shop in the phone book and thought I knew the way, but I'm afraid I got lost and had to drive around a bit before I found it."

Lawton shook his head. "Okay, this is all a little too weird," he said. "Mr. Winslow, are you going to object to a gunshot residue test? One of these officers can do it right now."

Harry shrugged. "I have no objection," he said.

One of the uniform officers stepped forward and asked Harry to hold out his hands, palms upward. When the old man complied, the officer took some adhesive strips and rolled them over his hands. Each strip went into a separate plastic bag that was then sealed, and he ended up with eight separate bags.

Lawton watched the process in silence, but when it was finished, he looked up at Harry, and then to Sam and Kathleen. "I'm afraid I'm going to need you all to come down to the station. I'm going to need complete statements from all three of you, and we'll need to know what tobacco shop that was you went to, as well."

Harry and Sam looked at one another, and then Harry nodded. "Of course, Detective," he said. "We are happy to comply."

16

Kathleen's cell phone chose that moment to ring, and she answered it to find her daughter on the line.

"Mother!" Beth shouted, and Kathleen could tell she was crying. "Mother, they just called me, the police called, and they said Daddy is dead! Mom, what on earth is going on? Is it true? Is it really true?"

"Honey, I just found out a bit ago myself. There's a detective here now, talking to Harry and me, but I really don't know anything more than you do. Let me try to find out and..."

"Mom, was it him? Was it your boyfriend? Did he kill my dad?"

"No, Beth," Kathleen said, "he didn't. I don't know exactly what's going on at the moment, but you've got to stay calm. I promise you, I'll call you as soon as I know more."

"But he had something to do with it, right?" Beth demanded through her sobs. "I mean, come on, what are the chances something like this could happen the day he shows up and ruins all our lives?"

"Beth, stop that," Kathleen said. "Listen, honey, I know this isn't going to be easy, but I'm afraid you're going to be finding out some things over the next few days that are going to be hard to swallow. I know that you and Harold are going to have a hard time with some of it, but I have to ask you to trust me."

Beth made a scoffing sound. "Trust you? Do you mean the way Dad was supposed to be able to trust you?" There was a loud bang, and the line went dead.

Kathleen lowered her phone and looked at Harry. "Beth heard," she said. "Of course, she's blaming us."

Harry nodded. "I suppose it's natural at the moment," he said. "Of course, the one bright spot in all of this is that we are now free to reveal the truth, I suppose."

"Which is precisely why we're going down to the station," Lawton said. "If I've gotta be honest, that's the very thing that makes you my number one suspect, Mr. Winslow."

"Of course, sir," Harry said. "I completely understand, though I can assure you I had nothing to do with his death." He grinned. "Besides, if you speak to any of my former coworkers, they'd tell you that if I killed Michael, I would have made sure there was no evidence that pointed at me."

"Oh, yeah," Lawton said, "you were a spy, right? Some kind of secret agent dude?"

Harry continued to grin at him. "Yes," he said. "I was exactly that."

Kathleen's phone rang again, and she knew instantly it would be her son. "Hello," she said.

"Mom," Harold said, his voice shaky but controlled. "Beth just called and told me that Dad is dead?"

"Yes," she said. "The police contacted me a little while ago, and there is a detective here now. Beth thinks Harry did it, but I..."

"Can't say I'm not thinking the same thing," her son said to her. "I mean, it would seem like an awfully big coincidence, wouldn't it? We find out you have a boyfriend, and the same day our dad is killed?"

"Harold, I'm sure it must seem that way, but it's not like that. Listen, right now we have to deal with the police, but I'll call you as soon as I can. Please, try not to believe the worst."

She listened to whatever Harold said next, then hung up the phone. Her face reflected how upset she was, but she didn't say anything.

Lawton sucked in his cheek and just looked at both her and Harry for a moment, then insisted they head down to the station. Sam picked up the keys to the Buick that Harry had laid on the bed when he returned, and the three of them followed the detective out to the parking lot.

As they climbed into the Buick, Harry caught Sam's eye in the rearview mirror. "I left the pistol you gave me under my pillow in the hotel before I left, Sam. If it turns out Michael was shot with a thirty-two, you can produce the gun and allow them to do a ballistics test. It won't match."

"I was gonna ask where it was," Sam said.

"And while we're at it," Harry went on, "you might want to hold onto this for me." He passed something up between the seats and Sam opened his hand to receive it. He glanced down to see what looked like a gold, tubular cigarette lighter. It was about four inches long and quite heavy.

"Your lighter," Sam asked. "Sure, no problem."

"It's not just a lighter, Sam, boy," Harry said. "If you open the lid backward, you'll see what I mean. It's a single-shot thirty-eight caliber pistol. The trigger is the big fake diamond on the side. Just open the cover, that takes off the safety, then point it at the target and slide the diamond toward the base. One shot, and it's only good inside twenty-five or thirty meters, but it'll get the job done if you're up close and personal."

Sam looked at it for another moment, then dropped it into his jacket pocket. "Harry, forgive me for what I'm about to ask, but did you go and kill Michael? And if you did, be honest with me, I'll still stand beside you and swear you didn't do it."

"I'm afraid I can't say I did, Sam," Harry said with a grin, "because I didn't. I'm as shocked about this as anyone, but whoever did it certainly picked the perfect moment, didn't he? Is there any doubt in your mind I'll be arrested before this day is over?"

Sam swore under his breath, something he rarely did. "Not a whole lot," he said. He started the car and followed Lawton out of the parking lot, turning toward downtown. "So, the problem now is how do I prove you're innocent? I'll go down to the tobacco shop and show photos of you, try to get someone to say they remember you being there at the right moment, but you've been a professional killer in the past. Lawton is going to say you had plenty of time to go back to the house, kill Michael and still make it to the tobacco shop. And unfortunately, he's correct. Unless that tobacco shop was in Orlando, you probably did have time."

"I certainly had time," Harry said. "But I just as certainly didn't do it. Naturally, I've no idea who did, but I can tell you some things about him." He held up a hand and ticked off points on his fingers. "Number one, he was either in the house this morning when we were or he has it bugged. Michael was killed in his own home, only hours after the most likely suspect there could ever be was sitting across the room from him, and facing down a gun, I might add. Number two, anyone who knew or worked with Michael should have expected him to be out of the country today, but our killer was apparently certain he'd be home and alone. Number three, whoever did this has actually had it planned out for some time, but seized upon an opportunity to give the police an easy target. Number four, the killer wanted Michael found as quickly as possible, probably because he wanted to be sure I was discovered and named as a suspect right away. And number five..."

Sam looked at him in the mirror again. "Number five? Go on."

"Number five," Harry said after a moment, "the killer is almost certainly a spook, like me and Michael. Which means that he's not going to take any chances about me having an alibi. He's either going to kill me, or that poor young man at the tobacco shop."

Sam's eyes snapped wide open as he looked at his old friend in the mirror. "What was the name of the shop again?"

"Clearwater Pipe and Cigar, McMullen Booth Road," Harry said. "Why..."

Sam floored the Buick and raced up alongside Lawton while honking his horn. The detective looked at him, surprised, but pulled over when he saw Sam waving frantically. Sam pulled to the curb behind him and jumped out of the Buick, running up to the detective's car.

"You need to send officers to the Clearwater Pipe and Cigar store on McMullen Booth Road," Sam said in a hurry. "I have reason to believe the killer may go after the clerk there."

Lawton stared at him for a moment, then picked up the microphone attached to the radio under his dashboard. "Dispatch, this is twenty-six," he said.

"Go ahead, twenty-six."

"Dispatch, send a car to Clearwater Pipe and Cigar, McMullen Booth Road. Make sure the clerk is okay."

"Twenty-six, ten four."

The dispatcher ordered a patrol car to go to the store, while Lawton looked up at Sam. "Wanna tell me what that was all about?"

"Mr. Winslow believes the killer might well be an intelligence agent, and could possibly be tailing him. If he's correct, the killer won't want Harry to have an alibi. He'll want Harry to be the only possible suspect, and that means eliminating any witness that could put him somewhere else when Reed was killed." Sam closed his eyes and smacked his hand on the detective's door. "If he's right, that kid is probably already dead."

Lawton's mouth was hanging open again. "Do you even realize how crazy you sound right now? Just where did you get your PI license, out of a Cracker Jack box?"

Sam scowled at him. "Ten years with the Denver Police Department, six of them as a detective. Don't get cocky, Lawton, because it's quite possible this case is going to turn out to be way over your head." He smacked the door again, then turned and walked back to the Buick. He slid behind the wheel and put it back into gear as Lawton pulled out from the curb.

The Clearwater PD was on Pierce Street, not very far from the hotel, but traffic and one-way streets caused the drive to take almost 20 minutes. Sam pulled in the parking lot behind Lawton and found a space that wasn't reserved for official vehicles. Harry and Kathleen slid out of the backseat as Sam got out of the front, and they all followed Lawton into the building and directly to his office.

No one said a word until they got inside the office and Lawton shut the door, and then the detective turned and looked Sam in the eye. "You called it," he said. "Our officers arrived at the tobacco shop and found the clerk, a twenty-four-year-old man named Jim Clayton, who happened to have a wife and two little kids, dead and stuffed under the counter. His neck was snapped, but the door was open and there were customers wandering around the store. They didn't even know he was there. CSI should be there any minute, maybe we'll get some answers."

Sam shook his head. "Dammit," he said. "I spoke to him a few minutes before you arrived, to ask if he remembered Harry. I wish I'd known to warn him, he might still be alive."

Lawton cocked his head. "You called the tobacco store, but you didn't mention that while we were at the hotel?"

Sam started to speak, but Harry cut him off. "He didn't mention it because the young man said he didn't remember me," Harry said. "The place was quite busy when I was there, and I'm not sure the lad even really looked at my face."

Lawton sat down in the chair behind his desk and pointed at three others scattered around the room. Harry, Kathleen and Sam pulled them closer and sat down.

"So, Mr. Private Eye, you already knew your client had no alibi at that point, right?"

Sam shook his head. "No," he said. "I only knew that the clerk didn't recognize Harry from my description. That didn't mean he wouldn't remember him from a photograph, or that another customer in the store might not be able to confirm Harry's presence there."

Lawton grinned, but there was no humor in it. "And now I've got two murders on my hands, but still only one suspect. Six years you were a detective, you said? Well, I've been doing this for more than ten. Don't try to teach Grandpa, Junior. No alibi is still no alibi, no matter how you try to cover it up."

Sam started to bristle, but Harry put a hand on his arm. "Detective," Harry said, "might I suggest that you verify my story about my past before we go any further. If you would simply call the DHS headquarters in DC, the personnel division can confirm that I have just retired from there. If you identify yourself as a police detective and give your badge number, they'll connect you with someone who can confirm that I have been an active intelligence agent in the past."

Lawton looked at him. "And that's supposed to tell me exactly what? I don't care if you used to be the President of the United States, right now you're a murder suspect, and you'll be treated like every other murder suspect."

"Young man," Harry said softly, "no matter what you might think of me at this moment, I can assure you that I still pull enough weight with the federal government to make your life quite miserable. Now, I have no intention of doing anything to interfere with your investigation, but I will be damned if I am going to be treated with such disrespect by a small-town policeman whose opinion of himself is way too high. You can either make the call I've asked for, or I shall make it myself. If I do, somebody is going to want to know why you haven't confirmed my identity, and that is probably going to become quite unpleasant for you."

"Oh, I'm scared," Lawton said, his face a mask of mock fear. He stared at Harry for a moment, then shook his head and reached for the phone. "Fine, what's the number?"

"Oh, don't be an idiot," Sam said. "Either call directory assistance or google the number for yourself. If you dial a number Harry gives you, you could claim he had someone waiting to answer."

Lawton glared at him, but then turned to a computer and typed for a moment. He dialed the number that came up on the screen and identified himself when someone answered.

"I'm sitting here with a Mr. Harry Winslow, who claims he used to be a spy." He listened for a moment, then nodded his head. "Yep, that's him, white hair and all. Yeah, I can hold."

The hold music was apparently loud, because Lawton held the phone away from his ear for a moment. The rest of them could hear it playing, a fairly recent hit song by John Legend. A moment later, the music ended suddenly and Lawton clamped the phone back to his ear.

"Yes, that's..." Lawton trailed off as the voice on the other end began speaking. He listened for several seconds, then tried unsuccessfully three times to interrupt before he finally got to speak. "Okay, look," he said, "I'm currently interviewing Mr. Winslow as a suspect in a murder investigation. He's giving me some long-winded story about how the victim, Michael Reed, stole his wife thirty years ago and he's just now found out she wasn't dead and buried." He listened again for a moment. "I'll let him call you when I'm..."

The voice on the other end of the line suddenly became louder, and Lawton's face grew dark. "Fine," he said testily. "Here he is." He held the phone out to Harry and glared at him. "They want to talk to you."

Harry leaned forward and took the receiver, putting it up against his ear. "Harry Winslow," he said. He listened for a couple of seconds, then smiled. "Jonas, you old goat, how have you been? Yes, it's true. I found out that Michael Watkins actually convinced her I was dead and that the KGB was going to come after her and the children. He took her to Brazil and got her a new identity all set up, and they got married sometime later. She found out I was alive after the Lake Mead incident, and then he started threatening her if she tried to contact me. I found out *she* was alive just a few days ago, when Michael left something inside my apartment to bait me into coming after them. I hired Sam Prichard—yes, that Sam Prichard—to help me track her down, and we showed up at her door this morning. Shortly after we sat down to talk, Michael came in and pointed a gun at us, but we talked him into a deal where we keep our mouths shut and he would get to keep the fortune they built together. Kathleen and I left, and I can assure you he was alive and well at that moment." He listened for another moment, then chuckled. "Whoever did it seems to have seized upon the opportunity to let me take the fall. Even the only possible witness who could swear I wasn't there at the time is dead under suspicious circumstances, so this is going to be quite a conundrum, I'm sure. This young detective doesn't seem to want to believe any of this, so you might put a bug in his ear."

Harry listened for another moment, then passed the phone back to Lawton. The detective put it to his ear. "Lawton," he said. "This is all really true?" He listened to whatever the other man was saying for a moment, then closed his eyes and shook his head. "All right, fine," he said after a moment. "None of that changes the fact he's currently the only suspect we've got. Frankly, it seems to me that if somebody had stolen my wife that long ago and I found out about it now, I might want to kill the son of a bitch, myself." He listened again for a couple of minutes, not even interrupting once, and his eyes slowly got wider. When he finally spoke, it was simply to say goodbye and hang up.

"Well, well," he said. "According to that fellow, who claims to be in charge of classified employee records, you used to make James Bond look like an amateur. Of course, that doesn't mean a whole lot right at the moment, but I guess I should at least listen to what you got to say. You want to tell me more about this whole crazy wife-stealing situation?"

17

Harry started talking, then, with Sam and Kathleen adding in details as needed. Lawton sat at his desk and made notes, but the look on his face was one of total disbelief. The whole story took almost an hour, and then another half-hour for Lawton to type it up for their signatures.

"At the moment," Lawton said, "I don't have anything to hold you on. We are interviewing the neighbors around Reed's house, and tracking down everyone we can find who's been to that tobacco store today, to see if maybe they saw anything. Could be you're correct about that clerk, that somebody killed him so he couldn't give you an alibi, or it could be you whacked him yourself so he couldn't tell us you were there an hour earlier than you claimed. Whatever the case, I don't want you leaving Clearwater. There's no doubt in my mind I'm going to have more questions for all of you before this is over."

Harry extended his hand, but Lawton refused to shake it. After a couple of seconds, Harry simply shrugged and walked out the door with Kathleen and Sam following. They got back into the Buick and Harry suggested they go find some dinner.

"Hey," he went on, "at least I wasn't arrested. That's got to be something good, right?"

"It's good at the moment," Sam said, "but if we don't find the real killer soon, I'm afraid your luck isn't going to hold out much longer. Lawton wants to close this case, and he isn't all that concerned about making sure he's got the right guy, as long as he's got somebody who looks guilty. Right now, that somebody would be you. I'm not a lawyer, but I'm pretty sure I wouldn't want to try to defend you on this case."

"Sam, boy, I know plenty of lawyers if I need one. What I need right now is the best private eye in the world, and that's you. There is a killer out there, and he's got to be caught before he manages to frame me completely."

Sam nodded as he made a left turn. "I agree," he said, "but at the moment, I haven't even got the slightest idea where to start looking. Kathleen, do you know of anyone in particular who might've wanted Michael dead?"

"Besides me, you mean?" Kathleen asked. "I'm afraid not. Of course, there's always the people he dealt with in his dark work. That's what he called it when he did special jobs for the CIA or NSA, 'dark work.' I always thought it sounded a little egotistical, you know?"

Sam chewed the inside of his cheek for a moment. "I don't suppose he kept any kind of journals or records about that work, did he?"

"Oh, no," she said. "Keeping any kind of record of his clandestine assignments would be a violation of security. There's no way he would ever do that."

Sam shook his head. "Harry, is there anybody you could contact who might be able to give me leads? Someone who might know what kind of people Michael might have pissed off in the last few years?"

"I can certainly try," Harry said. "I'll get on that as soon as we get back to the hotel."

"Good, you do that," Sam said. "Kathleen, I'm going to need to speak to your kids. Would you see if you can arrange that? Under the circumstances, it would be best if I could meet them somewhere else, but they could always come to my hotel room if necessary. You can be present if you want, but I'd want Harry to stay away."

Kathleen nodded. "They're upset," she said, "but I'm sure they'll be willing to cooperate with you. I doubt either of them really knows anything about this, though."

"I agree, they probably don't," Sam said. "The thing is, sometimes people know things they don't even realize they know. I'm just looking for a starting point, something to nudge me in a direction that might do some good."

She shrugged her shoulders. "I'll get them to sit down with us, but then the rest is up to you. I don't think either of them is very happy with me at the moment."

"That might change when they learn the truth," Sam replied. "I realize it's going to be hard for them to accept, but they're going to need to know just who Michael really was, and what he did to your family. And I can tell you without a doubt it will be better coming from you than letting them learn it from the news."

Sam suddenly turned the car into the drive-through lane of a fast food restaurant. "Tell me what you want," he said. "I don't think we have time to go sit down anywhere; I need to talk with your kids tonight, and pretty soon."

Sam relayed their orders to the teenager behind the intercom, paid for and picked up the food and headed on to the hotel. He parked the car, but it was suddenly mobbed before Harry and Kathleen could get out. A half-dozen reporters who had been hanging around the front door had spotted the Buick, and some of them had obviously talked the desk clerk into revealing what kind of car they were driving. The car was surrounded, and questions were being shouted.

"Mrs. Reed," yelled one reporter, "did you kill your husband?"

"Did you have someone do it? Did you hire one of these men to kill him?"

Sam climbed out and pushed a camera out of his face. He flashed his ID for just a second, then spoke loudly. "Back off, back off, or you could be charged with interfering in a police investigation."

"Shove that," said a burly man. "Haven't you ever heard of the freedom of the press?"

Sam shot him a look that could have peeled paint. "Of course I have," he said. "Haven't you ever heard of keeping details out of the press so that only the perpetrator will know them? These folks are under orders not to say anything at this time, so you can all go home for a while."

"Yeah? And who are you, their lawyer?"

Sam grinned and reached into his pocket for a stack of business cards. He passed them out to the reporters. "I'm not an attorney," he said, "I'm a private investigator. This gentleman is my client, and it's my job to prove that neither of these people had anything to do with the death of Michael Reed. Unfortunately, I am still not allowed to say anything at this point, but I promise to call a press conference as soon as I know something tangible."

"Prichard," mused one of the ladies. "Oh my gosh, Sam Prichard from Denver? You're the one who stopped the terrorists from nuking Lake Mead, aren't you?"

"Yes, but I don't talk about that one either," Sam said. The reporters tried to ask more questions, but he brushed them off. They had to settle for passing him their own business cards and begging him to call when he was ready to give the press information.

That got most of them to back off so Harry and Kathleen could get out of the car, although their pictures were taken a few more times before they got inside the hotel. From the way the desk clerk avoided looking at them, it wasn't hard to figure out who had tipped the press about their car, but Sam let it go. They hurried to the elevator and up to their rooms, then gathered in Harry's room to eat quickly.

They were hungry, so the burgers and fries disappeared rapidly. As soon as they were done eating, Kathleen took out her phone and dialed her son first.

"Hello?" Harold answered.

"Harold, it's mom," she said unnecessarily. "I need your help."

"My help? Are you hurt?"

"Oh, no, no, nothing like that," she said. "The police have just released us, but Mr. Prichard, the private investigator, he'd like to talk to you and Beth. The police detective is so sure Harry did this that they're not even bothering to look at anybody else or any other possibilities, so Mr. Prichard is doing everything he can to find the real killer. He's hoping maybe one of you kids can give him some kind of insight into what might have led up to this."

"Wait, what? I thought Prichard was working for Dad? Isn't he the one that found out you were having an affair and told Dad about it?"

"Son, I'm afraid that's only the tip of the iceberg when it comes to the lies your father told you, and forced me to tell you today. I'll explain it all when you get here, I promise, but we desperately need your help to prove Harry didn't kill him."

Harold was quiet for a few seconds. "Let me get this straight," he said slowly. "You want me to try to help the man who the police think is the number one suspect in the murder of my dad?"

"No," Kathleen said. "I want you to help Mr. Prichard." She took a deep breath. "And when you come, there are a lot of other things I need to tell you, as well, things I need to say to you and your sister at the same time. Do you think you could round her up and bring her along?"

"Shouldn't be too hard," he said. "She's sitting across the room from me now, crying her eyes out. Where are you? I'll bring her along, the kids can stay with Janine for a bit."

Kathleen gave him the name and address of the hotel, along with the number of Sam's room, and he promised to bring Beth and be there within half an hour. Kathleen hung up the phone with a deep sigh.

"I'm about to turn their entire world upside down," she said. "Do I really have the right to do that?"

"You're not the one who's doing it," Sam said. "The truth is that Michael did it, years and years ago. It's just that the repercussions haven't managed to catch up with anyone until now."

"Sam is right, Kathy," Harry said. "None of this is your fault, you must remember that. You, the kids, me—we are all Michael's victims. What we have suffered all these years, what these kids are going through now, all of that is his doing."

She tried to smile, but it looked more like a grimace of pain. "I know," she said. "I know you're right, but that doesn't make it any easier at this moment. My God, Harry, Beth didn't even really know you when it all happened, and Harold was only three; it didn't take long before his memories of you merged with the new memories he was making with Michael. As far as these kids know, he was the only father they ever had, and it just never seemed like a good idea to tell them he wasn't. I was always afraid it would confuse them, cause them trauma they couldn't handle. It's not going to be easy to get them to accept the truth, now."

"They'll accept it," Harry said. "Beth already noticed the resemblance between me and her brother, and he said I seemed familiar. All that will make sense to them once you tell them the truth."

Harry gave Kathleen the envelope with the letter and photos in it, and she and Sam went over to his room to wait. Sam busied himself with the little in-room coffee maker for a moment, and then they waited at the little table with the sounds of percolation in the background.

The coffee was ready just a minute before there was a knock on the door, and Sam opened it. Harold and his sister stood there, and Sam motioned for them to come on in. Since there were only two chairs at the table, Kathleen had moved to sit on the bed and she patted the surface beside her, inviting Beth to join her. The younger woman sat down beside her mother, and Harold sank into one of the chairs.

"I just made coffee," Sam said. "Any takers?"

"I'll have a cup," Harold said. "Just black, nothing in it."

"Nothing for me," Beth said. The look in her eyes told him that she was in no mood to accept any kind of hospitality. She wasn't there to answer questions as much as to get answers. Sam was sure he could understand. He poured a cup for himself and Harold and then sat down at the table.

"I do need to talk to you both about what's happening right now," he began, "but before we get into that, your mother has some things she needs to tell you." He raised his eyebrows at Kathleen, and she let out a sigh as she lowered her eyes to the floor for a moment. When she raised them again, it was with a look of determination in her face that would have done credit to a soldier on the battlefield.

"What I'm about to tell the two of you," she began, "is going to sound very far-fetched, but I swear to you that it's the absolute truth. This is all going to come as a shock, and I wish—oh, how I wish I could make this easier for you, but I can't."

Harold cocked his head to the right and lowered his eyebrows as he looked at her. "Mom? Whatever it is, just spit it out."

"Oh, God," Beth mumbled under her breath. "Mom, don't tell us you were involved in Dad's death. Please, tell me that's not what you're about to say."

"No, of course not," Kathleen said. "Good Lord, I almost wish it was that simple." She took a deep breath. "Harry, Beth, no matter what you think of what I'm about to tell you, I need you to just sit there and listen. Don't interrupt me right now, don't ask questions just yet, just listen. Can you do that?"

Both of them nodded, so Kathleen steeled herself to go on.

"Michael Reed was not your father," she said slowly. "Harold, you were three and Beth, you were just two, when Michael came to me one day and said that your father, your real father, had been killed on a secret mission for the government and that the KGB—those were Russian bad guys, back in the days of the Soviet Union—he said the KGB was out to kill all of us, because that's how they punished foreign agents. If they caught or killed an American agent, then they would send a death squad to wipe out his family, as well. In order to protect you kids, he said it was necessary for us to disappear that very day, and he had made arrangements to take us to Brazil and get whole new identities."

"Wait a minute, just wait a damned minute," Beth interrupted. "Are you going to tell us that old man you're running off with is our father?"

"Of course he is," Harold said. "Same name as me, and you noticed how much I look like him. I can even see his eyes and his chin on you, Sis. You even hinted at it this morning."

"Yeah, but I was just being a smartass," Beth said. "I thought Mom was gonna say she cheated on Dad back then, too, and that's where you came from." She turned it to look at her mother again. "But this..."

"Yes," Kathleen said. "Harry Winslow is your father. He was also...No, he *is* also my husband, and the only man I ever truly loved. When I thought he was dead, when I thought he'd been killed and left us at the mercy of the KGB, when Michael was standing there yelling at me that the only thing I could possibly do to protect you was to disappear with him at that moment, I—I panicked, I was overwhelmed. I didn't know what to do, and there was no one else I could turn to. We packed up a few things and got into Michael's car, and two hours later we were in the air on a diplomatic flight to Brazil. We started our new lives that day, with Michael there every single minute, watching over us, taking care of us, playing with you kids. He stayed with us for two weeks while I got settled in, then he had to leave for a few days. He was gone almost a week, and I'll tell you in a minute what that was about."

Tears began to run down her cheeks. "After a while, when the shock and pain and grief started to wear off, I buried myself in you kids. You were all that mattered to me, then, and I was so very grateful to Michael that he had kept us safe, that he was almost always there for us. When it hurt the worst, those first few weeks when I just couldn't function very well, he even brought in a nanny to take care of you whenever he had to be away. All I saw was how wonderful he was being, so when I finally started to feel like I could survive and live through it all, it seemed natural for us to sort of gravitate into being a family. It wasn't long before Michael and I were lovers, but I didn't want to present that kind of example to you kids, so I suggested we get married."

"I know you said to hold our questions," Harold said, "but I have to ask one. If this is true, then where has old Harry been all this time? I mean, didn't he even bother to come looking for us?"

Kathleen smiled sadly. "Michael was thorough," she said. "I only found out the truth year before last, when Harry turned up in the news. I was in shock, I couldn't believe he was still alive, and I asked Michael how it could be...That's when he told me the truth. Not only did he convince me that Harry was dead, but that week he was gone, he also made Harry believe that we were. Our house had burned down a couple of days after he left, and the fire department found three bodies inside. A woman, a little boy and a baby girl. Michael said they were bodies he got from the morgue, and that the CIA had manipulated medical and dental records so they would be identified as us, so when Harry got back from his mission, Michael was there to attend our funerals with him. Of course, now we know that the CIA didn't have any idea what Michael was doing, but that's what he told me at the time. Still, for more than thirty years, Harry has thought we were dead."

"Then how the hell is this happening?" Beth demanded. "Why has he suddenly shown up in our lives again, now?"

18

Kathleen reached under the pillow on the bed and withdrew the envelope Harry had given her. "For the first few years, I always had it in mind that someday I would tell you about Harry. I used to write him letters, and I'd put pictures of you kids in them and talk about what was going on in your lives, and I thought that maybe someday I'd give you all those letters and let you see just how much he meant to me. This is one of them, from when we were still in Brazil." She swallowed hard, then went on. "When I found out Harry was alive, that's when Michael showed me who he really was. He told me that if I contacted Harry in any way, he would kill Harry and then he would kill me. He even threatened you kids, and I can tell you that he was cold-blooded enough to hurt anyone if he thought it would benefit him."

"Dad? Come on, Mom," Beth said, "Dad wouldn't ever really hurt anybody."

Kathleen smiled, but scoffed. "Sweetheart, let me tell you how little you actually knew about him. Michael Reed wasn't his real name; it was Michael Watkins. Just like Harry, he was an American secret agent; that's how he was able to forge all the paperwork and pull off all the necessary magic to do all this. He's been working for the CIA or some other agency since before you kids were even born, and one of his main jobs is to force people to go along with what our government wants, even if that means he has to kill them or someone close to them. Trust me, he was a killer. Before you kids came to the house this morning, he had a gun pointed at me, Harry and Mr. Prichard. He shoved it down into the chair he was sitting in just before you arrived, but he made sure we knew he could get it out in a hurry if he needed it. Yes, if he thought it was necessary, he could have killed any of us."

She shook her head to get back on track. "Anyway, I started sneaking off on little trips to DC. I wasn't going to contact Harry, but I just wanted to see him, I just wanted to see with my own eyes that he really was alive and well. Well, Michael found out, and somewhere along the line he decided that he wanted to bring all this to a head." She waved at the envelope in her hand. "He took this out of the box I kept it in up in the attic and went to DC, broke into Harry's apartment and left this for him to find." She handed the envelope to Beth.

Beth opened it, and Harold rose and stood so that he could look over her shoulder. They read through the letter together, and then looked at the photos of themselves and their parents. Harold sat back down without a word, while Beth simply looked up at her mother with wide eyes.

"Anyway," Kathleen went on, "when Harry found that, he went to Mr. Prichard. Mr. Prichard is a private investigator, like we told you, and he managed to track us down. They showed up at our door this morning, because Harry just wanted to know what had happened. Michael was supposed to be on his way to Japan, so I let them come in and sit down so we could talk, but then Michael showed up with a gun. At first, he said he was going to have to kill Harry and Mr. Prichard, and maybe even me; he said he'd kill all of us before he would give up everything he built with the yacht business. It was Mr. Prichard who talked him into the whole divorce idea, but once we assured him we'd keep our mouths shut—we weren't even going to be allowed to tell you kids the truth—and with the threat that something would happen to you or Mr. Prichard's family if we ever did talk, he finally agreed to let us go. That's when he made me call you both to come over."

Beth and Harold looked at each other for a moment, then Harold looked at Sam. "Not that I don't believe my mother," he said, "but I'm sure you can corroborate all of this? You've got evidence to back it all up?"

"I do," Sam said.

Harold nodded. "All right, then," he said, "but you don't believe Mr. Winslow killed my—killed Mr. Reed?"

Sam sighed. "I've known Harry for a couple of years now," he said, "and we've fought side-by-side on more than one occasion.

He can be as cold-blooded as anyone in his line of work when he has to, but I've never met a more honorable man. I'm convinced of two things: first, all he wanted was to be able to see your mother and get to know you two, and second, and this is from what I know of him personally, if he had killed Michael he would have made absolutely certain that he had an airtight alibi. He certainly wouldn't do it at the moment when he would be the only viable suspect."

Harold shrugged. "Or maybe he's counting on you believing that."

Sam shook his head. "That wouldn't make any sense. Just my opinion isn't going to be enough to keep him from being arrested for this murder. And as it stands right now, unless I find evidence that can clear his name, I have no doubt he's about to be arrested and charged."

"Maybe I don't understand how this sort of thing works," Beth said suddenly, "but isn't it that police detective's job to figure out who did this?"

"It should be," Sam said. "Unfortunately, Detective Lawton is more interested in solidifying his case against Harry than looking for any evidence that might clear him. Look, you guys, I'm not going to deny that Harry had motive. If somebody had done to me what Michael did to him, I'm not 100 percent certain I wouldn't track the bastard down and kill him, but even I would be smart enough not to do it the very day everybody finds out I'm around. Harry and Michael both had what they wanted, without bloodshed. Now, I'll admit it's possible that the two of them might have eventually come to the point where one of them had to go, but it wasn't going to be today."

"Unless old Harry thought maybe he wouldn't be a match for my dad, so he ambushed him," Beth said, her eyes glaring at Sam. "Maybe he was afraid Dad would come after him later, and decided to get rid of him now."

"Once again, I'll fall back on how illogical that is. Harry would be smart enough to know that if Michael turned up dead today, he's the only suspect that the police are even going to look at. What I have to do is find out who else might have wanted Michael dead, and I'm hoping maybe you can help me with that."

The two of them looked at one another, and then back at Sam. "Why in the world would we have any ideas?" Harold asked. "Look, Mr. Prichard, as far as I knew my dad sold boats. Now, if Mom says he was some kind of secret agent, then I guess I believe her, but you've got to remember that we never saw any sign of that side of him."

"I'm sure you didn't, and that isn't what I'm asking. I want to know if you can think of any other situation that might have left someone angry at Michael, maybe angry enough to be violent."

Harold looked at his sister. "Beth? What about Daniel?"

Beth rolled her eyes. "Daniel couldn't be violent with anyone who might be able to fight back," she said. "The one time he and Dad got into it, he just covered his face with his arms and started crying."

"That may be," Sam said, "but Michael was killed by a gunshot. Having a gun in your hand can make even the biggest coward feel brave and tough."

"I can't see Daniel ever even touching a gun," Beth said. "He was always scared to death of them, even when his father tried to take him hunting when he was a kid. He wouldn't even buy toy guns for our son, Reggie; he said playing with toy guns would lead to violence when he grew up."

Harold looked at her for a moment, then turned back to Sam. "I can only think of one person who might've hated my—Michael," he said. "About ten years ago, back when he first started dealing in yachts, he had a partner. Guy's name was Alan Ellison, and he wanted to keep the business small, but Michael was getting chances to list and sell some of the big, multimillion=dollar boats. He didn't want to pass up the chance at million-dollar commissions, so he found some way to force Alan to sell out to him. I was around a couple of times when they argued about it, and I remember Alan saying something about getting back at him someday." He shrugged his shoulders. "I never really thought the guy was violent, but I guess you never know for sure about people, right?"

"That's absolutely true," Sam said. "Any idea where I can find Alan now?"

Beth huffed. "I do," she said. "He was always kind of like an uncle to my kids, and he still drops by every now and then. He lives down in Bradenton." She gave Sam an address and phone number, and he wrote them down. "I can tell you he didn't do this, though, he's just not that kind of guy. I don't think he has a mean streak in him anywhere."

"And you're probably right," Sam said. "It still can't hurt for me to check him out, though. What about your ex-husband? Where do I find him?"

Beth rolled her eyes, but she rattled off another address and number. Sam wrote that information down as well, then looked at Harold once more. "Anyone else you can think of?"

"Not off the top of my..." He trailed off, and then looked at Sam with a curious expression. "You know, this might sound crazy, but I remember something Michael said a couple of months ago. He'd been out riding the motorcycle I gave him, and I guess he had a run-in with some motorcycle gang over around Melbourne. One of them wanted to buy his bike, but he said it wasn't for sale and I guess it started a fuss. I kind of laughed it off, because I remember him saying he left six outlaw bikers laying in the parking lot of a bar." He shrugged again. "If the stories you're telling me are true, then maybe that wasn't just an old man bragging."

"Any idea what club they were with? Or what bar it happened at?"

"No, I'm afraid not. Like I said, I thought he was full of crap so I just ignored it. Let's see, it would have been back in late June or early July. That's all I can remember, right now."

"Hey, I'll take whatever I can get," Sam said. "Maybe there was a police report about an altercation, something like that. Any other ideas?"

Both of them shook their heads, and Harold looked at his mother. "Mom," he said softly, "the one thing I want to say to you right now is that I'm sorry you went through this. I'm not sure what to think about old Harry right now, but if he really is our father, we probably need to at least give him the benefit of the doubt. I gather he's around here somewhere?"

Kathleen nodded. "Our room is next door," she said. "He's waiting for me there."

Harold looked at his sister and gave her a wry grin. "What do you say we take them both down to the restaurant and get to know our real dad a little bit?"

Beth glared at him for a moment, but then she seemed to deflate. "If everyone is so sure he didn't do this, I guess I can give it a try." She looked at her mother. "Don't expect me to call him Daddy or anything like that, though. Michael may have been everything you claim he was, but all I remember is how good he was to us. Whether he was really my father or not, he was still my dad, and I'm not going to stop calling him that."

Kathleen nodded with a smile. "That's completely understandable, Beth," she said. "I'm quite certain Harry will understand, as well."

Harold got to his feet. "Shall we?" His mother and sister rose and the three of them walked out the door together. Sam sat back in his chair, picked up the cup of coffee that had already gotten cold and swallowed it down, then took out his phone and called Indie.

"Hey, Babe," she answered. "How's it going down there?"

"It's going," Sam replied. "We got through the police interview without Harry getting arrested yet, but I suspect it's going to happen. Kathleen got the kids to come over and talk to me, so I got a couple possible leads to check out."

"Really? You think one of them might be the actual killer?"

"I doubt it. We've got Beth's ex-husband, who seems to be a typical bully except that he's afraid of guns. Then there's Michael's ex-partner, but the issue between them happened years ago so it's doubtful it would suddenly come up today. The only other thing I've got to go on is a possible altercation Michael had with a motorcycle gang some time back, but I can't see that leading to this type of a murder. Still, I got nothing else so I'm going to check them out."

"Yeah, at least it's something. If there's anything I can do..."

"Well, maybe you and Herman can figure out who I need to talk to about the motorcycle gang thing. From what Harold said, it must've happened in late June or early July over near Melbourne. Michael told him that he left several of the bikers laying in the parking lot, so there ought to be news stories or police reports on something like that." He let out a sigh as he flopped back onto the bed. "Indie, I almost feel like I'm out of my depth on this one. Michael was a spy; he undoubtedly had enemies we'll never be able to identify. The trouble is, if I don't figure out who really killed him, Harry is likely to spend the rest of his life in prison for a murder he didn't commit."

"Sam, come on," Indie said. "It sounds like all they've got to go on is the possibility that Harry had motive. Unless there's some kind of physical evidence you haven't told me about?"

"No, right now that's all they've got, but look at the news the last couple of years. Look at how many people have spent decades in prison after being convicted on evidence just as flimsy as this. It's great that a lot of them are being exonerated by new evidence now, but Harry doesn't have that many years left in him. I can't see him surviving years in prison while I spend all my time trying to prove he didn't do it."

"I know you, Sam," Indie said. "You'll figure it out, you always do."

Sam sighed. "I hope so. I almost hate to ask this question, but I don't suppose Beauregard has had anything to add?"

"Not that I know of. I haven't heard anything out of Mom today, and I'm sure I would have. Want me to call and ask her outright?"

"No need for that," Sam said. "Just let me know if the old spook decides to give us anything."

They spent a couple of moments exchanging sweet nothings, then Indie put Kenzie on the phone. Sam talked to his daughter for the three minutes her attention span permitted, then promised his wife he'd call her again before he went to bed, and hung up the phone.

19

This is the first time my family has truly been together in over thirty years, Harry thought. *My wife is beside me, my children sitting across the booth, but I feel like a stranger to all of them.*

"I know this has to be hard on both of you," he said aloud. "Despite everything, I can tell you that Michael was basically a good man. I know that you both loved him and have many fond memories of him, so you won't hear me speaking evil of him."

Harold shrugged his shoulders. "From what Mom says, you have every right. What he did to you was wrong. If something like it happened to me and Janine, I'm sure I'd be pretty bitter."

"Oh, I'm not saying I don't feel anger," Harry said. "I most certainly do, because I missed out on watching the two of you grow up, I missed out on so many things in your mother's life—I'm simply saying that I won't subject the two of you to that anger. No matter how I feel about Michael, he was obviously good to you. Those memories belong to you, and I have no right to tarnish them. If you will both allow, we will simply put the fact of what happened on the table, and leave my feelings out of that. It's not the past I want to talk about with you, it's the present and the future."

"God," Beth said suddenly, "this is going to be such a nightmare. How am I going to tell my kids about this? They loved their grandpa, they're completely devastated by his death. Now I have to tell them they have another grandfather that they've never even heard of before? How am I supposed to do that?"

"Well, I would certainly not expect you to do so today," Harry said. "Those children need the chance to grieve for their loss. Let's not confuse them right now; let them get through the funeral and start to adjust, and then we can tell them the truth together. Would that help?"

Beth looked at him, but her eyes revealed nothing of her feelings. "I suppose it might," she said. "It's still going to come as a major shock to them, though. I don't know if they'll ever really accept it."

"Of course they will," Harold said. "I'm not saying it won't take some time, but if there's one thing I've learned about people, it's that we adapt. We're just all going to have to work together on this. It's not something we can just throw out there and expect everyone to be on board with it instantly."

"I agree," Harry said. "There's nothing that needs to be rushed. It's certainly going to take some time for all of us to adjust to this."

Harold turned and looked at his mother. "You know," he said, "it just dawned on me that no one is asking you how you're handling it all. You doing okay, Mom?"

Kathleen smiled. "It's all been a little overwhelming, I'll admit that. There's something I need to say, though, and I hope it won't upset you kids too much." She glanced at Beth, then turned to look at Harry. "I fell in love with this man many, many years ago. Even hearing that he was dead didn't change that, and even though I did come to love Michael, I never stopped loving Harry." She turned back to her children. "But you both need to understand that when I found out Harry was alive and that Michael had deceived me for all those years, any love I felt for him simply faded away. Michael told me he did this because he was so in love with me that he couldn't bear the thought of us not being together, but the pain-and-suffering he put me through—no, that he put us through, because you kids were devastated when your daddy was suddenly gone—that isn't what you do to someone you love. When I learned the truth, I wanted to leave Michael right then and let Harry know that we were still alive, but he told me that he would kill me and Harry if I tried. He even told me that, if I managed to contact Harry and let him know, then he would kill the two of you to punish me. Now, whether he would have carried out that threat, I really don't know, but simply hearing him say it was enough to make me hate him. Naturally, I promised never to contact Harry, and I didn't. I tried to be sneaky, though, and I got some fake IDs to use in traveling, so I could go and just watch him from a distance. I never would have contacted him, but Michael didn't believe that. He found out what I was doing, and he set this whole thing up to draw Harry here with the intention of killing him. If it hadn't been for Mr. Prichard, Harry at least would be dead, and probably me and Mr. Prichard as well." She looked down at the table between them. "Like Harry, I'm not going to try to ruin your memories of Michael. I simply need you to understand that I do not share your feelings of loss, now that he's gone. To me, frankly, it's an incredible relief. If that makes you hate me, I can't help it, but you deserve to know the truth."

Harold cast a glance at his sister, raising his eyebrows. "Sis," he said, "I don't know about you, but I think I can understand where Mom is coming from. I don't believe she'd lie to us, but I'll admit I'm having a little trouble reconciling my memories of Michael with the man who would do these sort of things." He looked back at his mother. "Still, just the fact that we are all sitting here right now tells me that there are probably a lot of other things we don't know."

Kathleen looked from Harold to Beth. "Beth? Can you understand?"

Beth had the paper wrapper from a soda straw in her fingers, slowly ripping it into tiny pieces. "I guess I can," she said. "It's just so hard for me to imagine Dad doing these things. I mean, all my life, as far back as I can remember, he's been the kindest, gentlest man I've ever known. It's hard for me to believe the things you're telling me, but I'm like Harold; I don't believe you would lie to us about it. That makes it all even more confusing."

Harold nodded his head and then leaned forward to put his elbows on the table. "Okay," he said, "so all of that is out of the way, for now. Harry, why don't you tell us a bit about yourself?" He grinned. "Whatever you can, anyway, I'm sure there are plenty of things you're not allowed to talk about."

Harry chuckled. "I see you inherited my sense of humor," he said. "Yes, there are some things I can't tell you, but what I can tell you is this: you and your sister were the two best things that ever happened in my life, after meeting and falling in love with your mother. Harold, you were my little cowboy. I used to get down on my hands and knees in the floor, and you would jump onto my back and ride me like a pony. Whenever I was home, you were always right there with me, and some of the best parts of me came from trying to be the best example I could possibly set for you." He looked over at Beth. "You were my princess. Your mother used to get so frustrated at me, because every time I went somewhere I'd come back with another stuffed animal for you. There were times we couldn't find you in the crib, because I piled them up in it and you would pull the whole pile down on top of yourself. I remember a particular stuffed bunny rabbit that you just adored, and you would keep it cuddled close to you just about all the time. When you started walking, you would come to me in my chair in the living room and throw the bunny up into my lap, and that was your way of telling me it was time to pick you up. I'd pull you up into my lap and hold you close, and you used to grab hold of my mustache and pull it, and the only way to make you let go was to give you a kiss. The whiskers would tickle you, and you would start giggling so hard, and it was just delightful."

He paused and looked at his hands, folded on the tabletop. "Those memories, they're what got me through that first few months. Whenever I wasn't working, I'd just sit and remember those times with the two of you. I think about when the four of us would sit down to eat dinner, with Beth in her high chair and Harold sitting in a chair beside me, sitting on a couple of big books so that he could reach the table, and you, Kathy, straight across from me with that beautiful, loving smile you always wore."

"I'm sorry you went through that," Beth said softly. "I can't imagine how I would survive if something happened to my kids. I can't imagine that I'd want to survive."

"Oh, there were times when I didn't want to. I thought about ending it all, more than once, but it always seemed to me that would be dishonoring your memories. The three of you had brought such joy into my life, I didn't feel that I had the right to end it just because you were gone. I owed it to you to keep you alive in my memories. That was all I could give you, at that point, so I suffered through the pain and forced myself to smile whenever I thought of you."

Harold shook his head. "This is so weird," he said. "I'm sitting here listening to you, and it sounds like the sort of things a man would say as he sat in a cemetery, looking at the graves of the people he loved."

"Yes, it does, doesn't it?" Harry asked. "Can you imagine how strange it feels to me? I'm saying those things that would normally be said at a grave, and yet my lost loved ones are actually getting to hear them."

Beth looked at him, her eyes softening slightly. "Yeah, it must. Like I said before, I don't know how I can handle it if I were you." She turned her eyes to her mother. "Mom, why didn't you tell us? Why didn't you ever tell us that he wasn't our real dad, that Harry was really our father?"

"When Michael came to me and said Harry was dead," Kathleen began slowly, "he had all this paperwork about how the KGB—they used to be notorious for hunting down and killing people, back then—he said the CIA had evidence they were going to come after us. In order to avoid that, we had to go into something like witness protection. We would each be given new identities, but it meant we had to completely abandon the past. Everyone we knew had to think we were dead, and that had been arranged. He explained that our house would burn down and that bodies would be found in the ashes, bodies that had died in accidents and such. They would be positively identified as the three of us, so that meant we could never go back and take up our old lives again. I wasn't allowed to even speak of my family, or of Harry, not to anyone." She shrugged her shoulders. "Unfortunately, that included both of you. That first few months, whenever you would cry and ask for your daddy, I just told you he went on a trip. When Michael was around, he would spend a lot of time with you kids and you gradually started to think of him as your dad. When I realized that, I suggested to Michael that we should get married; he'd been asking me for a while, and I finally gave in. After that, you both called him Daddy and there was just no way to explain it to you without causing confusion or, as I believed at the time, putting us at risk."

"But you said, those letters, you were planning to give them to us someday and tell us about Harry, right?"

Kathleen smiled sadly. "Yes, that's what I thought at the time," she said. "The thing is, as you both grew into young adults, I started to think that telling you might be cruel. I mean, as far as I knew, Harry was dead. You wouldn't be able to go look him up, you'd never get to meet him; there was just no way to ever give you any kind of closure on it, so I finally just put them away. I guess I should have gotten rid of them completely, but they were the only connection I had to Harry. I just couldn't quite give them up."

"Yeah, okay," Harold said, "I can see all that. What I want to know is why you didn't come to us after you found out Harry was alive and Michael threatened you. I would've protected you, Mom. I would've done whatever it took to keep you safe."

"Harold, I..." Kathleen trailed off, and Harry reached over and took her hand in his own.

"Harold, it wasn't herself she was worried about," he said. "She said Michael had threatened the two of you. She was worried that if she said anything to you, and he found out about it, he might actually harm you in order to keep his secret. She's your mother, she couldn't take that chance."

Harold spread his hands in a gesture of frustration. "Look, maybe I'm not a spy, but I'm a pretty tough guy. I think I could've handled it."

Harry grinned and cocked his head to one side. "How would you have handled it? Confronted him face-to-face? We're talking about a man who can kill someone twice his size with a single blow of his hand, a man who knows how to make dozens of essentially untraceable poisons, a man who can fire a killing shot from more than half a mile away or make a bomb out of stuff he could find in the average kitchen. If you had threatened him in any way, that would have made you a danger that he had to eliminate. I'm sorry, son, but you would have only put all of you in even more danger. She made the right decision in not telling you."

"Okay, maybe so," Harold said. "Still, we might've been able to help her in other ways. She said she was sneaking off to try to see you, but he found out. Maybe we could have helped her keep it a secret."

Harry shook his head. "If she had come to you for help with that, Michael would have found out about it. He would have seen it as a conspiracy working against him, and something terrible would've happened to all of you."

"Look," Kathleen said suddenly, "all of this is moot, now. Michael is dead and the truth is out. We can spend years thinking about what might have been, or we can simply accept this God-given chance to have our real family back together again. Who's with me on that?"

Harry immediately raised a hand, but surprisingly, it was Beth who raised hers next. Harold looked at her for a moment, then sighed and held his own hand up into the air.

"Look, Harry," Beth said, "this is all going to take some getting used to. I don't doubt what Mom has told us, but while you may be my father, I don't know you. The trouble is, that wasn't your fault; I mean, it's not like you ran out on us or anything. Somebody lied to you and told you we were all dead. I can't hold it against you that you weren't there while I was growing up, know what I mean? So, all that being true, the only thing I can do is say, yes, let's all get to know one another properly. I like what you said earlier about my kids, letting them get through the funeral and some of the grieving process before we spring this on them, but I don't think we should wait too long. Maybe a few days after the funeral, we can all get together for a cookout or something. How would that sound?"

Harry smiled and dipped his head. "I think that sounds wonderful," he said, "providing, of course, that I'm out of jail by then."

"Jail?" Harold asked, startled. "You actually think you're going to be arrested over this?"

Harry pointed toward the lobby entrance, and they all turned to see Detective Lawton standing in the doorway with two uniform patrol officers. "I'd say it's about to happen," he said. "That man in the suit is the detective in charge of the case, and the look on his face when he spotted me sitting here tells me that he hasn't dropped by for a friendly chat."

Lawton chose that moment to come walking toward him, the officers following dutifully. He stopped a couple of feet away from their table and looked directly at Harry.

"Mr. Winslow," he said. "You are under arrest for the murder of Michael Reed."

"So soon?" Harry asked. "I thought it would take you at least another day to put together a case against me."

"And it might have," Lawton said, "if we hadn't found a witness who saw you enter the house only a couple of minutes before the gunshots rang out."

20

Sam was sitting at the table in his room, looking down at the pad on which he had scribbled a few notes. He'd spent the past thirty minutes on the phone, starting his effort to clear Harry's name.

Alan Ellison had answered the phone on the first ring, but it only took a few minutes for Sam to eliminate him as a possible suspect. Ellison worked for the state of Florida, and had been giving a presentation on boating safety in Miami all day. His presence there was easy to confirm, so Sam thanked him for his time and ended the call.

Daniel Jacobs had been a little harder to reach, but Sam had left a couple of voicemails for him and he called back about ten minutes later.

"Mr. Prichard?" Daniel asked. "Daniel Jacobs. On your message, you said it was urgent that I call you. What can I do for you?"

"Daniel, thanks for calling me back," Sam said. "I'm a private investigator, and I'm working on a case in Clearwater. I'm sure you knew Michael Reed?"

"Yeah, I know that SOB," Daniel said. "What's he done now?"

"Daniel, Mr. Reed was murdered sometime earlier today. I understand that you and he had had some altercations, and I wanted to ask if you had any ideas about who might have wanted him dead."

"Murdered?" Daniel asked, the surprise in his voice sounding quite genuine. "Holy cow, that's a shocker. I can't believe anybody could manage to do it, he was one tough bastard. Any idea what happened?"

"All the police are saying right now is that he was shot through the head," Sam said. "I don't suppose you went to pay him a visit today, did you?"

"Me? You gotta be kidding. The one thing I always make sure of is that I'm as far away from him as I can be! We got into it one time, and he beat me half to death, and then..."

"And then what?" Sam asked. "Did something happen between the two of you after that?"

"Man, are you sure he's dead?" Daniel asked. "I don't want to be opening my mouth if he's not dead, you feel me?"

"Yeah, I'm pretty sure he's dead. One of my best friends is probably going to be arrested for the murder, even though he didn't do it."

Sam heard Daniel curse under his breath. "Okay, it was like this," he said. "Me and my ex got into an argument, it was over something stupid. Freaking Reed was my father-in-law, he just happens to show up while she's yelling at me in the front yard, and next thing I know I'm down on the ground and he's kicking the snot out of me. Cracked five ribs, broke my wrist, busted my nose, had both eyes swollen shut—I mean, I was in some serious pain! One of the neighbors called the cops and they came down and arrested him, asked me if I wanted to file charges and I said hell yeah, and they loaded me in an ambulance and took me to the hospital. Want to guess what happened three hours later? Michael freaking Reed comes walking into my hospital room just as free as a bird and shoves a gun in my face and tells me if I ever yell at my ex again, he's gonna blow my head off. And then he says if I tell anybody he came to see me, he'll kill me for that, too. He's one crazy bastard, man."

"Yeah," Sam said. "Sounds like it. Somebody treated me like that, I might decide to go after him and put a bullet through his head."

"Do what? Man, don't be talking crazy like that. I didn't kill him, I can guarantee you that. You can check, man, I've been at work all day."

"I'll check, can count on that," Sam said. "I think I remember you worked at the hospital, is that right?"

"Hospital? Hell no! I manage the gas station at Tarpon Springs Road and Tampa Avenue. And if you don't believe me, check the security cameras. I had to be there all day because I'm training a new guy."

"Okay," Sam said. "You still didn't answer my original question. Do you have any idea who else might have wanted Michael Reed dead?"

"Just about anyone who knew him, probably," Daniel said. "A guy like that, he's bound to make enemies. I mean, he actually threatened to kill me, and man, if you'd been there you'd be just as sure as I am that he really freaking meant that! That dude is crazy, man, or at least was."

"But you can't think of anyone in particular? Never heard of someone else who had a serious problem with him?"

"No, man, sorry. I just pay my child support and visit my kids when I'm supposed to, and stay as far away from him as I can."

Sam thanked him and hung up the phone. The possibility that it had been either of these two men who killed Michael had been slim to begin with, and Sam had known they were long shots, but he had to eliminate all possibilities.

He dropped his pen onto the table and leaned back in the chair, rubbing his eyes. This part of detective work was always time-consuming and frustrating. Working a murder investigation was bad enough when you had the resources of an entire police department to work with, but a private investigator was limited. Sam thanked God every day for Indie and Herman, and he even grudgingly acknowledged an appreciation for whatever kind of aberration Beauregard truly was—because, as much as he hated to admit it, Beauregard's tips actually paid off—but the majority of the work and the deductive process had to be on him.

Back home, he was usually lucky enough that he could work with one of the local police detectives on a case; the chances of getting Lawton to cooperate with him weren't going to be very good, though. Sam needed information about the crime scene, any kind of information about Michael's past, business associates, etc. and these were things that the local police were likely to deny him access to.

His phone rang suddenly, and he picked it up. There was a local number on the display but he didn't recognize it, so he answered gruffly. "Prichard."

"Jerry Lawton," said the familiar voice, "the police detective. Where is your boy Winslow?"

"Downstairs in the restaurant," Sam said. "Why?"

"Because we got a witness who described him perfectly, and saw him go into Michael Reed's house just minutes before the gunshots were heard. He's got a concrete motive and now we can place him at the scene of the crime as it was happening, so the State Attorney got the judge to go for a warrant. I'm coming into your hotel right now to arrest him."

The line went dead and Sam jumped up quickly. He had kicked off his shoes and taken off his shirt while he made his calls, so he hurriedly pulled the shirt back on, buttoned it and tucked it in, while sliding his feet into his shoes. He grabbed his phone and slipped his jacket on as he went out the door. The elevator chimed as he got to it and an elderly couple stepped out. Sam smiled at them as he slipped inside and hit the button for the ground floor.

When it opened again, Sam hurried out and headed for the restaurant, but he was too late. Harry was being led out in handcuffs already, and Sam saw Kathleen trying to follow. He spotted Lawton and stepped in front of him.

"Who is this witness?" Sam asked. "I'm gonna want to talk to all of your witnesses, you know that."

"Prichard," Lawton said, "you go bothering any witnesses, I'll charge you with obstruction of justice. I don't need you interfering and messing up my investigation."

"What investigation? Doesn't it strike you a little odd that you even have a witness who claims to have seen Harry? You're talking about a man who spent many years slipping in and out of foreign countries and accomplishing missions that most people wouldn't even believe, but he's gonna be stupid enough to let a witness spot him while he's trying to commit murder?"

"Yeah, yeah," Lawton said. "Look, maybe he was some kinda superspy back in the day, but now he's old. Ain't you ever heard of Alzheimer's? Happens to you when you get old, makes you forget things. Maybe he just forgot to put on his superspy disguise."

"Oh, good grief," Sam said. "Let me ask you this: you said you had a witness who saw him go in. Did anyone see him leave?"

"What would that matter? All we need to know is that he was seen going in just before Reed was killed."

"Think for a moment, would you? You've got witnesses who claim to have heard gunshots, and what's the normal reaction when you hear a gunshot? You look in the direction it came from, right? So, now you've got witnesses who heard gunshots and looked in the direction they came from, did they see anyone leave the house? Did any of your witnesses see Harry leaving the house?"

Lawton glared at him. "At the moment, all we got is that he was going in just before the gunshots. Nobody saw anyone leave the house afterward, no. Hey, I got it, maybe Mr. Superspy suddenly realized there might be people watching, so he snuck out through the back. That would make sense, right?"

"Only if Harry was an alligator. Reed's backyard was pretty small and backed up right to the water. You need to be asking yourself how witnesses could see somebody go in, but not see them leave. I'm pretty sure you're dealing with a professional killer, here, somebody who could show up looking like Harry in order to throw suspicion on to him, then disappear without a trace."

Lawton shrugged and gave Sam a wide-eyed look. "Well, isn't your old buddy there supposed to be a professional killer? Sounds to me like he's guilty as hell, and using you to try to build him a reasonable doubt defense. If you can convince a jury he wouldn't do things this way, he might walk." Lawton grinned suddenly. "But I wouldn't count on it."

Sam grimaced and shook his head. "What about bail?"

"He'll be arraigned tomorrow morning on the nine o'clock docket," Lawton said. "I would imagine bail will be pretty stiff, though, we're talking about capital murder."

The detective turned and walked away, leaving Sam standing there with Kathleen beside him. Her children had come out of the restaurant and were standing just behind the two of them, but neither had said a word. Sam watched the police car drive away with Harry in the back, then turned to face Kathleen and her kids.

"What was that all about," Harold asked, "with that detective?"

"He says they've got a witness that saw Harry go into Michael's house just a short time before the gunshots were heard. I was pointing out to him that if people hear gunshots, they naturally look in the direction they came from. That would make you think that one of them should have seen Harry leaving, but nobody did. Makes me think it wasn't Harry they saw, after all. Why would he take a chance of witnesses seeing him? For that matter, why would he use a gun that people could hear, when I happen to know that he has a pistol with a sound suppressor? If he was going to commit murder, that would probably be the gun he would want to use, but he left it in the hotel room when he went to get his cigars."

"Did he have any other guns?" Beth asked. "Maybe he just thought, 'oh, hey, I'm out by myself, why don't I go kill Michael?' Maybe he just took a chance and it blew up in his face when somebody saw him."

"No, the only other gun was mine, and I've had it the whole time. I realize you don't know him yet, but if you understand Harry, none of this makes any sense at all."

"So what can you do, Sam?" Kathleen asked. "How can you help him?"

"I don't know, yet," Sam said, "but I can promise you I won't give up until I find a way."

"I'll pay you whatever it costs," Kathleen said suddenly. "If Michael is dead, then I'll end up with most of everything. We both had wills, and I doubt he had a chance to change it today."

Sam put a hand on her shoulder. "Harry's got me taken care of," he said. "We'll go to his initial appearance in the morning, and you might be able to bail him out. I would imagine your house is probably closed off for now, as a crime scene, but you can contact the police department to find out when you can go back inside. I'd really like to get a look in there, see if I can spot anything this CSI team might have missed."

"Well, I have a key. Do we actually have to have permission to go in there?"

Sam nodded. "Until the police crime scene tape is removed, yes. They should be done by sometime tomorrow, I would think. For tonight, we might as well just get some rest."

"Mom," Beth said, "do you want to stay here at the hotel, or come home with me and the kids? They're pretty upset about Dad—about Michael, I mean, but I know they'd love to see you."

"No," Kathleen said. "I think I just want to stay here tonight. I'll go with Sam to the initial appearances in the morning, and I'll call you both afterward."

Harold and Beth gave her hugs, and Harold shook Sam's hand. "Mr. Prichard, if there's anything I can do..."

"I might take you up on that," Sam said. "Thanks for keeping a cool head through all this. I think it's helped your mother and your sister a lot."

Harold shrugged. "Sometimes," he said, "you just have to deal with whatever reality the world hands you. It isn't always easy, but it's still reality."

21

Sam went back to his room and called Indie to tell her the news. She was naturally upset, but understood that, under the circumstances, it was logical for Harry to be arrested. She wished Sam luck on finding the real killer, cautioning him to be careful, and then the conversation turned to simpler things.

When he got off the phone, Sam took a shower and climbed into bed, even though it was not yet nine o'clock. He often did some of his best thinking in bed, and this case was giving him plenty to think about. Unfortunately, he didn't have any great epiphanies during the night, so he rose early the next morning and got dressed and ready for court, then called Kathleen next door.

She answered on the first ring. "Hi, Sam," she said.

"Hey," Sam replied. "Feel like going down for breakfast?"

"I'll have to pass. Detective Lawton called before you did, and they're sending a car to pick me up to take me to the Medical Examiner's office. I have to identify the body."

"Oh, crap, I should've thought of that. Call Lawton back and tell him I'll bring you."

"It's too late for that, I think. You go on and have your break-fast, then do whatever you can think of to help Harry. I'll get a cab afterward and meet you at the courtroom, okay?"

"Are you sure you don't want me to at least go with you? Identification—it can be pretty rough."

"I'm a big girl, Sam," Kathleen said. "I can handle it, trust me. You need to be concentrating on figuring out how to prove Harry didn't do this."

Sam sighed, but nodded into the phone even though she couldn't see it. "Okay, I'll see you at the courtroom, then."

Sam went down to the restaurant and ordered breakfast, and tried to think of what his next step should be while he ate. He thought about calling Indie, but he didn't have any news to give her yet. Better to wait until after court, at least then he could tell her something.

When he was finished with breakfast, he drove to the courthouse and found Kathleen waiting for him in the lobby. "How bad was it?"

"Worse than I imagined, but I got through it. I had to identify him by a tattoo on his arm and a couple of scars; his face was simply destroyed when he was shot."

Sam shook his head. "I'm sorry you had to go through that," he said.

"Like I said," Kathleen said with a shrug, "I'm a big girl. But it might give me nightmares for a few days."

They found their way to the proper courtroom and waited for it to open, then filed inside with dozens of others and managed to find seats in the front row, right behind the defense table. They had been sitting there for almost 20 minutes when a number of handcuffed and shackled prisoners wearing orange jumpsuits were led in and seated in the jury box. Harry was among them, and smiled when he saw them sitting there.

The judge came in a few moments later and they all had to stand, but then they were told to sit down once again by the bailiff. Various cases were called, and it was almost 10:30 by the time Harry's name was called out. He was brought from the jury box to the defense table, where a young woman stepped up beside him. The two of them whispered back and forth for a moment, and than the woman told him to stand and face the judge.

"Please state your name for the record," the judge said.

"Harold Winslow," Harry said.

"This is a capital murder case," the judge intoned, "State of Florida versus Harold David Winslow. According to information filed by State Attorney Benjamin McCall, there is sufficient evidence to charge Mr. Winslow with the murder of Michael William Reed yesterday afternoon, and to establish not only motive, but opportunity." He looked up at Harry. "Mr. Winslow, do you understand the charge you're facing?"

"I most certainly do, Your Honor," Harry said.

"If you are convicted of this charge, you could become eligible for the death penalty. Do you understand this as well?"

"I do."

The judge looked at the young woman standing beside Harry. "Ms. Bigelow, is this your client?"

"No, Your Honor," she said. "I was simply appointed for the initial appearance."

"Mr. Winslow, do you have an attorney of your own?"

"Not yet, Your Honor," Harry replied. "I haven't had opportunity yet to try to secure one."

"And are you seeking bail, Mr. Winslow?"

"I would certainly like to, Your Honor."

The judge turned and looked at the State Attorney, sitting at the other table. "Objections?"

McCall looked at Harry for a moment, then turned back to the judge. "Your Honor, we feel that bail would not be advisable in this case. Mr. Winslow is a former government agent, and we therefore consider him quite a flight risk."

The judge glanced down at the file in front of him, then looked back up at McCall. "According to the information you gave me, Mr. Winslow is retired from government service. At his age, I don't think he'd be all that hard to find if he tried to run away. Do you have any other reasons for requesting the court to deny bail?"

McCall sighed. "Not at this time, Your Honor."

The judge turned back to Harry. "I'm going to grant bail, and set it at 250,000 dollars. Can you afford that figure, Mr. Winslow?"

"I believe so, Your Honor."

"Very well, bail is so set. Upon your release, you will be required to provide a local address, because I'm ordering you not to leave the state of Florida. Arraignment will be set for thirty days from today at nine AM. That's a Monday, according to my calendar. If you fail to show up, of course, a warrant will be issued for your arrest and your bail will be revoked. You will be able to call a bondsman once you are returned to the jail."

"Thank you, Your Honor," Harry said. The case was dismissed for the moment, and Harry was led back to the jury box.

It only took another half-hour to get through the rest of the cases, and then the prisoners were led back out of the courtroom. Harry winked at Sam and Kathleen as he passed them, and made a gesture with his hand that indicated he would call shortly.

Since it was already after eleven, Sam suggested they go and find some lunch. Kathleen agreed, and directed him to one of her own favorite restaurants. It was close to the waterfront, so it took him a few minutes to get there, but when he saw the menu he was glad he had let her suggest it. Sam was a steak lover, and there were some on this menu that he never heard of before.

"Try the wildfire porterhouse," Kathleen said. "It's a little spicy, though."

"Spicy is good," Sam said. "I'm just not sure I can eat the whole porterhouse steak at the moment. What else is really good here?"

Kathleen laughed. "Absolutely everything. If you like it spicy but don't want a steak that big, they have the wildfire ribeye, as well. It's every bit as good."

"That'll work, then," he said. The waitress appeared and took their orders, hurrying back with their drinks.

"My phone has been ringing this morning," Kathleen said as they waited for the food to arrive. "Friends and some of Michael's business acquaintances; I've got about three dozen voicemails. His death is likely to shake up the yacht community, he was pretty well known in those circles. A lot of people really liked him."

"If Harry ends up going to trial, the whole story is going to get out. That could be pretty rough on you and your kids and grandkids."

Kathleen rolled her eyes. "We'll deal with it if we have to," she said. "At least my kids are somewhat willing to give Harry the benefit of the doubt. If you can find out who really did this, or at least prove that Harry didn't, I suspect they'll come to love him eventually."

"I'm certainly going to try. Harry's quite a character, but he's been one of my best friends for the last few years."

Kathleen smiled at him. "You're the kind of man he always gravitated toward. How did you meet Harry, anyway?"

Sam chuckled. "Believe it or not, our association started out at gunpoint. He was working undercover, actually running a drug ring back in Denver, when he got wind of a potential terrorist attack that could have killed hundreds of thousands of people. I was looking for a missing child at the time, and it turned out her father was involved with the drug ring. Harry had a partner in the undercover work who had gone bad, as he put it—tried to get his hands on this terrible poison that was slipped into the country along with the drugs they were naturally importing. Harry pulled a few fast dodges to try to keep it from him, sending that little girl's father off to Timbuktu with it while he tried to handle the situation, but I messed it all up when I tracked the father down in Arkansas. I ended up with the poison and no idea who to trust, so Harry kidnapped my—well, she was just barely even my girlfriend at the time, her and her daughter, and used them to force me to meet him. When I did, he started telling me that he was the good guy and I could trust him, but it was when Indie told me he had actually handed her his gun that I decided to give him a chance. He took us all to a safe house, but then the other guy attacked with some mercenaries and Harry and I managed to fight them off side-by-side. We caught the bad guy, got rid of the poison and Harry finally told me the truth about who he was. Since then, he's called me in a couple of times when he had a situation that required, as he put it, 'the Sam Prichard touch.' He's had my back every time, and we became pretty close."

Kathleen was nodding. "That's Harry," she said. "Once he considers you a friend, he's a friend for life. And if he actually calls you in on things like that Lake Mead situation, it's because he sees in you something far above what normal men can do. He told me yesterday that you are better than any agent he has ever worked with."

Sam blushed a bit and shrugged. "You just do the job that's in front of you," he said. "I learned that from Harry."

An hour later, Sam reflected that she had been absolutely correct. The steak was delicious, and his mouth was still tingling as they walked out to the car.

Sam's phone rang as he was getting behind the wheel, and he answered it to find Harry on the end of the line. "Come get me, boy," the old man said. "They can't handle me here, they're kicking me out."

"You made bail that fast?" Sam asked. "Back home, it would have taken you at least six hours."

"Like I said, they want rid of me. I think someone told them my history, and the guards here are a little scared of me. The bondsman did his part, and I've already signed out, so I'll be sitting out front on the bench. Can you believe they wouldn't let me have my damned cigars in there?"

Sam laughed. "We'll be right there, Harry!" He started the car and headed for the jail.

Sure enough, Harry was sitting on the bench in front of the jail puffing on a cigar when they pulled up. Kathleen hopped out and opened the back door, then slid inside so Harry could sit beside her.

"I suppose you haven't miraculously found the killer yet, am I right, Sam?" Harry asked.

"Not yet," Sam said. "I've talked with Beth's ex-husband and Michael's ex-partner, but both of them have legitimate alibis. Harold told me something about Michael having some sort of clash with a motorcycle gang a couple months back, I've got Indie working on that angle. I don't really put much stock in it, though. My gut feeling is that whoever we are looking for is a professional, somebody on the same level as you and Michael.

That naturally makes me think of a foreign agent, and I wouldn't even know where to start looking for somebody like that."

"I'll call some friends at Langley, see if there had been any rumors that might involve Michael Reed. The problem is that I don't have an official security clearance anymore, so they may be reluctant to tell me anything. At this point, I'll confess I'm a lot more interested in proving my own innocence than finding out who killed him."

"I'm feeling the same way," Sam said. "I'll take us back to the hotel, then I'm going to call Lawton and try to convince him to let me see whatever he's got. There might be something in there that will help me prove you didn't do it. If that fails, I'm going to go try to bully my way into the crime scenes at the house and the tobacco shop. Maybe I can spot something they missed, something that will at least cast doubt on their case against you."

"There is one way I can help," Harry said. He took out his cell phone and dialed a number with his thumb. "Jonas? Harry Winslow again. Listen, I...Yes, that's true. I made bail this morning, right after my initial appearance in court. Hell, no, I didn't do it! That's my problem. If I had, I'd know what evidence they had against me and could fight it. As it stands now, we don't know anything, and that's why I'm calling you. That detective, Lawton? He's not showing any signs of willingness to cooperate with my private investigator. Think you could put a bug in his ear? Get him to share information with Sam Prichard?" He listened for a moment, then smiled. "I think that'll work, Jonas. Listen, I appreciate it. What does this make now, about a dozen favors I owe you? Well, call me whenever you need one of them paid back. I'll be ready."

He put the phone back in his pocket and looked at Sam in the rearview mirror. "You've just been designated a Special Investigator for the Department of Homeland Security. That gives you all the authority you need to demand access to Lawton's case files. If he refuses, all you got to do is speak to his captain."

Sam grinned. "Harry," he said, "you just made my day."

22

Sam dropped Harry and Kathleen at the hotel, then called Indie as he drove toward the police station. "Hey, Babe," he said. "Well, Harry's out of jail. He's been officially charged with murder, but the judge granted him bail. Any luck on the motorcycle gang angle?"

"Well, yes and no," Indie said. "I found the incident, but it turns out all six of those bikers were arrested that same day, and they're all still in jail. It seems every one of them had warrants outstanding for them, mostly for petty stuff like selling pot or shoplifting. These aren't the kind of bikers you normally think of in connection to something like murder. They'd be more like wannabes, I think."

"Well, it needed to be checked out anyway," Sam said. "Harry called somebody at DHS, and he got me appointed as a Special Investigator. I'm on my way to the police headquarters to talk to the detective in charge of the investigation. I want to see the case file, maybe I can spot something they haven't."

"Good luck," Indie said. "I checked out that detective, Lawton, and you might like to know that he's been reprimanded twice for improper procedures and once for failure to cooperate with federal authorities. This is a guy who doesn't play well with others."

"I already figured that out about him. With this appointment, though, I can go over his head if I have to. I'm pretty sure I'm gonna get what I want, and maybe I can actually figure out what's going on, here."

"Okay, I hope so. Hey, Kenzie wants to talk to you."

"Hi, Daddy," Kenzie said. "I miss you and I love you."

"Oh, sweetie, I love you and miss you too. Are you taking care of Mommy for me?"

"Uh-huh," she said. "We're gonna go get pizza for lunch, and then we're gonna go shopping."

"Pizza, wow. That sounds like a lot of fun."

"Uh-huh, here's Mommy..."

Indie came back on the line. "Well, that was short."

"Yeah, I guess talking to Daddy takes a backseat to going for pizza. You guys have fun and be careful, okay?"

"Same to you, Babe." They said goodbye and ended the call, and Sam turned into the parking lot of the Clearwater Police Department.

He showed his ID to the receptionist at the front desk and told her that he wanted to speak to Detective Lawton. She didn't even bother to call ahead.

"Go through that door," she said, pointing at a door to the right, "and he's in the fourth office on the left."

Sam smiled and thanked her, then opened the door and stepped through. His hip twinged as he did so, and he started to wish he had brought his cane along, but he had left it at home. Most days he could get by without it, and it hadn't given him any problem in several days, so he just limped steadily along and bore through the pain.

Lawton was at his desk and didn't look a bit pleased when Sam stepped through the door.

"I'd ask what I owe this pleasure to," he said, "but seeing you is no pleasure. What do you want, Prichard?"

"You should have been notified by now that I've been appointed Special Investigator for the DHS on this case against Harry Winslow. I'm here to look at your case files."

"Yeah, I got a phone call. You want to see my file? Fine, come on in and pull up a chair." He picked up a folder from his desk and thrust it out at Sam. "That's it, that's the whole thing, and everything in it tells me your buddy is my killer."

Sam took the folder, which was about an inch thick, and sat down in the same chair he had used the day before. "That's what I'm here to see," he said. He opened the folder and picked up the first sheet of paper, which was the initial report of the nine one one call.

Call received 12:41 PM from Mrs. Carolyn Garrett, 691 Bay Esplanade, who reported hearing gunshots from a neighboring house a few minutes earlier. Officers dispatched.

The next page was the report of the two officers who had entered the house. They had arrived at 12:56 PM and approached the door, finding it standing ajar. Officer Mendez, the senior of the two officers, had knocked on the doorframe and called out announcing their presence, but received no response. He knocked again, announced their presence once more, and when no response was received, he pushed the door open and stepped inside. He announced once more that police officers were present and then both officers began walking into the house with weapons drawn.

The living room was clear, so they moved further. A door at one end of the living room led into what appeared to be a den, and the officers spent a couple of moments looking around, then went back to the living room to another door that led to a hallway. A door directly opposite was standing slightly open, so they pushed it further and looked inside at what looked like an office. There were two desks, each of which held a computer and stacks of papers, but there was no sign of any human presence. They backed out and moved through the hallway again, coming to the dining room, which was also empty.

As they approached the kitchen, both officers noticed a metallic smell, as well as the odor of recently fired gunpowder. At the kitchen door, they saw a male figure lying on the floor, and saw a large pool of blood spreading from the area of his head. Officer Conklin, the junior officer, stepped into the room and carefully approached the prone man, then reached down to feel for a pulse on his throat. It was at that point that he got his first look at the victim's face, at which time he turned and ran out of the house to vomit on the front lawn.

Officer Mendez stepped forward and looked at the victim's face as well, and it was his instant opinion that the victim was deceased. He called his dispatcher and reported finding what appeared to be a dead body, the probable victim of homicide, and requested instructions. He was told to secure the scene and wait for paramedics, detectives and crime scene investigators to arrive.

The next item in the folder was a packet of photos, and Sam pulled them out to look them over. The first couple of photos were taken from a short distance, merely showing the body lying on the floor and the spreading pool of blood. The next photograph was taken up close, however, and Sam's eyes went wide when he saw that the face of the victim had been completely obliterated, just as Kathleen had said. It was nothing but a bloodied mass, and Sam estimated that it must've taken at least three or four bullets to do so much damage. It was no wonder she had to identify him by a tattoo.

He glanced at the other photos, and then put them back in the envelope. He read through Detective Lawton's initial report, and then read the CSI report. It told him there were apparently several shots fired, because a number of 9MM bullets were recovered from walls and cabinets. The medical examiner on scene had estimated that five shots had actually penetrated the victim's face, entering almost dead center through the left eye, just below the right eye, directly to the left of the nose, immediately under the center of the nose, and through the point of the lower jaw. All five bullets had exited through the back of the skull, though the lowest one had also shattered the top cervical vertebra and ripped through the spinal cord.

Well, Sam thought, *that explains the damage to the face. Whoever shot Michael apparently felt he needed to be wiped completely out of existence.*

The next couple of pages detailed Lawton's meeting with Harry, Kathleen and Sam, and the subsequent interview of the three of them at the police station. Sam skimmed through them and found that Lawton had been meticulous in his notes.

The next page listed the neighbors who had been questioned, including Mrs. Garrett. She only reported hearing the gunshots, but another neighbor, Caitlin Stoddard, reported seeing what looked like an elderly man with white hair entering the house just a few minutes before the shots were heard. She did not see a vehicle approach the house, nor did she notice one parked anywhere near it at the time. She said that she had seen a white-haired man with a beard walking across the lawn of the house and up to the door. She further stated that she had looked at the house after hearing the gunshots, but saw no one depart.

Another neighbor, Robert Seacrest, said he had heard what sounded like an argument coming from inside the house just seconds before the shots went off. He claimed he had been out in his yard, which was directly across the street from the Reed house, spraying for weeds at the time, and heard what he believed to be two men shouting at each other. He couldn't make out most of what was said, but was quite certain he heard the words "wife" and "mine," and thought he heard the name "Harry."

The next page was the report of Lawton's visit to Mrs. Stoddard. After his interview with the three of them, Lawton had gotten the report from the canvassing officers and immediately driven out to see Mrs. Stoddard. When he showed her a photograph of Harry Winslow, he said that she responded immediately that he was the man she had seen entering the house shortly before hearing the gunshots.

"That's sloppy, Lawton," Sam said. "You showed a witness a single photograph and asked if that was who she saw. Don't you know how unreliable eyewitness testimony is? A good defense attorney will tear her apart on the stand, and you along with her."

"We might not even use her," Lawton said. "Did you see the lab report yet? Remember the GSR test? Turns out your boy had gunshot residue on both hands."

"So does almost everyone else in this country," Sam said. "If you've ever fired a gun or shaken hands with someone who did, you've got gunshot residue on your hands. The damn stuff lasts almost forever and never washes off, which is why the FBI doesn't even bother to test for it anymore. If that's all you've got, I'd have to say your case is pretty weak."

"Weak?" Lawton squealed, leaning forward. "I've got a clear motive, I've got a witness who puts him at the scene at the time, and I've got gunshot residue on his hands. I've also got the fact that, by his own statement, he was at that tobacco shop right about the time the clerk was killed, so we're seriously considering charging him with that murder, as well. If I can find one witness who saw him there, that'll be enough to clinch it. You add all that together, I think I've got a pretty good case!"

Sam looked back at the folder. There was another sheet that said the fingerprints on the body matched those on file for

Michael Reed. Sam made a mental note to check with Harry about that, since it seemed to him that the fingerprints should come back to Michael Watkins, but then he remembered Harry's comment about there always being people who would alter records. Since they knew Michael was still doing work for the government, it was probably likely that his fingerprint records had been updated at some point to fit his new identity.

Sam suddenly felt a tingle in his gut, so he started going through the folder again from the front. Nothing had changed, of course, but he had a nagging feeling that he might have missed something. He looked over all of the pages again, carefully, but didn't see anything that jumped out at him. He closed the folder and started to hand it back, but then stopped.

He opened it again and took out the packet of photos. One by one, he looked them over carefully, and suddenly he realized what his subconscious was trying to tell him. He looked up at Lawton, his own eyes wide.

"This body isn't Michael Reed," he said.

23

Michael Reed stood at the picture window in his living room and watched as the Buick backed out of the driveway. Prichard had come through, just as he had expected the man to do. It had been touch and go for a few minutes, though, and Michael almost thought he was going to have to suggest the plan himself.

He was glad he had not needed to do so. That would have made it less believable when the news of his murder came out, at least to Prichard. The idea was to give everyone, especially his handlers at NSA and CIA, a firm and undeniable reason to believe that Michael was dead, and there was nothing that could convince them of that as well as a legitimate motive in the hands of a man who would be capable of such a thing.

Yes, Michael Reed was about to die, and Harry Winslow was going to spend the rest of his life in prison because of it. Michael felt no sympathy for his old friend, however; there was no room for empathy in his line of work, and especially not at this point.

He took out his phone and dialed the number from memory. "Ron? It's time," he said. "Are you ready?"

"Yes, I'm ready," Ron said. "To be honest, I've been ready for a while. The pain is getting pretty severe, lately."

"Well, it'll be over soon. See you at the Gator House?"

"You bet. Give me an hour or so, sometimes it's hard to get a taxi."

"No problem," Michael said. "When you get here, I'll go ahead and do the final money transfer. Once you've seen that, we can conclude our business."

"I'm looking forward to it," Ron said.

The two men said goodbye and Michael slipped the phone back into his pocket. He had at least forty minutes before he needed to get into the boat again, so he went to the bar and poured himself a drink. The whiskey went down smoothly, and as its warmth spread to his body he felt a sense of relief that it was all finally coming together.

Almost a year earlier, back before Kathleen had begun sneaking off to spy on Harry, Michael had been called up for a mission into Moscow. The job was a simple one: all he had to do was pick up a defector and escort him through the city and onto a diplomatic flight back to the States. It should have gone without a hitch, because the defector had been fully vetted. Langley and DC were both completely convinced that he was legitimate, and would be bringing information they desperately needed about Russian activities throughout the former Soviet Union. Satellites had captured enough troop movements to make it appear that war was imminent, and the type of war being rumored might well put the USSR back together again. The defector was supposed to have information that could help prevent that from happening.

Michael had gone in posing as a Russian businessman named Yuri Castronova, and had no difficulty with the insertion. He was dropped just outside the city shortly before sunrise with a collapsible hang glider. Once out of the low-speed, low-flying plane, he simply squeezed the trigger that caused its wings to slowly spread out. By the time they caught the wind, he was already moving horizontally and shortly was able to flare into a running landing. Luckily, the moon was just bright enough to let him see the ground before he became a permanent part of it.

The drop site had been prearranged, and a car was waiting for him not far away. He had memorized the route and drove quickly toward his target, arriving just as the sun came up. The defector lived in a small house, and it was he who answered the door when Michael knocked.

"Dmitri?" Michael had asked, using the codename he had been given. The defector smiled and nodded, welcoming him into the house. Michael stepped inside without hesitation, and wasn't expecting the feel of a gun barrel against the back of his head.

It all happened so quickly that he was taken completely by surprise. The man holding the gun had been behind the door and stepped out as it closed. Michael froze and held his hands out and to the side.

"What is going on?" he asked in Russian. "Have I come to the wrong house?"

"No," said the man with the gun, speaking English. "You are exactly where we want you to be. You are in no danger whatsoever, as long as you don't try anything. All we want is to speak with you, and to make you an offer we believe you might find quite lucrative."

Keeping his hands high and out, Michael turned slowly. The man with the gun stepped back a bit to allow it, and then motioned for Michael to sit down in a chair to his left.

Michael sat as instructed, and then laid his hands on the arms of the chair. "What kind of offer?"

"First, let us explain that we know who you are. You are Michael Reed, and you have for several years been involved with several different American espionage agencies. You may deny it, of course, but we are quite certain of our information."

With a gun pointed loosely in his direction, Michael didn't feel inclined to argue. His own pistol was still tucked in the back of his pants, but there was no chance of reaching it before he would be shot dead. For a moment, it seemed wise to simply go along with his captors.

"I won't deny it," he said. "Now, what kind of offer did you have in mind?"

"As I said, one that will prove quite lucrative to you if you accept. We know that you have been involved in a number of highly classified operations over the last decade or so, and so you certainly possess information we would like to have, and which your government would hope to keep from us. Most of the information we are looking for concerns things that have already happened, rather than anything to come in the future. We would be willing to pay quite well for answers to certain questions concerning that information."

"Do I look like a traitor to my country?" Michael asked. "If the alternative to cooperation is a bullet through the head, you might as well take better aim and pull the trigger. I'm not talking."

The man stared at him for a moment, then cocked his head slightly to the left. "Ten years ago, you were part of a rescue operation in the Sudan. In that operation, a high-ranking Sudanese official was killed by someone using only his bare hands. Our intelligence services believe that you were the one who performed that assassination, and that it was probably quite difficult to do. If you will confirm that information, I will give you access to a British bank account that contains almost one million American dollars. This is information that cannot do any harm to your country, but will help us to close a file that has been open for far too long."

Michael had been ignoring the gun and keeping his eyes on the man's face. The small telltale signs of deception did not seem to be present, and Michael was surprised to realize that the man was almost certainly telling him the truth. Since that was the case, there was still a strong possibility he would survive this encounter. Since it was also true that confirming his participation in the mission could not do any harm to American interests that he could see, he saw no point in passing up the opportunity to collect such a reward.

"It was me," he said. "Was it difficult? Yes, simply because the man you're referring to was large and powerful and an excellent fighter. I'll even admit that, for a moment there, I thought I was going to be the one left dead on the floor. If I hadn't gotten the chance to crush his larynx, he probably would've killed me first."

The man with the gun nodded. "That is exactly as we suspected. Thank you for confirming it." He looked at the man who had opened the door and nodded his head once. The fellow took a slip of paper from his shirt pocket and passed it to Michael.

Michael glanced at it. It contained the name of a bank in London, along with the account numbers and password that would be needed to access the account through the Internet. With that information, he could transfer any money in it to any other account he chose. The last line on the note showed a balance of just over 950,000 dollars.

He looked up at the man with the gun. "Hell," he said, "got any more easy questions like that?"

"Actually, yes, and each one will get you another such bank account." There proceeded from that point a question-and-answer session that lasted almost two hours, and left Michael with eleven separate bank accounts holding just short of nine million dollars in total.

"Now," said the man with the gun, "there is one more thing we should discuss. We should like very much to continue this type of relationship with you. You are a man with many talents, and some of those talents would serve our interests quite well. There are, of course, many situations in which it is ill advised to use our own operatives; since you are currently acting as a freelancer with the different agencies of your own government, we are hoping to entice you to take some work for us on the side. Will this interest you?"

"As I told you," Michael said, "I'm no traitor. I'm not interested in becoming your double agent, or acting against my own country."

"That is not something we would ever ask you to do. On this, you have my word. However, we have learned that you are a man who can produce information that others cannot, and can orchestrate situations so that they result in an outcome you desire. There will be occasional instances when we might need a source of such information, or a particular outcome to a troubling situation, and you have the requisite skills that we would need in order to achieve those goals. We would be willing to pay you quite well, as you can see."

Michael carefully dissected the things he had said, then looked into his eyes. "You referred to me as a freelancer," he said. "That's not actually correct. I'm still on government payroll."

"That does not concern us," the man said. "As you can see, the bank accounts we provide you will be untraceable. You can do with them whatever you wish, and we're certain that a man of your talents will find ways to access the money when you want to. Your government need never know about it."

The conversation lasted another couple of hours, and then Michael was allowed to leave with the "defector." This was a man who would provide the United States with certain information that they would consider valuable, despite the fact that it was of no genuine importance to the Russian government. He would use that information to insert himself into the American intelligence community, at which time he would be capable of sending genuinely valuable information back to Mother Russia. This, Michael was assured, was the only thing he would ever be asked to do that might in any way be detrimental to American interests. The addition of one more bank account containing another 10 million dollars convinced him to agree.

Of course, double agents, even part-time ones, are eventually discovered. Over the next few months Michael took care of three separate situations for his new friends in Russia, and he began to worry about the day he would be found out.

It was around this time that he began to admit to himself that he liked what he was doing. Working for his country had always been exciting, but he had felt like something was missing. He had tried to fill that void with business, amassing a fortune as a yacht broker, but the fear of discovery was ruining his enjoyment of his wealth. Add that to the issues he had with Kathleen sneaking off to peek at Harry, and he began to wish for a way to simply drop out of his life.

The problem with that was that the American intelligence services wouldn't accept his death unless they had what they considered concrete proof. Simply having a body wouldn't be enough; there would have to be a completely logical explanation for the how and why and when of his demise, and it suddenly dawned on Michael one day that Harry Winslow could do him one last favor.

If Michael were reported murdered, and at the hands of someone with an obviously clear and viable motive, even the CIA would be unlikely to doubt it. Michael knew that he was smart enough to create a situation in which Harry would be arrested and ultimately convicted, and then he would be free to assume yet another new identity, one that would bear no connection to any government agency, anywhere. That would leave him free to continue taking these freelance jobs, and he could even expand his clientele until he was available for hire to many different countries.

Of course, there still had to be a body. Michael had immediately started searching for someone who, in death, could play him convincingly, and he stumbled across the right man purely by accident. It was during a visit to his own doctor's office that he met Ronald Denham, and the look on Ron's face as he was walking out of the office caught Michael's attention. Ron was the right build, the right size and approximately the right age; without even thinking about what he was doing, Michael jumped to his feet and followed Ron out of the building.

He caught up to Ron in the parking lot and took him to a nearby coffee shop. There, he learned that Ron had just been informed that the cancer he had been fighting for years had come back after the last remission, settling in his kidneys but also spreading to other parts of his body. There was no hope, and he had a maximum of three to four months of life left. While they talked, Ron began to cry, talking about how his wife and children would have nothing when he died.

"What if," Michael had said to him, "there was a way you could provide for them that would last the rest of their lives?"

24

Lawton leapt to his feet. "Do what?" he demanded. "What kind of crap are you trying to pull? We ran his prints, there's no doubt that's him."

"Lawton, I sat face-to-face with that man while he held a gun pointed at me not three hours before he was supposedly killed. I got a good look at him, and as a former police detective, I have a tendency to carefully examine and just about memorize someone I'm having a weapon-involved confrontation with. The clothing on this body looks to be the same, but whoever did it missed something. Lawton's fingernails were freshly trimmed; it looked like he'd just had a professional manicure. Look at the fingernails on this body." He took the photograph he was holding and spun it around, shoving it in front of Lawton's face.

The right hand was in clear view in the photo, and it was easy to see that the nails had not been trimmed in some time. Each fingernail bore a white half-moon at its tip, about an eighth of an inch long. Lawton stared at it for a moment, then looked up at Sam with a sneer.

"What, you expect me to take your word for it? I told you, Prichard, we ran his fingerprints. They confirmed that the deceased is Michael Reed."

"Have you forgotten everything Harry told you? This is a man who can change identities the way most of us change our underwear. On top of that, we happen to know that he was still doing clandestine work for the NSA and CIA, so it probably wouldn't be very hard for him to get his fingerprint records altered. I don't know who this dead man really was, but he wasn't Michael Reed."

"So now you want me to believe that Reed is faking his own death? Now, considering this fantastic deal you all supposedly made with him yesterday morning, why would he want to do that? That would mean he had to walk away from all his money and his yachts and all that other crap he was so determined to hang onto."

"That must have only been a smokescreen," Sam said. "Whatever he's up to, there's no doubt in my mind he had this planned out. He admitted to us that he planted that envelope in Harry's apartment, as a way to draw Harry down here; we thought he originally wanted to kill Harry, but it's obvious now that what he was really after was someone to take the fall for his own faked murder. He went out of his way to reel in the best possible suspect, a man with as clear a motive as you could ever hope for, then arranged it to look like he'd been murdered and set Harry up to take the fall. Remember that lady said she saw a white-haired man go in, but never saw anyone leave? I can tell you why. It's because that white-haired man she saw was probably Michael in disguise. He wanted to be seen, he wanted a witness to say they saw Harry go in the house just before the gunshots were fired. Whoever the real victim was, he was undoubtedly already in the house and dressed in Michael's clothes at that point."

"But that's crazy," Lawton yelled. "If he killed somebody to make it look like he'd been murdered, how did the fingerprints match up?"

"That's what I'm trying to tell you," Sam said. "Reed had this all planned out. Whoever that poor schmuck was, he was somebody who looked like Michael Reed enough that, as long as you didn't see his face, you'd think it was him. Well, the face got taken care of, didn't it? Reed had to have picked this guy some time ago, far enough back to give him time to get those fingerprints switched. Somehow, this guy had the same tattoo and scars, but those can be arranged. He might have paid this guy a fortune to let himself be marked that way."

"Yeah, you can put a tattoo and a scar on somebody, but you can't change their fingerprints. This is stupid!"

"You don't have to change the prints on the body, you simply substitute that guy's fingerprints for your own in the appropriate databases. Witness protection does it all the time for people they need to hide. Trust me, there are people working for the government who can do that sort of thing, and some of them will for the right incentive. Reed would know them, and he would know how to get them to do it for him. Once Harry showed up and we all left, he probably called the guy over and found some excuse to get him into his own clothes, then made himself up as Harry and went outside, let Mrs. Stoddard see him, then went straight back inside and shot the poor man through the face."

Lawton was staring at him, and Sam could see the beads of sweat starting to form on his forehead. "I—man, this is crazy. Even if it was true, do you know what would happen if I went to the prosecutor with this? I'd end up in the loony bin, that's what. Nobody would ever believe anything like this, it's too crazy."

Sam scowled at him. "You think I don't know how crazy it sounds? Unfortunately, I've had to deal with these kinds of people before, so I don't get the luxury of pretending things like this don't happen. Trust me, they do, and that's what we're dealing with now. Michael Reed is not dead, he's your killer. He probably had a tracer on my rental car, so after he killed this poor guy, he checked out where Harry had gone. If Harry was at the tobacco shop around the time the victim was killed, that would be an alibi. That's why that kid at the tobacco shop had to die."

Lawton was staring at him. "Just assuming for the moment this makes any sense," he said, "how the hell do we find him? I'll tell you now, there's no way the State Attorney is going to buy this; if you're right, the only way to get the charges dismissed against your buddy is if we can produce this guy in court and prove this whole crackpot theory."

Sam sucked in his cheek for a moment. "It's not gonna be easy," he said. "This man is a master of disguise, and he can become just about anyone. I need to get back to Harry and see what kind of help we can get from the feds. I'd keep this under your hat, for now, but I'll be back in touch shortly."

He got up and walked out of the office without another word, leaving Lawton standing there staring after him. The detective picked up the photograph and looked at it again, then fell backward into his chair.

Sam got to his rental car, but then froze. If Reed was actually tracking the car, it was the last thing Sam wanted to be driving. He took out his phone and googled taxicabs, then called to have one pick him up. It arrived about ten minutes later and he slid into the backseat.

"I need the nearest car rental agency," he said. The driver nodded once and the car took off again. The ride lasted about ten minutes more, and then the cab pulled up in front of an Enterprise office. The meter said sixteen dollars, so Sam handed the man a twenty and got out of the car.

Fifteen minutes later, he drove out in a new Dodge Challenger and headed for the Marriott. As soon as he left the parking lot, he took out his phone and called his original rental company and told them where to pick up the Buick. Then he called Harry.

"Sam, boy? How's it going?" Harry drawled.

"Crazy as ever," Sam said. "Did you get a good look at Michael yesterday?"

"I did," Harry said. "Why might you be asking a question like that?"

"Did you happen to notice his fingernails?"

"Yep. Looked like he'd just had them done, didn't it?"

Sam breathed a sigh of relief. "Good, I'm not the only one who saw that. Well, I just got a good look at the crime scene photos of the body, and the nails haven't been trimmed in at least a week."

There was silence on the line for a couple of seconds, then Sam heard Harry mutter under his breath, "Son-of-a-bitch. We've been completely set up, Sam."

"And then some. The body looks like his, it has the same tattoo and scars, the fingerprints come back as his, but I know for a fact that the dead man they found in the kitchen floor is not Michael Reed, or Michael Watkins or any other Michael that we know of. It looks to me like he wanted to disappear again, but he wanted to make sure you were charged with his murder. I'm trying like mad to figure out a motive for this, but it's pretty much eluded me so far. Any ideas?"

"It means he's gone dark," Harry said. "He's sold out, gone rogue. Remember Long? He went dark when he discovered that there were factions in the CIA that were literally out to destroy our national sovereignty. In this case, Michael has probably sold out to a foreign power. He needs everyone, especially the CIA, to think he's dead."

"That's why he wanted you to find out about Kathleen," Sam replied. "After what he did to you, the police would naturally consider that sufficient motive for murder. All he had to do was put on a white wig and a Colonel Sanders beard and mustache, then add some looser clothes and a neighbor was happy to positively identify you as the man she saw sneaking into the house just before the gun went off. ME says the body was shot at least five times in the face, so there's no facial identification. He must've chosen the victim weeks ago, then got his prints and had them substituted for his own. Fingerprint identification would hold up in court with no problem, and between the witness, your motive, your lack of alibi and some gunshot residue they found on your hands, they probably have enough to get a conviction."

"Sam, get rid of the car," Harry said suddenly. "Michael must be tracking it..."

"Already did, already did," Sam said, talking over Harry to make him hear. "He's probably tapping our phones, too, so now he knows we're on to him. Damn, I should've thought of that!"

"Well, don't fret about it now. Do you have a different car?"

"Yes, and I'll be there in another five minutes. We need to get you and Kathleen stashed somewhere safe while I try to track him down."

The phone in Sam's hand beeped, and he glanced to see that Indie was calling.. "Hold on," he said, then switched over to the other line. "Indie? Everything okay, Babe?"

"Well, maybe," she said. "You told me to let you know if Beauregard had anything to say. Are you ready?"

"Yes, go ahead."

"He says, 'you already lost the first hand, but there are three more to play. The dealer has stacked the deck against you, but you have an ace in the hole. The last hand will be winner take all.' Any idea what that means, Sam?"

"Three more hands to play, but I already lost the first one? That explains the cigar store clerk; I just have to try to keep anyone else from getting killed, so that means I can't lose another hand. Any clue what he means by an ace in the hole?"

"Sam, you know he doesn't give any clear information," Indie said. "Mom just called and said I had to give you that message."

"Okay," Sam said. "Listen, I can't go into it right now, but this thing has gotten strange down here. I'll tell you when I can, but for now the less you know, the better."

"The less I know," Indie repeated. "Sam, are you okay?"

"I am for now," he said. "The trick is to stay that way. I'll call you when I can, Babe. I love you."

"I love you, too," Indie said. Sam clicked the phone back over to Harry.

"Harry? You there?"

"Right here, Sam. I was just bringing Kathy up to date, and she thought of something. Remember he mentioned that girl, the secretary, Heather? Out of all the people who have called Kathy today to express condolences or ask what happened, she should have been one of the first. Nevertheless, she hasn't called at all."

"Which could mean he either let her in on the plan, or he's used her up and she's quite possibly dead. Where does she live?"

Sam heard Kathleen's voice in the background, and then Harry said, "1371 Pine Brook Drive, in Clearwater. She lives with her mother, who was an old friend of Kathy's."

"Okay, I think it might be worth checking on her. I'll call you back in a bit."

"All right, but I'm taking Kathy out of here right now. Call me when you know something, and we'll meet up."

Sam cut off the call and punched the address into his phone's GPS system. A moment later, a woman's voice began giving him directions. He took the next right turn and made his way back toward Pine Brook Drive.

It took him almost 10 minutes to get there, and he pulled up in front of a small, pink stucco house. There was one car in the driveway, a small Nissan, and he parked behind it. Several dogs in the backyard began barking as he slid out of the car and limped toward the front door, then knocked on it when he got there.

There was a TV playing inside the house, but he heard no signs of movement so he knocked again, louder. When there was still no response, he tried to look through the small window on the door, but there was a curtain covering it. He made his way across the front of the house to a big picture window and looked inside, then leaned on the windowsill as his shoulders slumped.

There were two women sitting on a sofa, one of them obviously much younger than the other. The younger woman, whom Sam assumed to be Heather, looked like she'd been crying. He tapped on the window and the older woman turned and looked at him. She nodded when he pointed toward the front door and he made his way back to it.

The door opened and the older woman looked out. "What are you," she asked, "some kind of peeping Tom?"

Sam showed his ID. "I'm a private investigator, Ma'am," he said, "My name is Sam Prichard. Is Heather here?"

"Heather's not doing too well today, I'm afraid. She just found out her boss was murdered, and apparently they were a lot closer than I thought they were. I'm Annie, her mother, can I help you in some way?"

"It's actually Michael Reed's murder that brings me here. Mrs. Reed was concerned about Heather when she didn't call to offer condolences or ask what happened. The circumstances surrounding this case are very strange, and it's possible that Heather could be in some danger."

Annie looked at him for a moment then turned and called to her daughter. "Heather? There's somebody here who needs to speak to you." She stepped back and motioned for Sam to enter, then led him into the living room. He sat down in a chair across from Heather and looked at the girl, and it was obvious that she was grieving.

"Heather, my name is Sam Prichard and I'm a private investigator. I've been hired to look into the death of Michael Reed, and I understand you worked for him."

25

"What have you got in mind?" Ron asked. "I don't want to get involved in anything nefarious..."

"No, no, nothing like that," Michael had told him. "Look, Ron, I'm a man who's simply unhappy in his life. I'm very wealthy, but that isn't making it any better, and if anything, it makes it worse. What kind of challenges are there in life if a man can afford anything he could possibly want? I need a challenge, but that means I need to just start over completely, with no ties to my past at all. The only way I could possibly do that is if everyone thinks I'm dead."

Ron looked him over for a moment, then grinned. "I think I know where you're going," he said. "You and me, we look a lot alike. You're thinking of me taking your place when I die?" He shook his head. "It's a pretty wild idea, but it would never work. Even if they are pretty sure they know who a body is, they still go through all kinds of identification procedures. Your family would have to come and identify your body, they'd run my fingerprints, all that kind of stuff."

Michael held up a hand to stop him. "Strangely enough, I can handle those things. I have contacts that could put your fingerprints into all the big databases in place of mine, so that would confirm that it was my body. I also have some scars and a tattoo, and we could duplicate those on you pretty well. The only thing is, your face wouldn't match up, so—I'm afraid I'd have to destroy your face."

Ron simply stared at him for a few seconds, as if thinking it over. "And what would be in it for me?"

"I'm thinking 10 million dollars," Michael said. "That ought to let your family live quite well for the rest of their lives, especially if you set it up in a trust and let them live on the interest, probably 300,000 dollars or more per year."

Ron's eyes had gone wide, and he swallowed hard. "How soon are we talking about? The doctor says I've got maybe four months left..."

"I'm going to be honest," Michael said. "We'd probably have to do it a little earlier, but not for at least a couple of months. I know a plastic surgeon who can do the scars, and getting a tattoo is no big deal. Look, Ron, the fact is that you're going to die anyway. I'm trying to give you a way to use it to make sure your family will be okay when you're gone. The only thing is, they cannot know anything about our arrangement. No one can."

It took Ron less than an hour to think it all over and decide to agree. The doctor had warned him that his last few weeks would be very painful, so the thought of checking out early wasn't necessarily frightening. As a sign of good faith, Michael transferred one million dollars from one of his hidden accounts to a new account he hurriedly set up in Ron's name, and gave him all of the access codes.

Ron would only tell his family that he had once made a very lucrative investment, something he had kept secret because he was saving it for a rainy day.

* * * * *

Michael finished his drink and slipped out the back door, then into the boathouse a moment later. He knew from past experience that none of his immediate neighbors were likely to be out in the back, so he didn't worry much about being seen taking the boat out. To keep noise down, he used the electric trolling motor until he was far enough away from his own home, then started the Johnson outboard and gave it throttle.

It was almost four miles to the Gator House, but the Johnson made short work of it. It was only as Michael was preparing to ease into a slip at the docks that he began to wonder if Ron would actually show, but his fears were unfounded. Ron was wearing the suit Michael had brought him and sitting on a bench not far from where he tied up the boat, and Michael climbed out to walk over to him.

"Ron?" Michael asked. "You okay?"

"Yeah. Like I said, it's just really starting to hurt. I'm ready to get this over with."

Michael nodded. "I understand," he said. He took his phone out of his pocket and punched an icon, then showed the screen to Ron. "If you're sure, all I've got to do is enter my pin number and the rest of the money will be transferred right now."

Ron looked up at the sky for a moment, then turned back to Michael and smiled. "I'm absolutely certain," he said. "And I appreciate you letting me see you do this part."

Michael smiled at him. "Not a problem." He turned the phone back to himself and entered the number, then hit the submit button. A moment later the screen displayed the transfer of five million dollars from one of his secret accounts to another account he had helped Ron set up. They had already left instructions with an attorney that would cause that money to be placed in a trust for the benefit of Ron's wife on the first of the following month.

Ron smiled back. "I thank you, from the bottom of my heart. Let's do this."

The two men got up and walked down the docks to the slip, and Michael helped Ron climbed into the boat. He started the Johnson again and backed out, then turned the boat and headed back toward his house. He pulled it into the boathouse with the trolling motor a short time later, and led Ron inside.

"Now, this has to be staged just the right way," Michael said. "I'm going to change clothes and sneak out by going through the backyard and the gate into my front yard. As soon as somebody sees me, I'm going to come on into the house and..."

"Put me out of my misery?" Ron asked with a grin. "Don't worry, I remember. We have to have an argument, and then you'll do it. Quick and painless, right?"

Michael nodded. "Yes," he said. "You'll die instantly with the first shot."

Ron nodded, still grinning. "I appreciate that. Besides, it's a good day to die."

Michael grinned back at him and left the room. He went into his office and opened a file storage box that sat on top of his credenza. He lifted out a stack of file folders and then pulled out the bag that was underneath it all.

Five minutes later, he walked out wearing a white wig and a false white beard. He went into his bedroom and put on a blue suit that matched closely to the one he had been wearing that morning, then stuffed the machine pistol into the back of his pants and slipped out the back door. He made his way across the back of the house to the small section of fence that separated backyard from front, then peeked through a gap between the boards. There was no one in sight at the moment, so he opened the gate and slipped through, then stood behind a bush until he saw someone come out of the house across the street.

That was perfect, he thought. That old biddy loved to spy on her neighbors, so he stepped out from behind the bush and made a show of creeping stealthily across the yard toward his front door. As he got up to it, he saw in the reflection of the sidelight windows that the woman was watching him closely as he opened the door slowly and put on an act of slipping inside. He pushed it almost closed and left it, then walked toward the kitchen where he had told Ron to wait.

Ron was leaning against the counter, one hand pressed to his lower back. "We all set?" he asked, and Michael nodded.

Ron forced himself to stand upright and turned to face Michael. "What the hell are you doing in here?" he shouted. "Get out, or I'll call the police."

"I'm here to kill you," Michael shouted back. "She's my wife, you can't have her."

Ron looked like he was trying his best to suppress a laugh, but even though there were tears flowing down his face, he delivered his final line perfectly. "Harry! Harry, put down the gun!"

Michael had one hand up under his jacket and suddenly pulled it out with the machine pistol in it. Ron let his eyes focus on the gun and a smile spread across his face.

As promised, the first bullet went through Ron's left eye, killing him instantly, but the weapon was set to automatic fire. Four more bullets obliterated his face, while a few others went wild and struck the cabinets and walls.

For Ron, it was all over. The pain, the worry about his family, all of that ended the moment Michael squeezed the trigger.

For Michael, on the other hand, a new life was just beginning. He snatched off the wig and beard, ran into his bedroom and gathered up the clothes she had been wearing earlier and stuffed all of these things into a trash bag. He took the bag with him as he hurried out to the boathouse, then took off the suit he was wearing, leaving him in a pair of swim trunks. He stuffed the suit and his socks and shoes into the bag, put on swim fins and a mask and snorkel, and slipped into the water.

It took him only fifteen minutes to swim down to the vacant house, towing the bag behind him as he went. He swam into the boathouse and climbed up inside, then used towels he kept there to dry himself as thoroughly as he could. Luckily, he kept his hair short, so it wasn't obvious that it was wet. He put on his suit again, then put his swim gear into the bag and carried it inside. He went into the garage, tossed the bag into the passenger seat of his Lamborghini, and then backed out into the street. The Chevrolet would eventually be discovered, but just like the house, there was no way to officially connect it to him. He followed Bay Esplanade up the coastline until it curved around, then turned onto Eldorado Avenue and made his way back down the island to the causeway.

Once he was back on the mainland, Michael picked up the tablet and checked the location of Harry's rented Buick. It was moving, and as he watched, it turned off the street and came to a stop. Michael pointed his car in that direction, googling the GPS coordinates to find that the car was parked at the Marriott, so he checked on where the car had been for the last hour.

Damn Harry. At just the time Michael's neighbor would swear she saw him entering the house, Harry was at some cigar shop. The last thing he needed right now was for Harry to have an alibi, and anyone who could confirm his presence at the cigar store at that moment would be one. There would have been no way he could make it from Michael's house to that store so quickly, and the sound of the gunshots would clearly establish the time of death.

It took him almost 20 minutes to get to the cigar store, and he quickly put the nasal expanders and glasses back into place as he got out of the car. There were only a couple of customers inside, but the clerk was occupied when he entered. Michael carefully reached over while the young man was diverted and turned off the open sign, then waited until the other customers left before locking the door.

Finally, and with no one the wiser, he was alone with the clerk. He pretended to look around for a minute or two longer, then walked up to the counter and smiled.

"Hi, there," the young man said. "How can I help you?"

"Like this," Michael said as he thrust a hand out quickly and grabbed the boy by his throat. He dragged the boy toward him, quickly stepped around the counter and snapped the kid's neck, then bent down and stuffed him under it. He glanced around and spotted the DVR that recorded the security cameras, pressed its eject button and snatched the tape as he stood and quickly hurried toward the door. He was out and back in his car only seconds later, and was on the street less than half a minute after that.

"Sorry, Harry," he said aloud. "No alibi for you, old buddy. You are going down for the murder of Michael Reed."

He drove the car across Tampa and into the old scrapyard he had purchased under yet another dummy corporation. The place had been shut down for a couple of years, but all of its equipment was still in operating condition, and it would actually reopen under his proxy company in about a month. His remote let him open the big bay door and he drove inside, then up a long ramp and onto the dump tray of an Arjes VZ950, a monstrous machine that was capable of shredding any vehicle into a million unidentifiable pieces. He turned off the ignition and picked up the tablet, then got out of the car and climbed down the stairs to start the 800 horsepower diesel engine that powered the behemoth.

The dump tray lifted the car and dropped it into the big wheels full of tungsten carbide teeth, and they began chewing at it. There were some muffled explosions as various parts full of fuel, oil or pressurized gas were crushed and run into sparks, but the machine was built to handle it. Michael didn't even look back as the 400,000-dollar Lamborghini Aventador was turned into trash, but simply crossed the building and got into the nondescript Chevy truck he had left there in preparation for this moment.

The police scanner Michael kept in the truck suddenly picked up the dispatcher's order for a car to visit the cigar store, and he felt a grin slide across his face. "Well, well," he said to himself. "I wonder which one figured it out first, Harry or Sam?" Ten minutes later, he heard the officers report back that they had found the clerk dead of a broken neck.

All he had to do now, Michael figured, was wait. "His" body had already been discovered and there was no doubt the police were already looking at Harry, especially if he and Kate were stupid enough to tell the detectives the truth. They would, of course, because that's just who they were. Michael caught himself chuckling, and not for the first time he wondered why he hated Harry Winslow so much.

He used to think it was because Harry had what he wanted, but that situation had ended thirty years before. He had wanted Kathleen, and he got her, but apparently no romance really lasts forever. They'd been happy for the first few years, but he had known Kate was disillusioned with him by their tenth anniversary. They hadn't really been the happy couple everyone thought they were for at least the last ten or twelve years, which was why

Michael always chose gullible young secretaries. They were so easy to manipulate.

All that was over, now, though. As far as the entire world knew, Michael was dead, and Jonathan Brandon was about to become a major international information broker. The whole world was his potential client list, now, since even the Russians were likely to believe he was dead. There was no one left for him to answer to, and that was exactly how he wanted it.

26

The girl nodded. "Yeah," she said. "I was his secretary and personal assistant. You know, answer his phones, set appointments, that sort of thing."

"Heather, had Mr. Reed been acting strange at all lately? Was there anything in his demeanor that seemed odd to you, maybe just a little off?"

Heather stared at him for a moment, then shook her head. "Not really," she said slowly. "He had to get ready for a trip to Japan, and he seemed a little anxious about it. Other than that, he was perfectly normal."

"Heather, just a few hours before he died, Michael hinted that you and he might have been involved in a romantic relationship. Is that correct?"

Tears that had been barely held back suddenly began to flow as the girl nodded her head. "Yes," she said. "He and his wife, they haven't been—well, getting along very well, for a couple years, I guess. We work together a lot, and one day things just—happened. He said they were going to be working out the details on getting a divorce, and then we wouldn't have to hide it anymore."

She sobbed. "This is so unfair, it's just not fair. He said I made him happier than he'd ever been."

Sam sat there and watched the girl for a moment, then reached into his pocket for a business card. He handed one to Heather, and another to her mother. "Listen, I know this is going to sound odd, but if either of you hears anything unusual about him, or about what happened to him, please give me a call. We're not really sure what's going on at the moment, but Michael wasn't the only one who was murdered yesterday. It's possible that you could be in danger. Please, if you hear anything at all, no matter how strange it seems, please give me a call."

"We will," Annie said, eyeing him curiously. When Sam stood to leave, she followed him to the door and stepped outside, pulling it shut behind her. "There's something funny about this, isn't there? Something you're not telling us."

Sam looked into the woman's eyes for a moment, then nodded his head. "I wouldn't say anything to Heather," he said softly, "but there is reason to believe that Michael is not dead. It's possible that he actually faked his own death, but we don't understand exactly why just yet. If we're right, he's going to want to eliminate anyone who might be able to give him away. Depending on how much she knows, that could include Heather. You might want to consider taking her out of the city for a while."

Annie stared at him for a moment, then slowly nodded. "I think that might be a good idea. I've been thinking about visiting my sister in Miami for a little while, now, anyway."

"Good. I'd suggest leaving soon, and if I were you, I wouldn't tell anyone where you're going. Be especially careful not to say it over the phone, okay?"

Annie swallowed, but nodded her head. "Sounds like good advice. Thanks for letting me know."

Sam nodded, then turned and walked back to the Challenger. He slid inside and fired it up, then headed toward town as he took his phone out of his pocket once more. He called Harry and the old man answered instantly.

"Talk to me, son," Harry said. "What did you find?"

"The girl is okay," Sam said, "but she's pretty torn up. Apparently Michael told her all the standard lies, he and his wife didn't get along and they were going to get a divorce so he could marry the poor girl. I got to talk to her mother alone for a couple of minutes, and suggested it might be a good time for a vacation. I think she's going to take my advice."

"Good, at least she's okay. We're looking for a place to roost for a bit. Kathy says you should meet us around six at the restaurant she took you to. We'll let you know then if we found a place."

"Okay, no problem. I'm going to stay at the Marriott for now. I'm trying to figure out how to draw Michael out. In order to save your ass, we've got to prove he's still alive. Can you think of anything your fed buddies might do to help us?"

"Already working on it," Harry said. "I got through to the director, my former boss, and managed to convince him to take this seriously. He's twisting the arms of people at the Company, trying to find any information we might be able to use. You know, a list of wounds Michael suffered over the years, medical record details that might prove the body they have is not him. He's also passing on the warning that Michael may have gone dark. Considering the things he would know, that's a frightening thought to a lot of people at Langley."

Sam nodded into the phone. "Okay, that could help. By the way, when Indie called, it was to tell me that Beauregard has spoken again. He says I already lost the first hand, which explains the tobacco clerk being killed. Unfortunately, he says there are three more hands to play, and I dare not lose any of them, but he also said I have an ace in the hole. Any idea what that could be?"

Harry laughed. "I would suppose it's me," he said. "I'm guessing it means you'll need me to give you pointers on how to deal with a spook. Kind of ironic, isn't it? A spook telling you to use me to help you find a spook?"

Sam grimaced. "You could be right, but I'm not sure. It's like there's something about this I should be able to figure out, but it hasn't hit me yet. What worries me is that he says there's three hands, which means at least three more lives are hanging on what I do next. Do you know what I'd give to be able to say that old soldier had been wrong in the past?"

"Sam, boy, I don't know where Beauregard came from, but considering how many times he's helped you save the day, I'm not going to even blink at taking his advice. Whether he's real or not doesn't matter; somehow, your mother-in-law manages to get advance notice on bits of what's going to happen and warn you about them. Do you have any idea what I would have given for something like that?"

"Yeah, well, you know what they say about a gift, right? Sometimes it's hard to tell one from a curse."

"Hold on a moment, Sam," Harry said. "Call coming in."

The phone went silent, and Sam drove along until he came to the hotel parking lot, then pulled in and shut the car off. He looked around carefully but saw no one watching, so he got out of the car and walked as quickly as he could with his cane to the front door, still holding the phone to his ear. He rode the elevator up to his floor, and was inside his room and sitting on the bed by the time Harry came back on the line.

"Sam," said, "that was Leon McCabe, an old associate and friend from my days at CIA. He had some information to give me, but it's off the record. Seems Michael has been making people nervous for a little while back at Langley. They've been using him as a facilitator, a guy who makes things happen without any connections to the government. Facilitators are pretty important in my line of work, but sometimes they can blow up in your face. You see, facilitators often learn things, things that can leave Uncle Sam and his people vulnerable. Michael knows where a lot of bodies are buried, both literally and figuratively. He has information that could compromise currently active agents in the field, or mess up some long-term operations, and unfortunately, that information is worth a lot of money in the right circles. I guess there's been talk lately that Michael isn't enjoying the trust of some of the people he works with up there."

"Well, that could explain a lot. Remember Grayson Chandler? He used information to build a power base that almost let him control the world."

"Yes, and it's funny you should mention him. There was somebody who helped us out in that situation, remember? Leon suggested he might be able to help us once again. He worked with Michael on a couple of things about ten years ago, just before he went rogue. After you helped him expose Chandler and stop his plans for world domination, Kenneth Long was welcomed back into the fold. He happens to be in Nassau at the moment, but he'll be flying in to Tampa at 7:30 this evening. He'll be expecting you to pick him up and fill him in, any problem with that?"

"No problem at all," Sam said. "You think he might know Michael well enough to help us find him?"

"Well, he's at least dealt with him a lot more recently than I have, and he understands how those who seek power actually think. From what I understand, the current director of CIA has been using him like an Internal Affairs agent; he keeps the different factions from building too great a power base, and he's the first one to go after any rogue agent. His participation is purely unofficial, mind you; Langley doesn't currently believe our hypothesis about Michael faking his death, at least not officially. Leon just happened to know how to reach him and asked if he might be willing to come and evaluate the situation. If you can convince Long, there's a good possibility Company HQ will get involved."

"And would that mean you're in the clear?" Sam asked. "Would that get the charges dropped against you?"

"Unfortunately, probably not. The CIA is prohibited from interfering in any domestic situations, especially those involving justice. They can go after one of their own while he's on US soil, but they can't so much as give me a letter of reference in this case. If Michael gets away, my survival will probably depend on finding a lawyer who can convince a jury of our theory, and without any physical evidence..."

"And all we have is my personal conviction, based on the fingernails of a corpse. What about those medical records? Think there's any chance we'll be able to use them?"

"If I were planning to pull something like this, and had the strings to get fingerprints changed, I can pretty much guarantee that my medical records would also confirm the identity of the corpse. I would even go so far as to make sure the dental records matched, and before you ask, I already had Kathy call Michael's dentist and request a copy of them. We get to pick them up tomorrow morning. She says he got a couple of crowns about three years ago, so hopefully the records will confirm that and be different from the dental work on that body."

"It might be hard to tell. Remember, the dead guy's face was shot up pretty bad, including around the mouth."

"Don't be such a pessimist, son," Harry said. "Surely he didn't blow all of his teeth out. If there's even one intact tooth, it can be compared against Michael's dental x-rays. That might be enough to back up our theory and get the State Attorney's attention."

"Then it's worth a try. I'm back at the hotel, now, I'm going to kick back for a little bit and try to think about how to draw him out. I'll meet you guys for dinner as planned, then head for the airport after that. It'll be good to see Ken again. Just hope he's forgiven me for that fiasco in Rome."

"Fiasco in Rome? The way I remember it, Rome was an unqualified success."

"Yeah, except for the part where I never got around to telling Ken about how I set it all up until after it was over. Don't worry, Harry, he and I are good. He came by and visited with us a couple months after all that, while he was finally making peace with his daughter. If anyone can help us figure this out, he's probably the one."

Harry agreed, and they ended the call. Sam suddenly felt himself yawning and figured he had time for a nap, so he set an alarm on his phone and stretched out on the bed. Falling asleep wasn't hard, considering how tired he was; his worry about Harry the night before had kept him from sleeping very well.

Sam had been asleep for half an hour when he was awakened by the ringing of his phone. He rolled onto his back and reached for it on his nightstand, then glanced at the display. The call was from a restricted number, so he answered cautiously.

"Prichard," he said.

"You arrogant bastard," he heard, and he recognized the voice instantly. It was Michael Watkins. "Do you honestly think you can stop me? There is absolutely no evidence to back up your ridiculous claim, I made certain of that."

"I'm sure you tried," Sam said, "but no plan is perfect. It's like they say in combat; a battle plan survives only until contact is actually made with the enemy. Well, guess what, you son-of-a-bitch! You have met the enemy, and he is me. After what you did to Harry and his family, setting him up to take the fall for your murders is just going too far. If it weren't for that, I would've been happy to let you get away with whatever you want, play your power games to your heart's content. But you messed with my friend, and that means you have to go down."

Michael laughed, and Sam's jaw clenched with anger. "Do you honestly think you have a prayer of catching me? I'll grant you, you've had some lucky streaks in the past, but you're out of your league with me. I know everything you're doing, and I'm always a step ahead of you. You went to see little Heather? You should know by now she meant nothing to me, she was just a convenient plaything. I'm not surprised you went to check on her, though. Kate has a soft spot in her, even for those who had betrayed her. You needn't have bothered telling her mother to get her out of town, she's in no danger from me. I'm finished with her, and there's no way you can use her against me."

"I'm glad to hear that," Sam said. "Now, the question is, what do you want? You must've called me for a reason."

"What do I want? I want you to back down, that's what. Remember, Sam, I can still get to your family; you need to let this go, and you need to let it go now."

Sam breathed heavily into the phone for about four seconds, forcing himself to stay in control. "If I didn't have enough motivation to bring you in before," he said menacingly, "you just gave it to me. I'm coming for you, Michael, and I'm going to bring you down."

"You see what I mean? You're arrogant, Sam. You apparently think much more highly of yourself than you should. Tell me something, Sam, just between you and me: did you already tell that idiot police detective about your theory?"

"Of course not," Sam said, "he'd never believe it."

"Oh, oh, Sam, I think I detect a fib. You hesitated for just a half a second or so before you answered me, which means you were trying to decide quickly what was the best thing to say. What was it your wife told you a while ago? Three more hands of poker to play, and you can't afford to lose any of them?"

27

Michael had called Sam after listening to the recordings from his phone. He'd gotten quite a chuckle out of hearing about the old ghost again; there definitely were stranger things in the world than man could conceive, and it was interesting to note that one of Sam's greatest assets was either a genuine ghost or a crazy woman who could see the future. It didn't really matter, though, since the ghost never seemed to make a lot of sense until you could look at his warnings in hindsight.

No, the real problem was that Sam was actually one hell of an investigator. Michael didn't believe he could actually be caught, but the last thing he needed was for Sam Prichard to come up with any solid evidence that he was still alive. It wouldn't take CIA very long to figure out exactly what was happening if he did.

Then there was the issue of Kenneth Long. He was definitely a formidable opponent, and Michael didn't need any further problems. Both he and Sam would have to be distracted, and Michael knew exactly how to do it.

He picked up his phone and punched a number. The voice that answered was the same one that had cleaned up the Hornsby mess. "I got another job for you," Michael said. "Prichard's family.

Shoot the wife, but don't kill her, and don't touch the child. If one of the other women gets in the way, try to disable, rather than kill."

"That means leaving witnesses," the killer said. "You know I don't like to do that."

"So don't let them see your face, nothing that could identify you. You know how to handle this kind of situation, and I'm definitely paying you enough, right?"

The killer sighed. "Fair enough," he said. "No fatalities."

Michael put down the phone and picked up the tablet once more, then clicked on the link that would allow him to hear the recordings that were made by Sam's phone while it was off. The app he had installed on all of the Prichard family phones was capable of using the phone's microphone to record all sounds within about twenty feet, even when it wasn't in the middle of a call or was tucked into a pocket. He skipped through a lot of the conversations between Sam and Harry and Kate, ignored the recordings from the courthouse and such, but then he heard Sam talking to Detective Lawton.

Harry had pulled some strings and gotten Sam appointed as Special Investigator on the case, which meant Lawton had to share information with him. That didn't worry Michael so much, until the point where Sam suddenly insisted that the body in the photos couldn't be Michael's. He actually felt a moment's frustration as he realized that he had forgotten to look at Ron's fingernails. Maybe Sam had been right, and there was always a mistake. Sam had pointed it out to Lawton, but the detective was at least smart enough to realize that the State Attorney wouldn't believe it.

He grinned. "See, Sam? I knew you were lying about that."

Still, it might be enough to make Lawton believe Sam's theory about Michael faking his own death. He put the truck in gear and headed toward the police station as he picked up his phone again and dialed a number.

"Detective Lawton, please," he said when the call was answered. The receptionist put him on hold for a moment, and then Lawton came on the line.

"Detective Lawton. How can I help you?"

"Actually," Michael said, disguising his voice to sound younger, "I think maybe I can help you, Sir. You know that guy who was murdered yesterday? I've been afraid to come forward, but there was an old man who called for an Uber ride and had me drop him off right at that guy's house, just a little while before he was supposed to have been killed. Could you maybe meet me in your parking lot in about ten minutes? I'm a little scared to come inside the station, you know what I mean?"

"Yeah," Lawton said, "I can meet you out there. What's your name?"

"Um, do I have to give it? Like I said, I'm kinda scared."

"Well, yeah, I really need it. Don't worry, though, I won't let your name get out to the press or anything. You have my word on that."

Michael let out a sigh. "Okay," he said. "My name is Steve, Steve Jamison. I'll be there in about ten minutes, I'm driving a white Chevy HHR."

"No problem, Steve," Lawton said. "I'll be out there waiting for you. Just pull right up when you get here, and I'll get in the car with you so we can talk privately."

"Okay, thanks," Michael said, and then he ended the call. A moment later, he parked on the street just across from the parking lot of the police station, taking care to stay out of the line of sight of any security cameras, and reached behind his seat to pull out the sound-suppressed AR-15 that was stashed there. He kept it down and out of sight until he saw Lawton appear, then looked around to make sure no one was watching. There was no one else in sight, so he quickly raised the rifle and sited on Lawton through the scope, squeezed the trigger once and then dropped the gun into the passenger floorboard. He had the truck in gear and was moving again only five seconds after firing the shot.

* * * * *

Indie was sitting on the sofa watching TV with Kenzie and her grandmas when she heard the cars pull up into her driveway and immediately reached for the snubnosed .38 she kept in a drawer of the end table as she headed for the door. Sam had purchased a few of the small pistols and placed them around the house, then showed each one to Kenzie and explained to her clearly why she should never touch them, and he had taken Indie out to the firing range and taught her to use them. He often bragged that she was a better shot with them than he ever would be.

Someone knocked on the front door as she approached, and she carefully peeked through the peephole, then breathed a sigh of relief and shoved the gun into her pocket. George, the gray-haired black man who had been Harry's personal driver while he'd been stationed in Denver, stood on the porch with a smile on his face. There were five men with him, and Indie could tell they were security types. She opened the door and smiled back at George.

"Well, if you're here, I'm guessing Harry sent you?"

"Indeed he did, Ms. Indie," George said. "This is unofficial, mind you, but a lot of us in the local office are still loyal to Mr. Harry. He called a bit ago and asked us to make sure you and your family are taken somewhere safe, right now."

Indie blinked, but didn't argue. If Harry Winslow thought they needed to be hidden, there was no doubt in her mind that Sam would approve. "Have I got ten minutes to pack?"

"Yes, but we need to move pretty quickly. Mr. Harry believes there is a clear and present danger."

"No problem," she said. She turned around and saw her mother and Grace watching her. "Grab your bags and give them to George, then get Kenzie and go with him. I'll get our stuff and be right behind you."

The women did as they were told and they were all in the armored limo less than five minutes later. George slid behind the wheel as two of the security men climbed in with them and a third got into the shotgun seat up front. The other two were in a separate vehicle, a Ford Expedition, that followed behind them.

"So, where are we going this time?" Indie asked. "Back to the cabin?"

"No, Ma'am," George said. "Mr. Harry says the man that they are dealing with has been watching you folks for a while, so he would probably know where that is. We're going to a safe house Mr. Harry set up one time that's never even been used. Nobody else could possibly know about it, so anyone he sends after you would never find you there."

"Does it have a TV?" Kenzie asked suddenly, and George chuckled.

"Yes it does, Ms. Kenzie, and I've got a whole stack of new Disney videos for us to watch."

Kenzie squealed with happiness and clapped her hands. She and George shared a love for Disney movies, and every time they had spent time with him, the two of them parked on the couch and watched as many as they could.

Kenzie was in her car seat, squeezed into the big back seat between her mother and her grandma Kim, and Indie looked down at her precious little daughter. "You like Disney movies, don't you, sweetheart?"

"Yes," Kenzie said. "Me and George like them a lot."

"Yes, I know you do. Tell me something, Kenzie, what would you think if maybe Mommy and Daddy were to have a little baby brother or sister for you?"

Kenzie looked up at her with a smile on her face. "I think I'd teach 'em to watch Disney movies!"

* * * * *

Michael was certain no one had seen him shoot Lawton, or drive away, so he didn't worry about ditching the truck. He drove for about fifteen minutes, then pulled into the parking lot of a shopping center and made sure no one was watching again as he put the rifle back behind the seat once more. He was about to pick up the tablet again when his phone suddenly rang, and he recognized the number of the killer in Denver. "Yes?"

"I went to do what you said, but there's been some interference. Just as I got there, I saw the women and the kid get hustled into a limousine, with enough high-powered security I can't get near them. What do you want me to do?"

Michael swore. "I want you to get a bullet into that woman, but if you can't do that, at least follow them and find out where they're going. Maybe you'll get an opportunity, just keep your eyes open."

The killer ended the call, and Michael swore once again. Damn Harry! He had anticipated what Michael would do and gotten in the way.

He looked at the tablet in his lap and tapped the icon to check where the Buick was at, and then became frustrated when he realized it was back at the rental agency. Sam had obviously figured out that he was tracking it, and had already gotten rid of it. There was no way to tell what he might be driving, now, and he would surely be smart enough not to use a credit card Michael could trace.

Michael wasn't out of tricks just yet, though. He brought up another program that tracked the GPS information on Sam's phone, and saw that it was moving. As he watched, it came to a stop at what proved to be a shopping center, and a quick inquiry on Google told Michael that the main store there was an electronics shop that sold computers and cell phones. Sam was undoubtedly buying a throwaway phone, which meant Michael wouldn't be able to listen in on calls he made with it.

Not being able to listen in on his phone calls wasn't that big a handicap, though. At least Sam still had his original phone in the car, so he could keep tabs on where it was at. He decided to sit tight for a while. Sam, Harry and Kate were planning to meet up for dinner, and Michael knew where they were going. He could make a point of being there before they arrived, and maybe that would put an end to the whole mess. By the time Kenneth Long arrived, it might already be over, and without Sam to fill him in, Long wouldn't even really have any clue about what was going on.

Yeah, things were looking up. He could afford to take a few minutes to let himself rest and relax, so he leaned the seat back and allowed himself a short nap. He'd be awake in plenty of time to carry out the next phase of the plan, of that he was certain.

28

The phone had gone dead, and Sam immediately called Harry. He hurriedly told the old man what Michael had had to say, while Harry tried hard to get a word in edgewise. When he finally stopped talking, Harry began.

"I expected this, Sam," he said, "which is why I took the liberty after we last spoke of arranging for your family's safety. I had to call in a few loyal old friends, but they are all currently headed to a safe house that even the CIA doesn't know about. Indie will contact you once they get settled in, but Michael won't be able to get to them."

"That doesn't change the fact he threatened my wife and daughter," Sam said. "Harry, if we don't find him, we'll be looking over our shoulders for the rest of our lives. I can't handle that, and neither can my family."

"I agree, Sam, boy, we've got to take him down. This tells me, however, that he's still in the area. He wouldn't be trying to bully you into backing down if he was already gone. That means we've got a little time."

"Maybe a little," Sam said, "but remember that he's probably listening to every single thing we say. He knew what Indie had told me on the phone earlier, about playing poker. I'll call you back, I need to get hold of Lawton as soon as possible."

He ended the call and immediately dialed Lawton's cell phone number. It rang seven times before going to voicemail, so he ended the call and dialed the police station instead.

"Clearwater Police Department," said the receptionist. "How may I direct your call?"

"I need to speak with Detective Lawton, please," Sam said. "It's urgent."

There was a moment's hesitation on the line, and then the receptionist said, "One moment."

A man's voice came on a moment later, but it wasn't Lawton. "You're looking for Detective Lawton?"

"Yes, and it's very important I speak with him immediately. My name is Sam Prichard, I'm a private investigator. I was in to see him earlier, and..."

"What is your business with Detective Lawton?" the man on the line asked.

"That's between me and him," Sam said. "Is he available?"

There was another slight hesitation. "Look, Mr. Prichard," the man said. "I actually know who you are, but I needed to be sure it was really you. Detective Lawton is currently on his way to the hospital for surgery. He was shot in our parking lot about ten minutes ago."

"Shot?" Sam almost shouted. "By who? Did you get the shooter?"

"We're not releasing any information at this time," the man said. "You can understand that, right? I'm Detective Embry, and I'm heading the investigation into the shooting. As I said a moment ago, I know who you are, that you're working for DHS at the moment; you said you were in to see Lawton today?"

"Yes, just a few hours ago. We were talking about the Michael Reed murder."

"Yes," Embry said, "I've been going through his notes on it. Maybe you can enlighten me about something. One of the last things he scribbled down is a puzzler. It looks like he wrote RIP, then drew several lines through it, like he was trying to scratch it out. Any idea what that would be about?"

Sam started to answer, and then suddenly froze. If Lawton had been shot, there was no doubt in his mind that Michael had done the shooting, but that would only make sense if Michael somehow knew that Sam had told him the body couldn't be his. He held his phone away from his ear for a moment, then pulled it back. "I'm afraid not," he said as calmly as he could. "That wouldn't make any sense to me, either."

"Well, I thought I'd ask while I had you on the phone. I understand you were appointed by DHS because the suspect in that case is a former agent of theirs?"

"Yes, that's correct. I do some work for them occasionally, and they called me in on this because Mr. Winslow is also a close personal friend of mine.."

"Yeah, I caught that. Listen, I may need to talk to you again. Is this your cell number?"

"Yeah, that's it. Sorry to hear about Lawton, and call me if you need anything from me, or hear anything I might need to know."

Sam hung up without saying anymore, and looked at the phone in his hand. There were, he knew, numerous ways to use your own cell phone against you. There were even ways to turn it on from a distance, so that you weren't aware someone was listening in to what was happening around you.

He slipped the phone back into his pocket and headed into the bathroom to freshen up, then grabbed his gun and jacket and headed down to the elevator. When he got to the ground floor, he walked straight out of the building and to the Challenger, got into it and drove quickly out of the parking lot. There was always the possibility that Michael had discovered it and put a tracker on it, but he wasn't as worried about Michael knowing where he was as about who he was talking to and what was being said. He tossed the cell phone onto the console and kept his eyes peeled for an electronics or cell phone store.

Thirty minutes later, Sam had bought a cheap throwaway phone and activated it using a credit card number that Harry had once given him. He hadn't even been sure it would work, but it did, and meant that there was almost no way anyone could find out about the purchase or activation. He carried it out of the store and stood some distance from the car as he used it to call Harry.

The call went to voicemail. Sam used his best impression of Harry's southern drawl to leave a message.

"Harry, old son? This is Walter Sweeney, an old friend of Beau's. Just wondering how you been, old buddy. Give me a call when you get this." He knew the number of the burner phone would show up on the caller ID, so he ended the call and hung up.

He stood in the same spot for almost 15 minutes, but then the phone finally rang. As cheap as it was, it had caller ID but Sam didn't recognize the number that came up on the display. He answered it in the hope that Harry had gotten the message, and was rewarded when he heard the old man's voice.

"Since you took the trouble to call me on a burner," Harry said, "I have to assume that you heard about Detective Lawton."

"Yeah, I did," Sam said. "The fact that he was shot at this time is too big a coincidence. It tells me that Michael is almost certainly able to listen in through my phone, even when I'm not actually on it."

"Indeed he can. There's actually a pretty simple way to do it, remind me to teach it to you one of these days. In the meantime, however, we have bigger problems. I'm currently using a cell phone I liberated from the purse of a lady walking down the street, so we need to speak quickly. Are we still on for dinner?"

"Yes, but let's change the location. If he's been tailing me or tracking the Buick, he'd probably know where Kathy and I had lunch. Let's try somewhere else." He looked around for a moment and spotted a billboard. "Clear Sky Café, on Mandalay Avenue in Clearwater Beach. We'll meet up there."

"All right," Harry said. "See you there at six. No, wait—let's make it 8:30, and you can bring along your friend. We won't starve if we wait a couple extra hours. And, incidentally, Kathy and I have both removed the batteries from our cell phones. We'll put them back in periodically, just to check for messages, but we thought it a good idea not to give Michael an ear on what we're doing."

"That sounds like a good idea," Sam said. "I'll see you then."

Sam hung up from that call and immediately dialed the number of the burner phone Indie always kept in her purse. It rang six times before she answered, and she sounded out of breath when she finally did.

"Sam?"

"It's me, Babe," Sam said. "Keep this number, it should be good for a little while."

"Okay, good," Indie said. "Now, can you tell me what on earth is going on? Harry sent some people down to grab us up, and we're on our way to a safe house somewhere. George was with them and said we should leave our regular phones at home, so we did."

"I know," Sam said. "Harry told me, but not until after he'd done it. We are dealing with a pretty bad situation down here, and we both wanted to be sure it couldn't get to you." Sam took a deep breath. "Okay, here's what's going on. After we met with Michael yesterday, a witness saw someone fitting Harry's description going into his house just a few minutes before gunshots were heard. When the police arrived, they found a body on the floor with its face blown away. Fingerprints identify the body as Michael Reed, but while we were face-to-face with him, I happened to notice that he recently had his fingernails neatly trimmed. This morning I got to look at the crime scene photos of the body, and the nails were long and un-manicured, so it can't be Michael. It was a hell of a job, though, because Kathleen had to go down this morning and identify the body. Without knowing any different, she confirmed it was Michael based on a tattoo that he wears and a couple of scars, which seemed to be perfect. I told the police detective what I suspected, and now he's been shot. I think Michael has been tapping my cell phone, even listening in when I'm not using it. That's about the only way I can imagine he could have known for sure that I shared my theory with the detective."

"Oh my God, Sam," Indie said. "I'm getting scared, Babe."

"Well, I've got some help coming. Remember Kenneth Long? One of Harry's friends knew that we'd been involved with him in the past, and found out he was in the Bahamas. He gave him a call, and Ken is flying in tonight to help me with this."

"Okay, well, that will make me feel a little bit better. At least I know he's probably just as bad as Michael when it comes to all the intelligence stuff. Or maybe I should say he's just as good."

Sam chuckled. "I think you could get away with saying it either way. Anyway, I know for sure that Michael is alive, because he called me a while ago. Of course, there's no way to prove it, but he tried to make me back off by threatening all of you again. By the time I called Harry, he had already anticipated it and made the arrangements you were talking about. When Ken gets here, we are all going to go and sit down and talk this over."

"I'm going to text you a link," Indie said, "to an app that will automatically record every phone call you get. Put it on your phone in case he calls again."

"Good idea, but I wish we'd thought of it sooner. Probably too late, now, though. Odds-on, Michael is reading my text messages as well. If he sees a link to an app like that, he probably won't call me again."

"True. Okay. So, I take it you lost another hand? That's why the detective was killed?"

"I assume so, but the last I knew he wasn't dead. They said he was going into surgery, so hopefully he has a chance. I'll try to find out more in a while, but I just wanted to touch base with you on a secure line."

"I'm glad you did, I was getting worried. Sam, this means you've got only two hands left. Hey, real quick, did you know a local PI named Frank Hornsby?"

"Hornsby? Yeah, he's a sleaze ball. Why?"

"Probably nothing, really, but I heard on the radio a while ago that he was found dead this morning. I guess the mailman saw him laying on the floor and called police. His neck was broken, so they are calling it a homicide."

"I can't say that's going to be any great loss," Sam said, "and he probably had plenty of people who wanted him dead, so I doubt there's any connection to this case. Just let me know if you hear anything else, though, okay?"

"I will. Did you ever figure out what was your ace in the hole?"

"Not for sure," Sam said. "We're thinking maybe it's Harry himself. As far as I can tell, he's the only thing I've got going for me right now. The police aren't going to believe that Michael is alive, not as long as those fingerprints keep saying he's dead, and I'm not sure how I can draw him out to catch him. I'm not even sure I would know him if I saw him; he's undoubtedly capable of disguising himself beyond my meager ability to recognize him."

"Well, you talk to Ken and Harry, maybe the three of you can come up with something. I'll be somewhere safe with Kenzie and our moms, and I've got my computer with me if you need anything."

Sam's eyes suddenly went wide. "Your computer! Michael said he had managed to hack into it, and could track it anywhere. You need to hide it someplace, Babe, till this is over."

"He said what?" Indie said incredulously. "Don't worry, as long as I don't let it get online, it can't be traced. If he put any kind of a tracking bug in it, Herman can find it and root it out. I won't chance going online until I know I've cleaned it up."

Sam sighed. "Okay, Babe, you're the expert on computers. Just be careful, all right? I couldn't stand it if something happened to you, to any of you. And if Beauregard has anything more to say, call me on this number immediately."

"Really? You're willing to accept his advice now?"

"Let's just say Harry had a talk with me, and made some good points. As many times as Beauregard has saved my ass, maybe I need to give him a little more respect. Whatever he is, everyone of us owes our lives to him at least once. Even Harry, in a way."

"We-ell, since you said that, I should probably tell you that Beauregard just a few minutes ago said the final bet in the game will come when you have to choose the exact right moment to squeeze your trigger, and that you shouldn't be afraid to bluff."

Sam blew a breath out in a rush. "Harry said that too," he said, "about not being afraid to bluff. Damn. That means it's going to come down to him or me. Babe, do me a big favor. When Kenzie says her prayers tonight, make sure you both say one for me."

"Sam," Indie said, "we always do. And this time, I can promise you we are going to say some extra ones. You have to come home, Sam, you have to come home safely."

Sam's eyebrows lowered half an inch. "Indie? Is there something you're not telling me?"

She hesitated just long enough for Sam to be certain she was lying, but he decided to trust her and didn't push. "No, no, of course not. It's just that I love you, Sam, we both do, and we need you to come home safely. Promise me you will?"

Sam smiled into the phone so that she could hear it. "Of course I will," he said. "Just ask Beauregard."

29

Sam got back into the Challenger and just cruised around for a while. A glance at the clock on the stereo told him it was only 5:30, so he had two more hours to go before picking up Long at the airport. He cruised around the city, just taking in the sights.

After an hour of that, he picked up his regular phone and called the police department again. Detective Embry, the receptionist said, was out on a call but she would relay the message and ask him to give Sam a call when he got a chance. His phone rang again in less than ten minutes, and he answered it to find Embry on the line.

"Thanks for calling," Sam said. "I just wanted to check on how Lawton is doing."

"He's out of surgery," Embry replied, "but he's in the ICU. This is all off the record, of course, so keep it to yourself. He was hit three times, twice in the chest and once in the head. The head wound may have done some brain damage, they're not sure yet. The one that almost killed him was the one that nicked his aorta. The doctors said it was a miracle he didn't bleed out internally before they got him into surgery."

"Is there any prognosis?"

"Well, they think he's going to survive, but a lot depends on the brain damage. The bullet apparently caught him as he was falling, and basically just took a small chunk out of the top of his skull, but it did some damage to the top of his brain, too. The doctors say it's possible he won't even notice the bits they had to take out, but we won't know for sure until he's awake and actually starting to recover. They say that won't be for a day or two, at least."

"Man, I'll be saying my prayers for him. Does he have a family?"

"Jerry? Yeah. A wife and three kids. His youngest is only four."

"Damn. All right, thanks for letting me know. Any further developments?"

"Nothing concrete. A witness popped up who claims to have seen the shooter, but we don't know if it's legitimate or not. According to the witness, the shooter was around fifty, about five foot ten and 160 pounds, and fired the shot from a pickup truck across the street."

"Just curious, but why do you have doubts? That sounds like the kind of thing a shooter might do if he was going after a cop."

"Because the witness also said the shooter had pale white skin and pink eyes, like an albino. I'm having trouble believing that there could be an albino cop killer, considering that almost every albino is so nearsighted they're essentially blind. If the shooter was parked across the street, we're talking about 100 meters. That may not be much, but it would at least require some reasonable eyesight."

"Yeah, I guess I see your point. Still, it would've probably been a disguise. Maybe the albino part was a mask, something that could be snatched off in a hurry."

"We're considering that," Embry said. "I'll let you know if there's any news—oh, wait a minute. I got the autopsy report back on Reed a little bit ago. The guy would have been dead within a month, even if he hadn't been shot. Seems his insides were eaten up with cancer. Medical examiner says he would have been terminal."

Sam's eyes went wide. "Well, go figure," he said. "Any sign of that in his medical records?"

"Just got the order from the judge to get them. I'll let you know, but it probably won't be before tomorrow."

Sam thanked him and said goodbye, then hung up the phone and stuffed it into the box the disposable had come in, wrapped it up in the bag and shoved it into the glove box. He should still have been able to hear it if it rang, but that should have been enough soundproofing to keep Michael from being able to listen in on it when it was inactive.

He was letting his mind wander as he drove around the city, and it finally came around to Beauregard's latest utterance.

The final bet in the game is when I have to choose the right moment to take the shot. That sounds to me like a face-to-face confrontation, with each of us aiming at the other. If I choose the right moment, I get my man and still manage to live through it. If not... Sam let that thought trail off.

He said I shouldn't be afraid to bluff. What in the world could that mean? What kind of bluff can I pull that would draw him out into the open?

He rolled a dozen different scenarios around in his head, but nothing seemed to fit the concept of a bluff, at least not to the point that he believed Michael would expose himself over it. He decided to discuss it with Ken and hope the old assassin could come up with a viable idea.

At seven, he pointed the car toward the airport and followed the signs to get to the terminal parking lots. He parked and limped inside just in time to see the arrival of Ken's flight posted on the board, so he made his way to the debarking area, where passengers would come down into the terminal before heading for baggage claim. He wondered if he would even recognize Ken, but it turned out not to be an issue. Fifteen minutes passed, and then Ken came strolling toward him.

"Well, if it isn't my favorite private eye," Ken said. He broke into a smile and spread his arms, and Sam opened his own so that they could exchange a manly hug.

"Good to see you, Ken," Sam said. "I just wish it was under better circumstances."

"Yeah, me, too. Leon says this is off the books, because even he isn't sure he believes it, but I told him if Sam Prichard says it's so, that's good enough for me. What've we got going on?"

"Let's get your bags, then we can talk in the car. We're meeting Harry and his wife for dinner."

Ken hefted the thick carryon in his hand. "I travel light. Did you say Harry and his wife?"

"Yeah, it's a long story. Come on." He led the way out to the parking lot and to the car, and Ken tossed his bag into the back seat before climbing into the front. Sam got behind the wheel and started the car, then motioned for quiet as he approached the gate and paid the parking fee to get out.

Once they were out on the road, he looked over at Ken and grinned. "So, how much do you know?"

"Leon said Michael Reed was supposedly murdered in his home, and that Harry Winslow is the prime suspect. He also said that you have come to the conclusion that the body they've got at the morgue isn't Michael, even though every form of identification seems to say it is. You want to let me in on the rest of the story?"

"Here's the short version. Thirty-odd years ago, Michael Reed was Michael Watkins, and he and Harry were best buds. They worked together, and I gather they were pretty close, but Michael apparently had a thing for Harry's wife, Kathleen. He arranged for Harry to be sent on a secret mission into Cambodia or somewhere, and while he was gone, he told Kathleen that Harry had been killed by Russian agents and the KGB was coming to kill her and her children. Apparently he had whatever documentation was necessary to convince her, because she let him take her and the kids to Brazil and set up all new identities for them. A few months later, and remember that she thought she was a widow, they got married."

"Son-of-a-bitch," Ken said. "Are you sure Harry didn't kill him? I would have."

"I'm not sure he wouldn't have gotten the job done eventually, because—well, you know Harry. In this case, though, I'm absolutely certain he didn't kill Michael because Michael isn't dead. A week or so back, maybe less, Michael went to DC on the day that Harry was being retired and left an envelope in his apartment. Inside the envelope was a note Kathleen had written, sort of a 'making memories' kind of thing, and two pictures that showed the kids a few years older than they would have been when they supposedly died, and another picture of her and Michael all cuddly on a beach somewhere."

"I'll say it again, son-of-a-bitch! And this went on for how long?"

"More than thirty years. Harry went just a bit berserk when he saw that stuff, and then he came to me. It took Indie almost no time to track them down to their place here in Clearwater. Harry and I got into a private jet and flew down night before last, and yesterday morning we knocked on the door."

"And how did that work out for you?"

"Kathleen answered the door, and she was definitely surprised to see Harry standing there. She let us in, and told us how all this had gone down, but that she had found out Harry was alive back when he and I worked on that Lake Mead thing. I guess she confronted Michael about it, and that's when he told her that if she said anything or tried to contact Harry, he would kill both of them."

Sam paused for a moment as Ken shifted in the seat so he was facing him. "So Harry definitely had motive. Is there any actual evidence that he was involved in the killing?"

"Just a witness who claims to have seen someone fitting Harry's description go into the house just before the gunshots were. Anyway, while she was explaining all this to us, Michael walked in—I forgot to mention he was supposed to be on a plane, headed for Japan at the time—and pointed a gun at us all."

"You get yourself into the damnedest little messes, don't you? What happened then?"

"Well, we listened to him go on and on for a bit about how he decided to bring it all to a head, so that it would never come back to bite him in the ass. He wanted Harry and me to just walk away, forget all about it, and he made it plain that he wouldn't hesitate to kill anyone we were close to, in order to force us to cooperate. The thing is, It seemed to me that all he was really after was a way to keep the wealth and position he had built for himself, so I pitched the idea of him and Kathleen getting a divorce that let him keep it all, along with a pledge to never, ever tell anyone the truth. Since we all knew he could reach out and touch us anytime he wanted to, I figured there was a chance I could sell him on it, and he agreed. He even went so far as to tell Kathleen to come back next week to pack her things, just to take a small bag with her for the moment, and then he made her call her kids and bring them over to the house. She had to tell them that Harry was her boyfriend, that the two of them were having an affair and that Michael had found out, so they were getting a divorce."

"These kids are what, now, in their thirties? How did they take it?"

"Well, the daughter went a little nuts on her mom, but her son took it in stride. Everything seemed to be working out when we left, but then Kathleen gets a call—while Harry was out running around hunting for cigars, no less—that Michael had been murdered, and the police detective wanted to speak with her. She told him where she was, at the hotel, and he got there just a few minutes after Harry got back."

"Okay, I'm going to ask again, are you certain Harry didn't kill him? This is all pretty circumstantial evidence, I grant you, but it sure looks convincing to me."

"You want to hear the story? Then shut up and let me tell it. Okay, so anyway, we all talk to the police detective and Harry even admits he wasn't in the room when Michael was apparently murdered, that he was out running around town by himself. Next thing you know we're headed downtown, but we're talking on the way about how it looks like Harry has literally been set up to take the fall on this, and it dawns on me that the only witness that could possibly give him an alibi is the clerk at the tobacco store. If the killer wanted Harry to take the fall, there couldn't be an alibi. I got the police detective to stop, and he sent squad cars out to that tobacco shop."

"Let me guess," Ken interrupted. "The clerk was dead, right?"

Sam nodded. "Neck was broken, and he was stuffed up under the counter. So the detective interviews the three of us, and finally we leave to head back to the hotel. Kathleen calls the kids, who by this time knew that the man they knew as their father was dead, and they come over to talk. Naturally, they think Harry must've done it, so Kathleen and I talked to them alone for a while. Once they began to get a grasp of the real, true story, which didn't go over very well with either of them to be honest, they finally decided to give Harry the benefit of the doubt. They took him and Kathleen down to the restaurant to talk, and that's when the detective called and said he had a warrant for Harry's arrest, because of this witness who came out of the woodwork, somewhere, and said she had seen a white-haired old man with a white goatee going into Michael's house shortly before the gun-shots were heard. They had done a GSR test on Harry's hands, and of course it came back positive. Gunshot residue never goes away, you should know that."

"Right. FBI says they found it on people who have never even touched a gun."

"Which is why they don't test for it, anymore. Anyway, Harry got arrested and Kathleen got called to identify the body the next morning. She went to the morgue and looked at it, but the face had been completely blown away so she had to rely on iden-tifying marks. The body had a tattoo that she recognized, and some scars that Michael had, so she confirmed the identification. After that, she and I met at the courthouse to be present at Har-ry's initial appearance. The judge set bail, and Kathleen and I went to have lunch while we waited for the bondsmen to do their jobs. Harry called us right after lunch and said he'd made bail, so we went and picked him up and I took them back to the hotel. After that, I headed for the Police Department to look at the file on the case."

"Wait, what? The detective let you see the case file?"

Sam grinned. "Harry had called up to DHS and rattled some chains, so I was appointed as their Special Investigator for this case. I don't think the job pays anything, but it opens doors like a bulldozer. By the time I got to the station, the detective already had been informed that he was to give me whatever cooperation I wanted. He handed the file over without a bit of argument, and I went through it. Most of it was standard police procedural stuff, but the crime scene photos were there. Now, I had spent quite some time sitting within fifteen feet of Michael Reed while he pointed a gun at me, so I had pretty well memorized the guy. One of the things I noticed clearly was that he had just recently trimmed his nails. In fact, they were so perfect it looked like he had a manicure, and of course he's a rich guy so I figured maybe he did. The trouble was when I looked at the crime scene photos of the body, the nails were long and a little bit rough. They definitely had not been trimmed in at least a week."

"So? Everybody knows fingernails keep growing after you die."

"Actually, they don't. What gives that appearance is the fact that the skin around the ends of the fingers begins to shrink back as it dries out. And even then, that effect takes days to show up, not just a few hours later. Those fingernails are incontrovertible proof, to me, that that body was not Michael Reed. Unfortunately, I made the mistake of telling the detective what I believed. I don't think I actually sold him on it, but he at least reached the point that he was willing to consider the possibility. The only thing he did say was that he couldn't take my opinion to the prosecutor without getting hauled off to the crazy house, and I can understand why he felt that way. Fingerprints, personal identification, next of kin all said it was Michael Reed; who did I think I was to try to overrule all that evidence?"

Ken grunted. "If you tell me you believe Michael Reed is alive, I'm going to go with you. I've seen you in action, you don't miss much. Anything else?"

"Yeah," Sam said. "This afternoon, I get a phone call from a restricted number. Bet you can guess who was on the other end of the line."

Ken's eyes widened slightly. "Then we have confirmed that Reed is alive. I'm sure the police aren't checking missing persons that might match his description; they'd have to believe what you're telling them in order to do that. What's your game plan?"

30

Michael woke up at just before five, thanks to the internal alarm clock he had developed over the years, then climbed out of the truck and walked into a fast food restaurant to use the bathroom and freshen up. He was back in the truck ten minutes later, and headed toward the restaurant Kate had taken Sam to for lunch. He wanted to be inside before the rest of them arrived.

He got there with plenty of time to spare, then picked up a bag he had kept in the truck and began putting on a disguise.

They can do wonderful things with latex, nowadays. A skull-cap with dark brown hair in a male balding pattern went over the top of his head, covering his hair and fitting so snuggly against his skin that it would take very close examination to see where they met. His nose was covered by another prosthetic, but this one used adhesive to keep it in place, as did another that he stuck to his chin and jawline. That one even had stubbly whiskers, as if he hadn't bothered to shave that day. An inflatable cushion went down the front of his pants and he tucked his shirt in over it, and suddenly he was an entirely different person. Without the jacket of his suit, he didn't look anything like Michael Reed.

He withdrew a pistol from the bag and shoved it down the back of his pants, then climbed out of the truck. He checked once more to be sure no one had seen him make the transformation, then walked into the restaurant and let the hostess seat him at a table near the back. It was a good line of sight to the door, and he would be able to see them easily when they arrived.

For appearances' sake, he went ahead and ordered dinner, and when it arrived he realized that he was genuinely hungry. He hadn't taken any time to eat during the day, so he had been fasting since dinner the night before. He forced himself not to eat too quickly, though, so that he could stay long enough to see his quarry come to the door.

It was after 6:30 by the time he realized that they weren't coming. He should have expected it; he cursed himself for telling Sam that he was listening to his phone calls, because they obviously had changed their plans. He signaled the waiter for his check and gave the man 100-dollar bill, told him to keep the change and hurried out to the truck again.

He picked up the tablet and checked the GPS location on Sam's phone again, and realized Sam was just cruising around aimlessly. They had probably decided to let him pick Long up first, then meet for dinner somewhere else. Unfortunately, Michael wouldn't be able to get to the airport in time to spot Sam's new car, so he decided to scan the recordings from his phone again to see if there was a clue about where they might meet.

He picked up where he had left off, after hearing Sam's conversation with Detective Lawton, then skimmed through several minutes of nothing but engine and street noises before he came across another conversation. This one was with Heather and her mother, and Michael suddenly felt a chill. Heather had told Sam about her job and her relationship with Michael, which wasn't that big a deal, but if Sam were to think for a few minutes about what she'd said, he'd be back to ask more questions that just might create a problem. If that happened, Heather would become a potential star witness against him, and could easily confirm Sam's theory about the body not being Michael's.

It was time to do something about her. He allowed himself to feel the slightest twinge of regret as he put the truck in gear and headed toward Pine Brook Drive. Even that was going to take a while, since the restaurant was in Tampa, and he'd heard enough to know that they might already have left for Miami, but it was a loose end that had to be tied up. If she was gone, he had a contact in Miami that would have no trouble finding out where her aunt lived and taking care of the problem for him.

He got to the neighborhood about forty minutes later, and cruised slowly past the house. He was in luck, because there were lights on inside. Heather and her mother had not left town yet. He went around the block and came at the house again from another direction, stopping the truck at a point where he could see the house clearly, but where it would be difficult for anyone else to see him.

He thought about getting out of the truck and approaching the house, killing both women inside, but he could hear the dogs barking. They would almost certainly get even louder if someone came sneaking up toward the house, and the last thing he would need would be neighbors looking out to see why the dogs were making a fuss. He decided to wait a bit and hope for an opportunity to present itself, then reached behind the seat and pulled out the suppressed AR.

He waited almost 15 more minutes, and then Lady Luck smiled on him. Heather came out the front door holding a suitcase, but instead of going toward the car in the driveway, she put it down and sat down on a bench on the porch. It looked like she was crying, but Michael didn't let that stop him. He picked up the rifle and aimed it carefully, using the high-powered scope to draw a bead directly on her forehead.

He let his breath out slowly, then squeezed the trigger, but Lady Luck was fickle. Just as he fired—a three-round burst that was accomplished by a simple modification to the sear pin—Heather leaned forward and got to her feet. All three bullets penetrated the window behind her, and she suddenly screamed as she ran into the house.

Michael swore and dropped the gun into the floorboard, then started the truck and took off. He didn't plan on going far, but he didn't want to be parked so close when the police arrived in a few minutes. He drove down a few blocks and turned around, so that he could watch from the truck when they arrived.

Ten minutes later, when no police cars had come screaming toward the house, Michael began thinking about trying again. He was about to put the truck into gear when a car suddenly roared around a corner and slid to a stop in front of the house.

Even without being able to look to the scope, Michael was certain that the car held Sam Prichard and Kenneth Long. He was convinced of it a second later, when two men jumped out and ran toward the front door.

Seconds later, Heather's mother came running out and dove into the car, and immediately afterward Michael saw both men hustling Heather between them. They stood watch as she got into the back seat with her mother, then they hurriedly got into the car and it sped away.

Michael put the truck in gear at last and hurried to follow, keeping some distance between them. If they were taking Heather with them, he might get the opportunity to eliminate every possible threat to his plans all at once.

If he did, this little setback would be well worth it. He kept his eyes on the Dodge Challenger as it slowed down to the speed limit, but was careful to keep a couple of cars between them. The last thing he needed was for Sam to figure out that he was being followed.

Unfortunately, Sam Prichard was pretty sharp. It was only about ten minutes later when he made a surprise turn, but Michael was smart enough not to fall for it. He cruised past the intersection at normal speed, then found a place to pull over so that he could watch Sam's movements on the tablet.

Suddenly it occurred to him that Sam and Harry were no longer alone. With Kenneth Long on their side, the three of them made up a formidable force. It would be very difficult for Michael to take them all out, at least by himself.

He picked up his phone and dialed a local number. "Vito?" he said, once again disguising his voice. "You don't know me, but we have some mutual friends. One of them was Michael Reed, and I'm sure you heard he was murdered yesterday. Well, I'm zeroing in on his killer and the people helping him, but I need some backup. Yes, no problem. I can pay."

* * * * *

The limousine had driven all the way to Colorado Springs, and the killer had managed to keep it in view the whole time. Along the way, he had been formulating a plan, something so daring and crazy that he thought it might actually have a chance of success. When the limo and its escort had peeled off an exit, the killer had followed.

He had no doubt he had been spotted, but at this point he was counting on it. He hung back just far enough to cast a little doubt about whether he was intentionally staying with them, but by the time they had made three consecutive turns, he knew they would be certain. He wasn't a bit surprised when the escort car suddenly spun sideways and two men jumped out and aimed guns at him.

He didn't stop. Instead, he shoved his foot to the floor and laid down in the seat so that he was out of the line of fire. The old Dodge truck he was driving was pretty stout, and the two men didn't even have time to jump out of the way before it plowed into their SUV.

One of them was caught between the grill of the Dodge and the side of the SUV, while the other was crushed between his door and the car itself. The killer sat up and looked through his bullet-riddled windshield, then backed up and went around the wreckage of the car. The limo was just disappearing around another corner, as he picked up the Mac 11 submachine gun and used its barrel to break the rest of the glass away.

He pressed the accelerator all the way down once again and fishtailed around the corner, just in time to see the limo turn into a driveway. He slid to a stop just behind it as three more bodyguards leapt out, but the Mac made short work of all of them. None of the bullets penetrated the car, even bouncing off the glass, but once the guards were down, the killer put the truck in park and stepped out. He had picked up another Mac, along with a hand grenade. No matter how armored the body of the car might be, a grenade underneath it would almost certainly do the job.

He had completely forgotten his orders. The longer the chase had been, the angrier he had become. If his employer wanted Prichard to be distracted, he was pretty sure killing his entire family would get the job done. He kept the Mac pointed at the car as he approached, then put a finger in the ring of the grenade and prepared to roll it under the car.

That was when the driver's door flew open, and a pistol was thrust out through the opening. The driver was already squeezing the trigger, and while the first two shots missed completely, the third one caught the killer in the throat. He stumbled backward as he dropped the gun and the grenade, his hand going to his throat to try to stop the bleeding, but it was far too late. Only seconds passed before the loss of blood to the brain was enough to bring him down.

The limo door closed, and everyone inside stayed when they were until police arrived seven minutes later. At that point, George finally stepped out to speak to them, but first he bent at the waist, put his hands on his knees and vomited. It was the first time he had ever killed anyone.

Of the three guards who had been in the limousine, only one had suffered a fatal wound. The other two would survive, but the two in the SUV had also died. The police had their hands full trying to keep the scene secure with all the neighbors standing in the yard and trying to see, and it would be more than two hours before they finally had all of the information they needed.

George was allowed to sit back down in the driver's seat, and he finally looked at his passengers. They were safe, that was true, but he was terribly worried about what the little girl had seen.

"Ms. Kenzie," he said softly, "are you okay?"

The child looked up at him and George was astonished at the calm in her face. "I'm okay," she said, "and so are Mommy and my grandmas. Don't cry, George. You had to shoot that man, you just had to. You'll be okay."

George managed a smile through his tears. "As long as you are all safe," he said, "I'm sure I'm gonna be fine."

"You will. Sometimes my daddy has to shoot people, too, and sometimes he cries about it. But he says you just gotta do it, sometimes, and then he's okay again. You'll be okay in a little while."

George continued smiling, as he stared at the little girl in her mother's arms.

31

"Ha!" Sam said. "I wish I knew. Did I ever tell you about Beauregard?"

"Yeah," Ken said. "That's the ghost that tells your mother-in-law what's going to happen, right?"

"Right. Well, Beauregard says I'm playing poker with Reed, and that each hand I lose will cost a life. So far I seem to have lost two, and the first one cost me the tobacco shop clerk, the second seems to have been the detective, Lawton. Now, he isn't dead yet, but it's quite possible he's going to have enough brain damage that he might as well be. Still too soon to tell. Beauregard says there are still two more hands to play, which means at least two more lives hanging in the balance. And then the last message I got from him says the last hand will come when I have to decide when to shoot, and I shouldn't be afraid to bluff, but I can't figure out what kind of bluff would do me any good in this game."

"There's something about games with us, isn't there? When we first met, I used chess to explain to you what was going on, and now you're dealing with a highly trained government agent who might very well be either a traitor or a psychopath, and you have to consider your interaction with him as a poker game. Sounds like we got kind of a pattern going, doesn't it?"

"I don't care if we play monopoly," Sam said, "as long as I figure out a way to win. In this case, winning is going to mean proving Harry didn't kill this guy, but it could also mean bringing Michael Reed to justice. Harry thinks the reason he's doing this is because he's decided to go rogue. Apparently Michael knows where, as Harry puts it, a lot of bodies are buried both literally and figuratively, and could seriously cash in on that kind of information."

"Harry's probably right. When I went rogue eleven years ago, I never did stoop so low as to sell information that could hurt my country. I sold plenty of it back to my country, information they needed but didn't have any way to get on their own. A man like Michael Reed, though, he's going to be looking at turning all that information into his retirement account. He's out to accumulate an awful lot of money in a short time, then retire to Barbados, or the French Riviera, somewhere like that. He'll have yet another new identity, a small army to make sure nobody can get to him and enough money to live that lifestyle for 100 years."

"Sounds like a dream, but the price is too high. Ken, we've got to stop this guy if we possibly can."

"We can," Ken said. "He's just as evil as Chandler, but not nearly as smart. I worked with him once, so trust me when I say that. This guy isn't nearly as smart as he thinks he is, even if he is brighter than the average person. He's got a weakness, and we have to find it. Any women in his life, other than the one he stole from Harry?"

"His secretary," Sam said. "She's a sweet young thing, early twenties I would guess, and he seduced her. The usual lies, about how he and his wife were going to get a divorce and he was going to marry the pretty young girl, but I've seen her and I'm convinced she has no idea he's still alive. He even told me himself that he was done with her, so I don't think we can consider her any kind of weakness."

"Okay, and he doesn't have any other family. He's walking away from everything he had in this life, so we can't use any of that against him. Damn, he isn't making it easy, is he?"

"Not even a little bit. So far, the only mistake he's made that I can find is forgetting about the manicure. If the nails on that body had been neat and trimmed, I never would've figured it out."

Ken stared out the windshield for a moment, then turned to look at Sam. "There's got to be something else, something we can use. Something even the police can't turn a blind eye to."

"I agree, but I don't know what it..."

He was interrupted by the ringing of his cell phone, the one inside the glove box. He put a finger to his lips to tell Ken to be quiet, then reached over and snatched the glove box open, grabbed the bag and dumped it out in his lap. He got the box open by the fourth ring and answered the phone.

"Sam Prichard," he said.

"Mr. Prichard? This is Annie Keller. You said to let you know if—if anything came up about that man?"

Sam's eyes went wide. "Yes. What's happening, Annie?"

"Well—listen, I know this might sound crazy, but I think someone just tried to kill Heather."

"What? What happened?"

"Well, we've been getting ready to leave to go visit my sister, but we had to make arrangements for the dogs and stuff, and Heather's been—well, you saw how she was this afternoon, she hasn't gotten any better. She decided to go outside and sit on the porch for a few minutes, but then she said it was too hot and wanted to come back in. Just as she started to get up off the chair out there, something came through the window right behind it, and now there are three little holes in the wall. She screamed and ran inside, and I heard a car take off really fast..."

"Are you still at the house?" Sam asked.

"Yes, but we were about to..."

"Stay put, and stay inside. I'm on the way. I'm only about two or three minutes away, I'll be there in no time."

Sam cut the call and shoved the phone back in the box, and Ken finished wrapping it in the bag and putting it back in the glove box. "What was that?" he asked.

Sam had whipped the car around and then fishtailed around another corner before he answered. "Heather Keller, the secretary? It seems somebody just took a shot at her. Michael had told me earlier that he had no reason to bother her, that she was in no danger from him, but he must have remembered something. We've got to get to her, and quickly, or she's going to be dead."

Ken reached under his jacket and pulled out a Glock nineteen, carefully checked to be sure there was a round in the chamber, and then kept it in his hand. He didn't say anything as Sam raced through the residential streets, and when Sam slid the car to a stop in front of the little house, he was out even before Sam got the car into park.

Sam followed, drawing his own weapon and looking around as he got out of the car, and the two of them quickly but carefully made their way to the house. When they got there, Sam knocked on the door.

"Annie? Heather? It's Sam Prichard. Come on, we need to get the two of you out of here quickly."

The door started to open, and Annie peeked out before swinging it wide. Heather was right behind her, still crying but looking terribly frightened.

"Annie, run for my car and get into the backseat as quickly as you can. Leave the door open, my friend and I will bring Heather right behind you."

Annie looked at them and their guns for a moment, then seemed to steel herself and rushed out the door toward the car. She snatched open the passenger door and flipped the seat forward, diving inside as quickly as she could.

Back on the porch, Sam and Ken each grabbed Heather by an arm and kept her tight between them as they hurried her along the walk. When they got to the car, they folded together behind her as she climbed into the backseat, and then Ken told them both to get down, to keep their heads down and stay out of sight.

Sam hobbled quickly around and got behind the wheel again while Ken got back into the passenger seat. The car was still running and Sam slammed it into gear without even bothering to put his seatbelt on, and they raced away with the seatbelt alarm ringing incessantly.

From down in the backseat, Annie cleared her throat. "Mr. Prichard, can you tell me what on earth is going on? Why would anyone try to shoot my daughter?"

"Because the person who shot at her is Michael Reed, himself. What I told you earlier turned out to be true. Michael is not dead, but he's already murdered at least two people and possibly more while taking his own death. He actually had the gall to call me earlier today, and he told me Heather wouldn't be in any danger from him because she didn't know anything that could hurt him, but I'm guessing there might be something after all."

Sam whipped the car around a couple of corners and kept watching to see if they were being followed, but there was no obvious sign of pursuit. He slowed down to the speed limit and started making his way toward his appointment with Harry and Kathleen once again.

"Heather," he said after a moment, "do you understand what I'm saying? Michael isn't dead, but he's faked his own murder. In order to do that, he had to kill someone, and he's trying to frame another man for it so he killed someone else to make sure that man wouldn't have an alibi. This afternoon, the police detective in charge of the investigation was shot and may die yet, simply because I told him what I knew, that the body they have identified as Michael's isn't him."

"Yeah," Heather said haltingly. "I understand, I just can't believe it. Why would he do that? Why would he kill anybody?"

"Sweetheart," Ken said, "something you need to get through your head right now is that your boyfriend never was who he claimed to be. He's actually a government agent, and one of those who sneak into other countries and kill people as part of their job. Killing someone, to him, that's like you making sure your files are all in order."

"But he was always so gentle. I mean, I never even saw him get mad at anybody. Never, not once. The closest I ever saw him come to getting angry was when his wife would call and interrupt something he was doing, but even then he would just make a face and go on like it was no big deal."

"Well, somehow or other," Ken said, "you've become a big deal to him, big enough that he figures he needs to kill you so it won't become bigger. Can you think of anything he might have said or done in the last few weeks that he might not want you to tell anybody about?"

"No, nothing. It's been nothing but business as usual. I mean, my job is one of the easiest jobs in the world. All I do is answer the phones and take messages, sometimes I set appointments for him, things like that."

"Well, keep thinking," Sam said. "Whatever it is he thinks you know could be the thing that brings him down."

Ken glanced over at Sam, and saw him watching the rearview mirror closely. "Somebody on us?" he asked softly.

"About three cars back," Sam whispered. "It's made the last couple of turns with me, and always backs off to let another car get between us."

"Normal surveillance technique. Try a surprise turn."

Sam nodded, then a moment later, just before it would be too late to make a right turn, he whipped the wheel around and cut to the north. He watched the rearview mirror until he saw the offending pickup truck continue straight on the street he'd turned off of.

He breathed a sigh of relief. "Just coincidence, I guess," he said. Still, he continued north for several blocks before turning east once more. His route took him to North Keene Road, and he turned south when he reached it. A few moments later he turned right again onto Highway 60, which would take them across the causeway to Clearwater Beach.

It was almost nine o'clock by the time they arrived at the Clear Sky Café, and the four of them got out of the car. They started to enter, but then Annie turned to Sam and held something out. "I don't have a pocket," she said simply. "Would you mind to hold these for me until we come out?"

Sam looked and saw that what she was holding out was a pack of cigarettes, and he reached out and took them from her without comment. He slid them into his shirt pocket and then they all walked inside. There, they were met by another surprise. Harold and Beth were sitting with Harry and Kathleen, but fortunately Harry had had the foresight to get a large table. The waitstaff had made it by putting two tables together, but it was big enough for everyone to sit down.

"Ken," Harry said as he and Harold rose to shake hands. "It's good to see you again, and I appreciate your coming to help."

"I owe you guys," Ken said. "You need me, I'm there."

Harry introduced Harold and Beth to Ken, Sam introduced Annie and Heather, and then they all sat down again.

32

"I've been bringing the kids up to speed on all this," Harry said. "Beth is a little skeptical, but Harold is just as observant as you and me. He saw Michael's fingernails as well, so..."

"So if the ones on the body they identified as Michael are noticeably longer, then you're right. It can't be him."

Heather looked up sharply at Harold, but didn't say anything. She seemed to be trying to figure out just where she fit into all of this, and seeing the widow of the man she'd been having an affair with sitting directly across from her wasn't helping. She lowered her eyes to the table in front of her once again, and kept them there.

Sam explained quickly about the shots that were fired at Heather, and Harry agreed that he had done exactly the right thing by going to grab her and her mother. "Obviously, the girl knows something that Michael considers damaging. If we can figure out what that is, it could be the key to solving this entire puzzle."

The door opened, and Sam looked up instinctively at the new customer. A chubby, balding man walked in and sat down in a booth near the door, and after looking him over carefully, Sam dismissed him. He turned back to the people at his table.

"We've asked, but she doesn't seem to remember anything significant."

Kathleen leaned forward and reached across the table toward Heather, extending a hand. "Heather, I need you to understand something. Michael was—he was something of a monster, and he was an absolute genius at getting people to do whatever he wanted. I hold no animosity toward you, none at all. I've known for several months that you were sleeping with him, but trust me when I tell you you weren't the first. Every time he's been in business, he's always made sure he had a pretty young secretary. It doesn't take a rocket scientist to figure out what a man like him wants from an office girl."

Heather kept her eyes down for a moment, but then slowly raised them to look directly into Kathleen's. "I figured you'd hate me," she whispered. "He said the two of you were unhappy, that you were going to get a divorce, and that all he was waiting for was for you to sign the papers. I'm sorry, I..."

"It's okay, Heather, really. No, we weren't happy together, but what you don't know is that Michael did some terrible things a long time ago that made me believe my husband—my real husband, this man sitting beside me—was dead, and that the only way I could keep my children safe was to flee out of the country with him. He managed to make it all so convincing that I fell for it, and I spent more than thirty years thinking that my husband Harry was dead, but a couple of years ago I found out the truth. Believe me, we were not happy at all after that. So, yes, I know exactly how he could manipulate a girl into doing what he wants."

Heather looked into her eyes for another moment, and then she began to cry softly. "Oh, I've been such a fool," she said. "He was just so nice to me, and it made me feel good. He never even tried to pressure me into—you know, sex. It all just sort of seemed to happen naturally."

Beth was staring at the girl, and suddenly she started shaking her head. "My God," she said, "we never knew him at all, did we? I never would have believed he would do something like this."

"Like I told Heather," Kathleen said, "she wasn't the first. Wealthy men seem to have a need to prove their virility by seducing younger women. It's just part of their nature, I guess, at least for some of them. Michael always had pretty secretaries, and he always found reasons to take them on trips with them. Like I said, it doesn't take a rocket scientist."

"So the man we thought was our father," Harold said, "is not only a philanderer, he's also a murderer and probably a traitor to our country." He shook his head. "I find myself wishing that he was actually dead."

"Well, he's not," Ken said. "I can tell you that makes him a direct and extreme danger to each and every person at this table. Harry, you have a vested interest in proving that he's alive, and the rest of you now know enough that his memory is ruined for all of you. Heather and her mother are in danger because he obviously thinks she knows something that can prove our case. Harry, are you armed?"

"Me? Why, I'm out on bail, I'm not allowed to carry a gun. Of course I'm armed, what kind of fool do you think I am?"

"Okay, so that makes three of us..."

"Four," Harold said. "I've had my CCL for years, I never go anywhere without a weapon on me. And before you ask, yes, I know how to use it."

Ken grinned at him. "Okay, four of us who can at least shoot back. Now all we have to do is figure a way to draw him out."

Everyone was silent for a few seconds, each of them thinking, but then Heather whispered, "Manicure."

Sam leaned toward her. "What did you say?"

"You were talking about his fingernails. That was another part of my job, because I used to be a manicurist. I had to do his nails every week, I just did them the day before yesterday."

Sam and the others all stared at her. "Heather," Sam said, "are you absolutely certain it was day before yesterday?"

The girl nodded. "Yes. It was the last thing he had me do before I left for the day, and we did it a couple days early because he was supposed to be flying to Japan the next morning and I would have a few days off."

Sam, Harry and Ken all looked each other. "That's it," Sam said, "that's the proof we need." He reached into his pocket for his phone, but the one he pulled out was the burner. "Crap, I need my other phone. Be right back." He stood and started toward the door, heading toward the Challenger to get his phone out of the glove box.

The customer who had come in looked up at him and smiled, and Sam smiled back. The man was holding the menu, and something about the way he was holding it struck Sam as odd. His fingers were curled against the back of the menu, so that it looked like his thumbs were simply clamping it into his fists. The incongruity of it made Sam glance closer, and he got a good look at the man's left thumb.

The nail on that thumb was perfectly manicured, and Sam suddenly froze midstep. His eyes shot from the thumb to the face, and suddenly he could see the features of Michael Reed under the rubber prostheses covering the nose, chin and forehead.

Michael saw the recognition and reacted instantly, flinging the menu into Sam's face as he swung his legs out of the booth. He was on his feet while Sam was still staggering back, his hip causing him to stumble, and Sam saw him reach behind his back and under his shirt.

He's going for a gun, Sam thought, and threw himself forward as hard as he could. He wrapped his arms around Michael and the two of them fell onto the table, breaking it and causing it to fall. They slid down it to the floor, but Sam lost his grip and suddenly Michael's gun was pointed at his face once again.

The door flew open again, and four men burst into the restaurant. Each of them was holding a submachine gun, but they seemed confused when they saw Michael pointing a gun at Sam's head.

Michael looked up at them and indicated the people at the table with his head. "Them! Get them," he shouted.

Back at the table, everyone was on their feet and Sam saw Michael glance up at them. The four men looked up, also, and out of his peripheral vision Sam saw each of them suddenly go wide-eyed. He turned his head to look and saw Ken, Harry and Harold all standing there with pistols leveled in their direction.

One of the men who had entered suddenly yelled, "Screw this," and then he ran out the door. The other three raised their guns and pointed them toward the table, but all three pistols fired at once. Michael's reinforcements dropped to the floor, and Sam knew that at least two of them were already dead from the size of the holes in their faces. The third one had taken a bullet in his chest, and was lying on the floor, moaning.

All three guns suddenly turned toward Michael.

"Ah-ah!" he shouted. "One wrong move, and Sammy here gets a third eye." He grabbed Sam by his shirt and hauled him to his feet, then reached under his light jacket and grabbed his Glock. He shoved it down his pants as the waitress and cook came rushing out from the kitchen, then hurried back inside when they saw the guns and the fallen men.

Michael pulled Sam in front of him and moved his gun to the side of his head. He looked around him at the others. "You all think you got it figured out, don't you? You all think this is going to be the end of it, right?" He laughed. "Hey, Ken, how have you been? I've got to admit I was surprised when I heard you were coming in on this."

"Michael," Ken said, "let him go and put the gun down. You know damned well that if you shoot him I'm going to kill you before you can get out that door. The only chance you've got to stay alive right now is to drop that gun and let Sam go."

"Oh, good Lord, you're still just as arrogant as you ever were. I got fifteen rounds and there are only seven of you. Only three of you have weapons, and with Sam here in the way, none of you can draw a bead on me. I could probably drop all three of you, then finish off the rest at my leisure, but this has gotten messy enough already." He pressed his gun harder against Sam's ear. "Now, all of you just need to stand right there. Me and Sam are going out the door, and if nobody gives me any trouble I'll let him go in just a minute. Understood?"

No one spoke, and Michael started dragging Sam backward. There was a quick bump as Michael's back hit the door, and then they were stepping backward onto the sidewalk. Sam could still see Ken and the others standing around the table with their guns drawn, but then Michael suddenly let go of him and stepped back. Sam turned around to face him and saw the gun pointed directly at his head.

"So much for letting me go, right?"

"That's how it goes, Sam," Michael said. "Don't worry, the rest of them will be joining you in a few minutes. Once I shoot you, they'll come running out. It'll be like shooting ducks at an arcade." He grinned and reached out with his free hand to thump the cigarettes in Sam's pocket. "Wanna light one up before you go? Those things will kill you, you know."

Sam glanced down at the cigarettes, forgotten until that moment. He looked up at Michael again. "Yeah, if I can," he said. Without waiting for an answer, he reached into the pocket and took out the pack, shook a cigarette out into his hand and stuck it between his lips. He patted the pocket for a moment, then started patting all the others. Finally he grinned and slipped his hand into his jacket pocket.

"Hey, now," Michael said, "pull that hand out slowly."

Sam did, and then held up the lighter Harry had given him the day before. He cupped his hands around it and put it up to the end of the cigarette, and flicked the cover a couple of times as if he was trying to get it to light. He looked up at Michael. "Just give me a second, it'll work," he said, then went back to clicking the cover.

I have to know when to take the shot, Sam thought, *that's what Beauregard said.* He was carefully watching Michael in his peripheral vision, praying for one moment of opportunity, and then it came. For a split second, Michael took his eyes off Sam and leaned slightly to the right as he looked toward the café door.

Sam flipped the cover open backward, then thrust his hand out with the lighter pointed directly at Michael's head and pulled the diamond back with his thumb. The explosion that resulted shocked him, and the recoil made him drop the lighter, but then he looked at Michael.

The man was still standing on his feet, still pointing his gun at Sam, but there was a streak of blood running down his nose from the neat round hole in the center of his forehead. His eyes rolled up, and the gun clattered to the sidewalk as all of his muscles relaxed at once.

Behind him, Sam heard the commotion as Harry and Ken fought to be the first out the door. Ken won, but just barely, and Harry and the others were right on his heels. Ken, Harry and Harold all had their guns in their hands still, but they lowered them when they got to Sam and saw Michael lying dead on the concrete in front of him.

"Damn, Sam," Ken said. "I saw him take your gun, what the hell happened?"

Sam still had the unlit cigarette hanging out of his mouth, and he reached up to take it out as they all gathered around him. Beth and Heather were whimpering, but the rest were simply staring down at the body of the man who was supposed to have already been dead.

Sam looked at Ken and held up the cigarette, then pointed down at the still smoking lighter-gun. "I bluffed," he said.

Ken's eyes were wide. "Yeah, you did," he said, "and it looks like you won the pot."

33

The police arrived fifteen minutes later, and at Sam's insistence Detective Embry was called out. When he arrived, Sam finally explained what the strange doodle on Lawton's notes had truly meant, that Michael Reed was still alive and had faked his own murder. The whole group was taken to the station for interviews, and it was Heather's statement about giving Michael the manicure Sam had noticed that finally got Embry to believe the story.

Both Sam and Harry suddenly got phone calls, and the timing couldn't have been more perfect since they came just as Embry finished with them. Sam answered his phone to find his wife on the line, and the first words out of her mouth almost gave him a heart attack.

"Sam," she said, "first I need you to know that we are all okay."

"Oh, God," he said, "what happened?"

It took almost 15 minutes for her to explain it all, how a crazed gunman had apparently followed them all the way from Denver to Colorado Springs, then launched a one-man attack that took out all of their security. The police had told her that they had recovered a hand grenade at the scene, and it hadn't taken her long to figure out what the killer had planned to do with it. Sam listened with his mouth hanging open through the whole thing, but finally he managed to close it when she told him how George had saved the day.

When he finally got off the phone, he saw Harry grinning at him. "Let me guess," he said. "That was George on the line?"

"Indeed it was," Harry said. "I gather Indiana has already told you what happened?"

Sam nodded his head slowly, and then walked over to Harry and pulled him into an embrace. "Thank you, Harry," he said. "Thank you for keeping my family safe. I'm so sorry about the men you lost, that was terrible, but thank you for my family."

"Now that we've proven our case, this whole thing falls under National Security. Those men died in the line of duty, and they will be honored for their sacrifice. Had Michael's killer managed to reach your family, you probably would not have been in any condition to handle him when the time came. Since you were the only one who could, those sacrifices were an unfortunate necessity."

Sam could only look at him, unable to speak any further.

Over the next few days, during which Sam was required to remain in the area and assist with closing the investigation, they learned that the fingerprints on the real Michael didn't turn up in any database, but even though the back of his head was blown away by the secret derringer, his face was still easily recognizable. Enough people could make a positive identification to settle the issue.

A search of missing person reports had turned up the fact that a Ronald Denham, who had recently been diagnosed with cancer, had disappeared a couple of months earlier.

Sam and Ken went to Fort Lauderdale to interview Denham's wife and children, his only surviving relatives, and learned that he had recently come into a substantial amount of money. He had given his wife a healthy sum, almost 100,000 dollars, and told her more would be coming soon. He and his wife were separated, but he had visited the family every few days and told them about some mysterious investment he had made that had made him the money he had already given them, and was going to provide for them after he was gone.

Gradually, Sam was able to put together a timeline. Michael had met Denham at the doctor's office on the day he had learned that the cancer was terminal. At that point, Michael appeared to have put his plan into action. They were able to find the tattoo parlor that had put the tattoo on Denham, and located a cosmetic surgeon who, after intense questioning, finally admitted to creating a couple of realistic-looking scars by scraping off the upper layers of skin and flooding the tissues with steroids.

It finally became completely clear that Michael had offered Mr. Denham a large sum of money to take his place in death. Kidney cancer is insidious, and people often don't even know they have it until it's far too late. Denham would have looked fairly healthy to those who knew him, but the autopsy had revealed that he probably had less than a month to live. With the money he got from Michael, he had established a trust fund that would support his family for many years after he was gone. The money was eventually found, but due to the vagaries of trust law, that money could not be touched and would still benefit his family.

Getting Harry down to Florida had been the trigger. By planting the envelope in his apartment, Michael was certain Harry would turn to Sam and that Sam would find him within a few days. He hadn't expected it to happen so quickly, but thanks to the fact he had someone recording all of Sam's phone calls and reporting to him, he was alerted in plenty of time to make the arrangements he needed. The police were able to find a couple of witnesses who had seen Michael picking up Mr. Denham in a boat on the day of the killing.

They also found Michael's abandoned scuba gear in the boathouse of the vacant place down the street. From that, they figured out that Michael had left his home by swimming down to the vacant house, and some barely visible tire tracks in the garage proved that his car had been parked there at some time.

They never did find the car, or any trace of it.

The only thing that had given Michael away was his failure to notice Denham's fingernails. If he had, he probably would've gotten away with it all and Harry would be looking at life in prison, or worse.

After a couple of days, the police department held a press conference to reveal what they had learned, and Sam was required to attend since he was the one who had actually figured out what was going on and taken Michael down. He stood beside Detective Embry as Embry read off the prepared statement, and then the reporters began shouting questions at Sam.

"Mr. Prichard, you've done a lot of work for the government over the past couple of years. Do they often call you when they have a rogue agent?"

"I wouldn't say often," Sam said. "I'm not at liberty to divulge any details, but this is not the first time I've had to deal with an intelligence operative who's gone bad. This particular case, though, started out as a simple matter of trying to help an old friend reconnect with his family."

"Mr. Prichard, is it true that Michael Reed deceived Mrs. Winslow? Was she ever aware that her original husband was still alive before all this happened?"

"Well, that's probably a question you should be asking her, but she actually found out he was alive about a year and a half ago, when Mr. Winslow and I were the subjects of a news program. I guess she saw his picture and recognized him, but Mr. Reed actually threatened her to keep her from making any contact with him. Mr. Winslow only found out that his wife and children were still alive about a week ago, and he came to me to help them track them down."

"Mr. Prichard, if it's true that Mr. Reed was a trained intelligence agent, how were you able to overcome him?"

"Michael Reed was actually holding me at gunpoint at the time, but I had a single shot pistol in my possession. I managed to get it out and use it when he took his eyes off me for a split second."

There were dozens of other questions, and Sam tried to answer them all, but Embry finally put a hand over the microphone and said that was enough. Sam followed him back into the police station, and they sat down together in Embry's office.

"How did I do?" Sam asked. "I hope I didn't overstep any bounds."

Embry chuckled. "Man, you did fine. I have stood in front of that firing squad so many times it's ridiculous, I was more than happy to let them get you in their sights today. You handled them like an old pro, but I guess that's pretty much what you are nowadays, right?"

"You'll never catch me admitting to back," Sam said. "Harry Winslow gave me some advice once, and it is probably the best advice I've ever received. He told me that all I ever have to do is do the job that's in front of me, and that's how I get through these things. I just look at the situation in front of me and do my best with it."

Embry nodded his head and grinned. "I don't think I've ever put it into words, but that's pretty much how I live, too. One day at a time, one step at a time, just deal with whatever the reality is at the moment. Because, sometimes, reality isn't what you think it is."

"Now you sound like the old pro," Sam said with a grin of his own. "Have you ever had to deal with spies and such before?"

"Not on the job here," Embry said, shaking his head. "I know a little more than the average cop, though, because both my father and my uncle were in intelligence in the military. I grew up hearing stories about what it was like to be an agent, and some of the things I've heard about you go right hand-in-hand with the stories I heard back then." He leaned forward suddenly and extended a hand. "Prichard, put 'er there. There aren't a lot of men whose hand I really want to shake, but yours is definitely one of them."

A week later, the charges against Harry were formally dismissed and the investigation was closed. Ken had stuck around through it all, and it was finally time for Sam to go home. Harry was going to be staying in Florida with Kathleen for a while, though she had decided to sell the house and share an apartment with Harry.

Sam wasn't finished in Clearwater, though. He had held onto the Challenger until he was ready to leave, so when the police were finally done with him he drove himself to the hospital and managed to convince a nurse to tell him where Detective Lawton's room was.

Lawton looked up as Sam walked into the room and scowled. "You come to rub it in? Do the old 'I told you so' bit?"

"No," Sam said with a chuckle, "but let's face it, I could. I just wanted to see how you're doing. I've been shot before, myself, and I know it ain't no fun."

Lawton shrugged. "The docs say I'm almost back to normal. Doesn't look like I'm going to suffer any real problems, even though your boy managed to blow out part of my brains."

"Yeah, but you're a cop. Everybody knows a cop doesn't need all of his brains."

"Up yours," Lawton said, but there was a bit of a grin on his face. "Listen, Prichard, I owe you an apology. You were right, and I was just too stubborn to see it. If I had actually listened to you, I might have smelled a rat when I got a call that lured me outside."

"You don't owe me anything," Sam replied. "Just, maybe try to learn something from this experience. You may never have to deal with people like Michael Reed or Harry Winslow again, but don't be so quick to think things are cut and dried if you do. One thing I've learned about government agents is that they are never what they seem to be."

"Now, ain't that the truth. I had a big fuss with the IRS a couple years ago, and those agents? Talk about monsters, I was wishing for stakes and garlic. Vampires, every one of them, I'm telling you."

"You think IRS agents are bad? Wait till you have to go into some other country and deal with the CIA and all the other alphabet-soup groups. Then you can talk to me about monsters."

Lawton seemed to shudder. "No, thanks," he said, "I'm planning to leave all that stuff for you. Don't even bother to call me for help, because I ain't coming."

Sam laughed, and stayed for almost an hour. By the time he left, he felt like he had gained another friend.

Harry, Kathleen and Ken drove Sam to the airport, where he was treated to a return flight on the private jet. They were able to go with him directly to the tarmac beside the plane, and then it was time to say goodbye.

"Ken, it's been good to see you again," Sam said. "I really appreciate your help through all of this."

"What help? Hell, I got here just as you figured it all out. Next time you call, I'm going to wait a couple days. By the time I get here, you'll be celebrating and I won't have to do anything at all."

Sam laughed and turned to Harry. "Well, Harry, I don't know what to say. Are you going to be staying in Florida for good?"

"Oh, it's definitely good," Harry said. "Don't you worry, Sam, boy, you can't get rid of me that easily. They may think I'm retired, but I'll guarantee you Uncle Sam isn't quite done with me yet. Trust me, they'll call me up for something or other, and I'll need your help once again."

"And I'll come," Sam said, "but can you at least try to leave homicidal maniacs out of the equation? I've looked down all the gun barrels I ever care to see."

"I shall certainly try," said Harry with a laugh.

Sam turned it to Kathleen. "Kathy," he said, "it makes me pretty happy to see Harry having so much. I wish you two all the best, especially with thirty years or more to catch up on. When I get home, I have to catch up on a week or so, and sometimes that takes me months."

Kathleen laughed heartily. "I know what you mean," she said. "That just means Harry has to stick around for another thirty years, so I can enjoy all the time I was supposed to have with him." She leaned forward quickly and kissed Sam on the cheek. "Thank you, Sam Prichard. Thank you for bringing Harry back to me, and thank you for not letting him be taken away. I will be forever in your debt, so if you ever need anything..."

"Thank you," Sam said simply.

He turned and walked onto the plane, taking a seat at the window so he could wave at them as its copilot closed the hatch and the plane began to move.

EPILOGUE

He was back in Denver in an amazingly short time, and it was a relief when he claimed his Corvette from long-term parking and headed for home. Kenzie came squealing toward the door as he entered, and he happily scooped her up into his arms for the hug he had been craving.

It was early enough when he arrived that they all sat down to dinner together, and then spent a quiet evening—well, fairly quiet, except for Kenzie's excited shouts—watching one of the latest Disney movies on television. Sam enjoyed every bit of her antics, but by the time the movie was over and Indie carried her up to bed, the quiet was welcome.

When Indie came back downstairs, she crawled right into his lap in the recliner and simply held him for a while. Sam closed his eyes and wrapped his arms around her, He was enjoying the company and comfort of his family so much that he didn't even bother to unpack until the next day.

It wasn't much later that Indie climbed back off of him and took his hand to lead him to bed. Sam didn't offer any resistance, and even less when they closed the bedroom door and she began removing his clothes. A moment later, he returned the favor by removing hers, and the two of them fell into bed with their arms, legs and lips all entangled.

The next morning, Sam was awakened by a kiss on his cheek, and he opened his eyes expecting to see Kenzie, but it was Indie who had kissed him. He opened his eyes and smiled, and that's when he realized that she was holding something in front of his face. It took him a second to focus, but then he saw the white plastic stick with a plus sign showing in bright blue.

His eyes went wide and he looked up at his wife. "Baby? Is that..."

Indie began nodding vigorously, her smile so wide that Sam was sure it must hurt. He threw his arms around her and pulled her down into the bed, and the two of them lay there together, cuddling and kissing, until Kenzie finally opened the door and peeked inside.

"Guess what, Kenzie," Sam said. "Mommy's gonna have another baby. Isn't that wonderful?"

Kenzie's face broke into a smile and she ran and jumped onto the bed, then began bouncing up and down. Sam watched her with a smile on his face, thinking that she was acting out exactly what he was feeling.

A few minutes later they all got up and got dressed, and Sam noticed his bag on the floor beside the bed. He picked it up and opened it, ready to toss the clothes into the hamper.

And that's when he found it. A small package was inside his carry-on bag, wrapped in simple paper and with a note attached. He opened the note with Indie standing beside him and read it.

I thought you should have this. I probably won't be needing it in the future, but you never know when you might need an ace in the hole again.

Harry

Sam smiled, and unwrapped the package. Inside was the shiny gold lighter that concealed a single-shot gun.

What'd You Think?

Thank you for reading Aces and Eights. I had a blast writing it, and I hope you had fun reading it.

If you enjoyed the book, please consider telling your friends, or posting a short review. Word of mouth is an author's best friend and is much appreciated.

All the best,

David Archer

Full List Of My Books Can Be Found Below

www.davidarcherbooks.com[1]

---

1. http://www.davidarcherbooks.com/

Printed in Great Britain
by Amazon